Connections

Reborn in the Perfect Fantasy World

Fantasy.Productions L.L.C.

4601 E. Douglas St.

STE 150

Wichita, KS 67218

For serious business inquiries only,

contact cristoph@fantasy.productions

REBORN IN THE PERFECT FANTASY WORLD

Thank you, to my wife, for supporting me through this series.

And to my daughter for brightening every day.

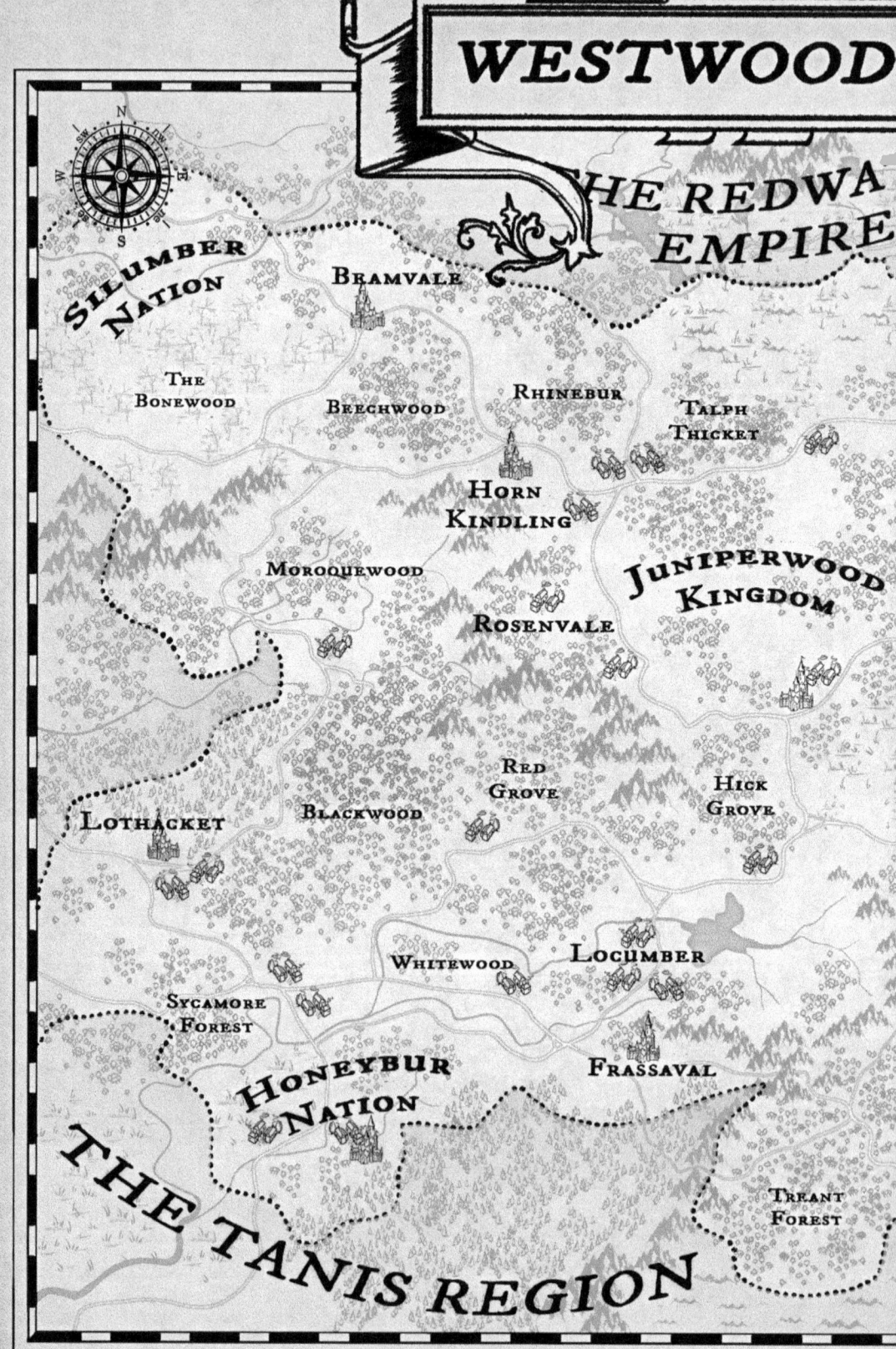

WESTWOOD

THE REDWA EMPIRE

SILUMBER NATION

BRAMVALE

THE BONEWOOD

BEECHWOOD

RHINEBUR

TALPH THICKET

HORN KINDLING

JUNIPERWOOD KINGDOM

MOROQUEWOOD

ROSENVALE

RED GROVE

HICK GROVE

LOTHACKET

BLACKWOOD

LOCUMBER

WHITEWOOD

SYCAMORE FOREST

HONEYBUR NATION

FRASSAVAL

TREANT FOREST

THE TANIS REGION

EMPIRE

KEY:
- Village
- City
- Mountain
- Road
- Border

MAPLE COPSE

OAKENVALL

LEAWOOD

THE SCARLET BOSCAGE

...ARCH ...VALE

JASPERWOOD KINGDOM

GRATHVALE

TULIP KINGDOM

JORISVALL

ASPWOOD

OBSIDIAN FOREST

HAWTHORNVALE

REDWOOD KINGDOM

CHERRY KINGDOM

PINVALE

BIRCHVALE

...OROUS ...OREST

ELM COPSE

WINDWOOD

FIRFONT

FIREWOOD KINGDOM

2,000 MILES

CHAPTER ONE
PREP

Finday, Polarae 23rd, 1735
[July 22nd, 2029]

BECOME MY CHAMPION are words you might hear a princess tell a knight. I think of those words at times when my mind wanders. In my case? The Goddess of Death, Eloria, uttered those words to me on my fourth birthday, by universal Standard. That moment wasn't exactly warm and fuzzy. Surprisingly, this was only the second most striking thing about my young life. The first had been finding out that death is a liar, when I was reborn on the world of Anfang.

It had been a year since then. A maid had just delivered my school uniform. Sarah, my lady's maid, usually helped me dress, but I was excited to change by myself today. I knew that my twin brother Oliver probably felt the same, because he'd surely find some new friends to train with at school. He's something of a battle maniac, even though we're only five. But on Anfang, some cultivating kids grow up quickly in ways that would be shocking on Earth.

I'd set up my privacy screens just as Sarah usually does, so I couldn't see Sarah when she entered as the door clicked. Calling to her, I said, "Sorry, I just couldn't wait to get changed."

Hearing no response, I called out again, "Sarah, are you there?" Still no response.

I must've been hearing things, I shrugged, and let it go while I admired my new outfit. The school uniform even included its own embroidered shift. While I found it odd, I didn't think too much of it. That was, until, I turned around after putting on my socks and caught a familiar face in the mirror. It wasn't Sarah. Instead, I saw a red-cheeked Marion Gideon Varn, my "fiancé" in the *acp hoth* we shared. It meant "child pact," which was why I'd been viewing it as a play engagement.

He wasn't fond of his first name. But I was annoyed and knew that using it would leave a bigger impact. "Marion," I chided, making clear eye contact.

He snapped to attention and averted his gaze. "Y-yes Anessa?"

"You know it's improper to enter a lady's room without announcing yourself first, right?" I said and deepened my voice to show my displeasure. "Turn around."

Hastily complying, he said, "I'm sorry."

Then my face heated up as it dawned on me that I'd removed my shift *after* "Sarah" entered. *How much of me did he see?* Thinking on it, I realized with dismay that the answer was probably quite a lot. I took a moment to swallow my thoughts on the matter and disregarded it. *I'm just a five-year-old bean-pole. Nothing to see here, carry on.* I took a moment to rearrange the offending screen, and patched the eye line to myself from the mirror.

Sighing, I thought, *He* is *almost thirteen. It's not unthinkable that he'd be interested in the fairer kind. Though I wish he'd use some common sense! Child pact or no, there's decorum to adhere to.*

It took some finagling for my tiny five-year-old hands, but I managed to finish dressing myself. Were I born a high noble I might even be prouder of such a simple feat, since my Lady's maid usually does most of the work now. Being born into "humbler" circumstances, she had only been helping me a little over a year.

Taking a few moments to check myself in the mirror, moving the privacy screen with me since I was still a little annoyed at my guest, I tightened my braid and did a pirouette. *Good. Now then... let's get back to my unannounced guest.*

Exiting the screened area, I fixed a stern gaze on Gideon with my arms crossed.

Gideon, who had apparently just been fidgeting nervously in place as I finished dressing, didn't seem to know what to do with himself. His eyes darted from the floor to me a few times.

When I'd judged he'd suffered enough, I said finally, "I'm not going to bite you. Please just don't do that again, okay?"

He nodded.

I asked more cheerfully, "What's up?"

Tilting his head, he seemed confused by the Earthen phrase, and momentarily gazed above my head. He shook his head and eventually said, "I was just going to tell you that our outfits are here, but you obviously already know that." He scratched his cheek. "Big surprise, huh?"

Holding out my arms, I repeated my spin for him. "How do I look?"

He blurted out, "Adorable." A blush bloomed across his face. "I mean… you look good."

Closing in on him, I leaned in, or up rather, since he was far taller than I. "Adorable, huh?" I smiled. "Acceptable," I nodded.

"It's still hard to believe," he said wonderingly.

"What is?"

He pointed between us. "That I'm in an *acp both* with the Imperial Duke's daughter."

16 CONNECTIONS

"Yeah, it's no picnic for me either." Furrowing my brows, I asked, "You still don't remember, do you?"

Gideon shook his head. "You've told me that we met at our Awakening Ceremony, but that entire day is just a blank for me."

Our engagement had been arranged in exchange for some stupid archaeological site that carries far more weight than my hand in marriage. I was cautioned about keeping this fact quiet due to the danger of the site's existence. Gideon could talk my ear off about the site when we first met. But my mother Lily, the Imperial Princess of the Westwood empire that we live in, said that his chatty exuberance about the site wouldn't be a problem. And it hadn't been. In fact, he stopped talking about it altogether.

Uncrossing my arms and deflating a bit, I sighed. "Your memory loss extends beyond just that day, doesn't it?" A worry had been pestering me over the past year; I strongly suspected that Mom had something to do with his sudden selective amnesia. *I can't exactly ask him, "Hey, what about that secret archaeological site on your family's land?"*

He nodded reluctantly, confirming my fear that he was missing a bigger swath of memory than he'd been letting on.

Without thinking, I recrossed my arms. "Well, why didn't you say anything?"

"It took me a while to realize how much was missing," he protested. "I don't look at the calendar every day, you know?"

I knew that pressing him would get us nowhere, so I changed the subject. I asked, "Did your mom, Una, get mad that you couldn't wear your first set of uniforms?" He'd grown from my height—thirty-nine inches—to almost five feet in a single year. All of those fancy uniforms that his family had paid for were unusable.

Shaking his head he said with a bit of disbelief. "No. She said it's no problem. In point of fact, the stipend mama-Lily agreed to is… more than generous."

I grabbed his hands, happy to think about the positives of his starting school later. "I'm glad she's not worried about it. Though the uniforms may not fit you, at least we'll still be able to start school at the same time."

My excitement was cut short when my lady's maid, the actual Sarah, coughed at our side, reminding me that *I* had now broken etiquette by holding his hands. *Crap. Where did she come from?*

Sarah didn't say anything, but she did give me a knowing look when I didn't immediately release his hands.

Give me a break, you surprised me! I thought. "S-so," I said with a fake laugh in an attempt to direct her attention away from myself. "What was that summons about?" Half an hour ago Sarah and all other personal servants had been called away for a meeting.

Her playful smile dropped and she stood a little straighter.

Uh-oh.

"I'm actually here to guide you, Your Imperial *High* Grace Anessa Carlyle, to the great room." Her corner of her mouth twitched. "Her Imperial *Lower* Grace Julilah Carlyle has returned, and requests your presence." After relaying the message, Sarah broke eye contact.

Crap. I knew that I could theoretically say no, since Sarah had emphasized our difference in rank. Julilah had not been granted an equal title like my father Roland because she was born a commoner. I'd even overheard some of the staff expressing surprise that Julilah's marriage to my father hadn't been annulled when he was promoted to an Imperial Duke. The promotion was due to my mother's lineage. However, while I might delay the inevitable, I knew that I wouldn't be able to avoid her forever.

With a sigh I said, "Okay. Let's get this over with." Looking down at my school uniform I added, "I'm not changing again, though. I just put this on."

Sarah gave a light bow. "Very good ma'am. Would you like me to guide you?"

"Yes, please." What I'd never told her, but I suspected she knew anyway, is I was quite directionally challenged. Even though it'd been a full year, I still couldn't find my way around the main estate without getting lost.

Embarrassing. Before we exited my room I turned back for a moment. "Gideon," I started, then I corrected myself with a sigh. As Sarah was using our full honorifics I should, too. "Excuse me. His Imperial Low…" I paused, trying to recall the correct term.

Sarah whispered, "Presumptive."

I laughed. "*Presumptive* Duke Consort Gideon Varn is joining us." The number of modifiers on Anfang made studying Earthen culture trivial by comparison. *Sheesh.* His status as Low reflected his origins from the lower caste and the presumptive state of his title.

She nodded.

Gideon stiffened. "It'll be difficult to get used to that title." He followed silently, although I occasionally caught him commenting about being an Imperial noble.

Join the crowd, buddy. It's new for me too!

Once we entered the great room, my eyes found Julilah almost immediately. Her typically extravagant attire granted her a pompous air. She sat at a side table, drinking tea with a severe expression. It was as though she'd been waiting far too long.

Dad was standing at her side, his focus on my mom, who was also waiting. When the lot of them noticed me, they shifted focus as one.

Julilah stood and approached me, which caused alarm bells to go off in my head. Luckily, before she was twenty feet away, I heard Dad cough and she stopped.

"Good morning Your Imperial High Grace, Anessa." Her usual fan was in her hands, and she gripped it with white knuckles before continuing, "I must apologize for my behavior. It was most unbecoming of me to try and mar your second birthday with a Genesis test." She bowed deeply to me. "I only hope that you can forgive my transgression."

Dad, behind her, gave me a discreet nod. It seemed he wanted me to forgive her.

Julilah was certainly being a lot more polite now than before. On my second birthday when she had roped me into that Genesis test, she'd been gleeful at the results. The test, which measured the number of children a person could have, gave her the impression that I was unable to have any, and she lost no time in declaring that I'd be ineligible to inherit anything. As it happened, she was wrong.

Mom only smiled, making it clear she didn't care what I did.

"It's fine, Mama-J." I said, and then my voice softened, "Please raise your head."

Julilah did so, and for the faintest of moments, a glimmer of violet flashed in her eyes. In a blink, it was gone. I'd seen some odd things on Anfang, but this was new.

What the heck, was that a trick of the light? I blinked. Her eyes were perfectly normal. *I must've imagined it.*

She smiled at my forgiveness, though I was certain it was a performance. The smile did little to dispel my frustration with the woman.

You see, I was certain she'd also talked my brother into attacking me when we were two. That might not sound too bad, but Oliver was a high-class cultivator. In other words, he had powers that would enable him to K.O. any Earthen M.M.O. fighter with a tap of his fist. He had tried to hit me with an outright full-face punch, which could've demolished a school bus. To avoid my head being pulverized like a watermelon, I'd reacted with a reflexive Gift Burst, a defensive manifestation of my own latent power. My counterattack nearly killed *him,* and would have gravely injured everyone around us were it not for the intervention of an actual angel. The whole thing was so surreal it sounds like I'm making it up, but unfortunately it had really happened.

Once she had departed with my parents in tow, Gideon approached me and whispered, "Man. Her smile was scary!"

I nodded. "I know," I murmured.

"It—" he paused, "It reminded me of the last smile my dad gave me when I was a kid."

Where's he going with this? The admission earned him an arched eyebrow. "Yeah?"

"That was just before he stabbed me."

"What?!" I shouted and covered my mouth.

"I got better," he added.

Yeah, you're here aren't you? Though of course I then had to ask, "Why would your dad stab you?"

He said, meekly, "I'd rather not talk about it, if that's okay."

"That's fine." I touched his hand. "I'm sorry you had to go through that."

Sarah coughed and politely reminded me to maintain a proper distance.

"Thanks" Sarah.

▼ ▼ ▼

"How about we go find Oliver?" I said after releasing his hand.

"Sure." He laughed. "I'm sure I know where he is."

We said at the same time, "Training with Kile." Our timing made us laugh. We both knew my brother all too well.

We headed into the interior courtyard, and sure enough a flurry of cracks rang out as my super-powered brother faced off against his equally-capable trainer. Between each strike was a hastily stated, "Point." Each and every score was Kile's.

Kile showed just how far Oliver had to go in gaining control over his own power. Though my twin brother had improved since we moved into our new home, he still hadn't landed a single blow on the older man.

Off to the side of the training arena was Mina, Oliver's fiancée. He technically had two other *acpę hoth*, or child pacts. As was often the case on Earth, Nobles on Anfang were frequently engaged at a very young age, for reasons that were largely political. Mina had been the most visible recently.

Pia and Roa have been showing up less and less.

They were twins. However, unlike Oliver and me, they argued with one another quite a lot, and my brother said the girls needed to figure their relationship out first before they could move forward with him. I found his view rather mature for a child.

He probably just hated the fighting.

Several additional clashes rang out.

Ironic. Considering.

Then I had an idea. "Kile," I called out. "Can I train, too?"

He didn't say anything for a few moments as he was focused on Oliver's latest flurry of attacks.

"Eloria said I was a cultivator," I added, then amended, "At the very least, I have essence vision." Though I'd been permitted to resume my training for the full year, the damned etiquette, lessons on manners, and all sorts of crap I was far behind on as a proper "lady" usually kept me too busy for the training grounds. *Since I'm here, I might as well take advantage of it.*

A particularly loud crack echoed across the courtyard as Kile smacked Oliver's sword out of his hand. The weapon embedded itself into the ground a few dozen feet from the arena.

Seeing his weapon was gone, Oliver sat down in a heap of gasping breaths.

Mina rushed to his side with a towel, which he took gladly. As she was over six feet tall, compared to his three foot ten inches, the sight was almost comical, making her appear more akin to a big sister. However, the way he gazed at her caused my heart to ache.

Don't grow up too quickly, Oliver.

Kile, in the meanwhile, was wordlessly setting up a mannequin for me to face off against.

"Great," I said with a sigh. "Another dummy."

As I wrapped my fists, the older man chided me, "Yes, another dummy. Until you gain a level of control over your own skills. I will not permit you to face off against a live opponent."

"Yeah, yeah." I hated to admit it but he was right. My skills were unpredictable and not as potent as my brother's. But they were plenty dangerous, and I couldn't control them. I turned my focus to the dummy. Though I hadn't trained with Kile, I'd practiced on a steel training post, or a *makiwara*, in my bedroom. A few dozen hits on the dummy later and I stopped. *Fifteen marks. But I only consciously used* that *skill five times.*

Scattered across the dummy's breastplate were five teeny pockmarks the size of a pea and as deep as a strand of hair is thick. Ten other marks on its surface were the size of a quarter and half as deep as one. A perfect semisphere had been gouged out by my unique and disturbing gift. *Yeah, those would hurt a lot.*

"Gideon," Oliver said, having gotten his breath back. "How about you and I both go against Kile?"

My fiancé held up his hands. "No thank you. While the gap between you and me is smaller than the gap between you two…" He exhaled. "I'd just embarrass myself."

"Damn it," I said aloud before covering my mouth and looking over to Sarah. My lady's maid merely shook her head firmly, meaning I'd likely be okay if I didn't curse again.

"What's wrong?" Kile asked.

"All I can do is put teeny pockmarks in this." I pointed them out, then pointed at one of the bigger spots. "And I didn't even mean to do these."

He took his thumbnail and ran it across my efforts, catching against the depression with a tinny click. Then placed his thumb in the deeper marks. "Don't discount yourself just yet. If you can get the hang of this, it'll be very useful." He gestured for Oliver to come over. "Remember that this is High Grade Third Rank Steel," he continued to me, "These marks may be small, but they're marks, nonetheless. Your brother can't even put a dent in this material."

Putting my hands on my hips I said disbelievingly, "Are you sure?"

Waving toward my brother who stepped forward, Kile stood back, and put his hand on my shoulder to move me back.

Oliver willingly unleashed a flurry of attacks on the steel, which rang with each hit. It was loud enough that I had to cover my ears. We all did, save for Kile and Oliver.

As he attacked, I followed the dummy's frame to the arena floor. It was anchored in place by a bar on each side. *So that's why it doesn't just fly out of the arena when he hits it.* Oliver wasn't levitating right now, instead he planted his feet on the flat plate the dummy was anchored to, probably for better leverage.

When my brother was done deafening everyone in the area, he stepped away. Sure enough. There wasn't so much as a dent on it.

"Third Ranked means suitable for those in the Sky Realm." Kile patted me on the shoulder. "High Grade means it'll withstand someone at the top of that Realm. So what you're doing is beyond a top-ranked Sky Realm cultivator. They can barely *dent* this stuff."

His words didn't inspire confidence. I thought to the goddess who had gifted me with so much. *Eloria has two monikers. That of Craft and Death. She told me that I am her champion of Craft.* I looked again at the divots gouged out of the nigh-impenetrable steel. Though they were small, they were real. The metal wasn't reshaped as you might expect from a crude crafting effort. The material was simply gone.

This doesn't look like a crafting effect. Touching the surface with my finger, I thought, *It seems closer to destruction and… Death.*

CHAPTER TWO
ENROLLMENT

Septaday, Zenthriae 12th, 1735
[August 28th, 2029]

AS WE CRESTED the nearest hill to our destination and the Maaka Institute for Cultivating Juniors came into sight, Gideon and I let out a gasp. The school was a literal castle built on top of a mountain, or at least what was left of it.

A forest filled the valley below. Our carriage plodded over a stone bridge built to cross the chasm. It seemed like a wildly impractical location for a school, but it definitely left an impression. *It would look amazing in a brochure.* The thought made me pause. *I don't think they have those here though.*

Mom told me we would start school in the month of Polarae, but that's just when we *departed.* The trip to the school actually took sixteen long and boring days. With no phone or apps to keep me busy, and the days being 54.6 hours apiece versus Earth's paltry 24, it was quite the trek. By the end of our journey, I knew every stitch of the carriage's interior.

"Anessa, turn back around and sit down," Sarah chided me. Gideon was sitting opposite of me, so he didn't have my visibility issue. My view was akin to a rear-facing third seat from an SUV. Providing little of note.

Harrumphing as I complied with her demand, I crossed my arms. "Fine." I had long since passed the point where I was being gracious about things.

An hour later, our carriage finally dropped us off and moved slowly away from my dorm's entrance.

"Isn't this all a bit much?" I said and gaped at the castle-like structure. *It's a quarter the size of the school itself!* Even Harvard's dorms looked humble in comparison. A twelve-foot-tall stone wall surrounded the "dorm." Past those doors was a gorgeous courtyard bursting with flowers, and a healthy reminder that the accommodations for nobles were vastly different from those intended for commoners.

"These dorms house up to fourteen Imperial Royals," Sarah explained as we approached a large fountain big enough to swim in.

Holding my arms out and gesturing over the building I asked, "You're telling me this entire building is for only fourteen students?"

She nodded. "And it's not full at present. Currently only you, Oliver, the heir presumptive Imperial Prince Lukas, Imperial Princess Rina and their two half-siblings are staying here."

30 CONNECTIONS

I wanted to ask why they'd waste so much space and have eight empty dormitories. Based on the size of the building, it suggested to me that the six staying here must have a lot of servants. *Then there's the issue of security. Allowing just anyone to stay here would be problematic.*

Sarah continued to say, "When you and Gideon marry in the future, he'll either stay in your dorm suite or be assigned one of his own."

Her words gave me pause and then I blushed furiously. *That's right: school lasts until I'm twenty-two years old. We'll definitely be married by then.*

"Anessa?" Sarah called.

Smacking my cheeks, I shook my head. "Sorry, just hadn't given a lot of thought to having a husband." I turned my attention to Gideon. "Not yet."

She nodded. "It is still eleven years away."

I'll be sixteen and he'd be twenty-three, almost twenty-four.

Then a teenage boy's harsh voice interrupted my musings. "And just who the Nether are you all?" he demanded.

The hairs on my neck stood on end at his tone.

Looking at the boy, I froze when I saw the coat of arms on his jacket. A pair of gilded dragons in a circle, chasing one another and swallowing each others' tails. There was a number "one" beneath the heraldic symbol. It was in an old-timey numbering system analogous to Earth's Roman numerals. The blazon made it clear who this was: the imperial prince, Lukas Q'Tar. Hence the attitude.

How should I talk to him? I fretted. He was higher-ranking than I, but we were peers of sort since he was my cousin. I decided to go with an informal approach. "Hi," I said in a chipper tone. "I'm your cousin Anes—"

Lukas cut me off. "My cousin needs to learn her place," his tone was dripping with contempt. His steel gray eyes narrowed on me.

Okay. Got it, he's an entitled prat. What little I'd read about him also indicated he was almost on par with Oliver as a cultivator. Given that I wasn't entirely sure what he could have done to me, I decided to hold my tongue and gave a shallow curtsy to him, which I held in place. "I'll endeavor to learn the proper form of address by the next time we meet, Your Imperial Highness."

Gideon wasn't bowing at all, and I briefly tugged on his sleeve, and gestured with my head. He did as I suggested, though his bow was almost forty-five degrees.

Behind us, to my dismay, the four guards who were supposed to be protecting me were all bowing as well. To my side Sarah had been frozen in a deep curtsy since Lukas first spoke. Her eyes were firmly on the ground... I think. *Come to think of it, I'm not quite sure what her eyes are doing most of the time.* From time to time, I had difficulty seeing her face clearly, and always had difficulty ever since we first met, though the observation tended to slip my mind like the features of her face.

While I was distracted, Lukas moved forward and knocked into me on purpose.

Charming.

As he did so, he said, "It seems you already know the proper way." He glowered at me. "Be sure to remember it, next time." He eyed Gideon scornfully. "Or I might not be in such a forgiving mood."

None of my guards budged an inch—*thanks for the protection guys*—and while I could have avoided falling, I had a feeling doing so would just anger him further. Consequently I allowed my rear to hit the ground.

What a complete asshat! Seeing my "guards'" inaction spoke volumes about the class hierarchy, and exactly where *I* stood in the pecking order right now.

Uh oh.

Gideon was making a fist at his side and was closing his eyes.

Please don't say anything Gideon. My heart rate increased, but I decided the best thing for me to do was to stare at the ground. *Lukas can do a lot more to you than he can to me.*

Lukas's earlier glare at Gideon said, quite clearly, that he would most certainly harm my fiancé. He'd probably enjoy it, too.

Heat suffused my chest and spread into my arms. I fought the stinging in my eyes because I didn't want to give Lukas the satisfaction of knowing his behavior was getting under my skin. However, it was all I could do to not scream at my oldest cousin.

Thankfully, Lukas turned away from us then, apparently feeling that he'd made his point. He continued out of the Imperial Royal dormitories. The heir presumptive's six personal guards followed. All of them avoided eye contact with us. It was hard to tell, but I didn't get the impression that they much cared for my cousin.

The feeling was mutual.

Once Lukas had exited the main gate, Gideon picked me up and sat me on my feet. "Are you okay?" he whispered.

I nodded and replied, "Thanks."

Watching my baleful cousin depart I said quietly to Sarah, "Make sure I avoid him as much as possible."

She nodded in silent assent.

"At all costs," I emphasized.

After we entered my personal dormitory suite Sarah dutifully wrote down my note about avoiding Lukas, though it didn't seem hard to remember to me. Then she busied herself directing the other three maids in unpacking my things. It seemed like a lot of fuss over one person's stuff, but this sort of thing goes with the territory of being an Imperial noble.

That still takes some getting used to. Before our family had been promoted to an Imperial Dukedom, I had generally been required to do many things myself. Now even the person who does things for me has people do things for her, placing her in more of a supervisory role. *Weird.*

This crowd of busy bees was avoiding one of my trunks, however. I approached it and lifted the lid, curiously looking inside. Though I didn't view the contents as terribly personal, what was inside were my shifts on top, followed by hosiery. Then my custom-tailored boyshorts were to the side, neatly flattened out.

Eying the boyshorts and shifts I thought, *Perhaps these are why.* I glanced at Gideon for a moment. *They view these as undergarments, and opening this with him around is a no-no.* As the date neared for me to start school, Mom had sternly encouraged me to either stop wearing hose or find some form of underclothes for them. Her reasoning was solid. If they were to tear during training I could be embarrassed to death.

Gideon asked, "What's in there?"

Immediately I closed the lid. "Nothing. Just personal stuff."

He reached toward the edge of the box, instinctively.

I smacked his hand. "Personal," I repeated sternly, "Stuff."

Holding up his hands he took a step back. "Got it." Looking around the room he said, "I should get checked into my dorm room, too."

He put his hand on my head and gently patted it. For some reason, I closed my eyes and smiled, then leaned into his efforts.

Then he took my hand and I opened my eyes, the one that had just smacked his, into his own. "Anessa," he said then bent a knee, though he almost threw me off balance doing so. Giving the top of my hand a light peck, his face instantly bloomed into a vibrant crimson blush. "My lady," he squeaked out before he stood again after the unsteady gallant gesture.

My earlier smile broadened at his awkwardness and embarrassment. Then the memory of a deeply disapproving scowl and steel gray eyes pushed their way into my head, and my smile dropped. I knew I'd be chastised for this next breach of etiquette, but I rushed forward and gave him a hug anyway.

"Stay away from Lukas," I whispered and added, "Please." As quickly as I'd embraced him, I let go.

Gideon nodded and promptly departed, but not before giving another deep bow.

Sarah explained later that his profound bowing was due to our vast distance in rank. It was a strange world in which he was permitted to pat my head, but must also bow so deeply as to nearly fall over.

36 CONNECTIONS

When the door to my dorm suite closed behind him, a very firm, "Anessa," came from Sarah.

Her cross tone told me she was upset and I ducked instinctually. "Yeah?" I said with a shaky laugh.

"Touching his hand is bad enough, and I politely reminded you by coughing." Her hands moved to her hips. "Giving him a hug is simply not permitted. You know that, right?"

"I was worried about him, though."

"Is it about Lukas?" she asked.

I nodded and sat down on the sofa. "Yeah. I assume he isn't likely to do anything to me because our statuses are relatively close, but Gideon does not have a title to protect him. Heck, as the son of a baronetess, he's barely gentry." Playing with my fingers I added, "Our Carlyle family are Highborn Peers and Lukas is an Imperial Royal. I just know with the way he looked at me, if he knew it would get under my skin, he'd probably do something to Gideon."

Sarah sighed. "I get it. But just remember if you were in public when you hugged him, although the act itself is simple, I would've been required to inform your mother, Her Imperial High Grace, Lily Carlyle." She brought me a cup of tea that someone had already brewed. "If you think I'm being harsh, just be aware that she would be even more so."

"I know," I said and breathed in the calming aroma of mint and apple from my tea. It was like a minty chamomile blend which I'd decided to call chamentalle. I closed my eyes for a second before turning back to her. "You know I wouldn't do that in public, right?"

"Perhaps not, but do be careful," Sarah said and picked up the tea tray. "There are countless nobles and Imperial nobles who would jump at the chance of–" She plucked a sugar cube then pretended to drop it. "–knocking someone in your family down a peg."

"Yeah," I said in frustration, equating her caution to cancel culture from Earth. Whether the person was guilty of indiscretion mattered little, what mattered was *opinion*. Though I didn't do it often, I took a moment to send a prayer to Eloria. *Please look after Gideon, and protect him from my idiot cousin.*

I hoped she was listening. Because deep down, I knew that if Lukas was so inclined, Gideon wouldn't survive the encounter.

CHAPTER THREE

SETTLING IN / ACCOUNTS OF THE DAY OF DEATH

THE FOLLOWING DAY I decided to explore the school library. Since classes hadn't started yet, Sarah followed me everywhere. While walking through the main courtyard of the Imperial Royal dormitories I saw that my cousin Rina, Lukas's sister, was sitting there drinking tea. Thinking of my encounter with her brother, a cool prickling sensation ran down my back and my stomach roiled. *Maybe she won't notice me.*

But my hopes of walking past her were dashed when she said, "Anessa."

I froze.

Knowing I couldn't brush the Imperial Princess off, I turned to her and gave her a carefully proper curtsy. "Hello, Your Imperial Highness."

To my surprise, she waved her hand at me negligently. "Don't be so formal. We're family."

Rina isn't baiting, me is she? Her demeanor is the complete opposite of her brother. I kept some of my guard up, and said politely, "How might I assist you today?"

Smiling she said, "First, please, take a seat."

I obliged.

"I wanted to apologize." She stood and gave me a deep curtsy.

Clearly this was unusual, because at my side Sarah gasped in surprise. I glanced at her, and she turned her eyes to the floor.

"My brother was out of line yesterday," Rina continued, her neck bent and her eyes turned down. "I'm sorry he put you through all that."

"It's fine," I said, and smiled. It was a relief to know that at least one of my cousins appeared to be sensible.

Rina straightened and sat down. "Thank you. Lukas has been a bit… temperamental since father hasn't yet proclaimed him as the heir apparent."

"What do you mean?" I asked.

She chuckled. "I guess you are only five, so you probably don't know. Traditionally, when the eldest heir turns fourteen, if there are no better heirs, they are announced as the heir apparent." Shaking her head she said, "No such proclamation accompanied brother's birthday celebration, and the omission did not go unnoticed."

A sigh escaped her lips. "That's not to say his behavior should be excused due to the circumstance." With a weak smile she added, "I figured some context might help understand him a little better. He's not making many friends lately, and I fear those who are taking to his side now may not have our empire's best interests at heart."

Lukas will *be the next emperor.* Her commentary had me worried. "Who's trying to get close to him when he's acting like... well, yesterday?"

Rina tapped her chin for a few seconds. "The Juntaro Imperial Duchy's secondary heir, for one."

I let a groan slip before I caught myself. "Isn't he known for being... kind of stabby?"

My blunt comment caught her off guard and she just blinked at me, twice. Then she snickered and laughed out loud. Afterwards, she promptly regained her composure and coughed. "Yes. He has been known to," she gave me a half smile, "do that from time to time." She held up a finger toward me. "Though don't let anyone else hear you say that. They might not find it as funny."

"What's so funny about him stabbing people?"

"It's not so much the act as it is the informality of the word. Have you ever seen the Imperial Duke's second son?"

I shook my head.

Rina held her hand up to her forehead. "He isn't even as tall as I am. He has a long, hooked nose, bad posture and thinning hair. His favorite weapon is a dagger his father gave him when he was six. There's even a light green tint to his skin, though no one knows why. Put it all together and he looks quite a lot like a..."

Finishing for her I said, "Goblin?"

"Yes, exactly. Nasty little critters. They're fond of sneak attacks and," she suppressed a laugh, "stabbing people."

Instead of trying to visualize him in my mind's eye I was more surprised that goblins were *real* on Anfang, though I didn't let it show. *Weird that there's an overlap with a monster from Earth.*

At our side, Sarah coughed gently. It was her polite way of telling me to change subjects.

Rina had a pair of lady's maids standing at her sides, but I didn't know either of their names. Both seemed to give a brief smile at Sarah's suggestion.

Taking Sarah's hint I asked, "How did you know I was five years old, anyway?"

Rina smiled. "You're family. As a member of my family, your arrival was something that I was informed of a month prior."

Her words were obvious, which was a little frustrating, but it was mostly my fault. *Did my run-in with Lukas blind me to what's right in front of me?*

"Not to mention," she added with a grin, "you're an Imperial Princess yourself."

"Really?" I said with surprise, and thought, *That's the first I've heard of this.*

She tapped the table with her ring. A pamphlet appeared on the table between us, conjured from the storage artifact on her finger. The page announced Oliver and my's attendance at Maaka, and included a fairly crude image of us. Though, with that said, the cartoonish picture definitely still resembled us. The document also listed us as Imperial Royalty, which is true, but didn't sink in for me until that moment.

Am I somewhat of a big deal? It wasn't too surprising, since we'd been treated like our own form of royalty at home, but it was interesting nonetheless. Then I amended my view, *It's not* me *that's a big deal, it's our family. Mom's family.*

"You can keep it," Rina said, gesturing to the pamphlet. "I have another one."

Returning her earlier smile, I said, "Thanks." I picked it up and handed it to Sarah, who stored it away in her own ring. *When I'm able to use one, I should get a storage ring for myself.*

"Oliver's arriving tomorrow, right?" Rina asked.

"That's right," I said, and then furrowed my eyebrows. "I hope he doesn't have a similar run-in with Lukas. Oliver would knock him flat. Or at least try to do so."

Rina giggled. "That might be fun to see. Lukas could do with a knock here and there."

I gasped at her words. "I'm just worried what Lukas would do to my brother. Afterwards, I mean."

Rina waved her hand. "No harm will come to Oliver." She placed her hand on her chest. "I'll see to that."

Talking with Rina put a smile on my face. If Lukas had been a cold bucket of water, she was a breath of fresh air.

Sarah and I resumed course for our original destination, the school library. The closer we got to the library, the more I sped up with excitement. At my side, my lady's maid carried the lightest of smiles.

"Why are you smiling?" I asked out of curiosity.

Her smile vanished. "No reason in particular."

"Come on. I'm not going to be mad. What is it?"

"Just your eagerness to go to their library. You're too young for romance books, and your academic pursuits already place you well above your peers. To be frank, you even give young master Gideon a mental challenge lately."

I'd like to think it's due to the nineteen years I've already lived on Earth in my previous life. However, she didn't actually say I'm equal to an adult, which means I still come up short.

Changing topics, I asked, "Why were you afraid to answer me a moment ago?"

Sarah checked for other people around us. Seeing no one, she replied, "It is not my place to respond emotionally to my charge. As a lady's maid my place is to remain quiet and as transparent as possible."

"You know you're allowed to speak freely to me," I said. "Please be sure to remember that."

She nodded. "I will do so. But I must also make sure it is in a socially appropriate context. Even your overt permission is insufficient to permit my freedom without possible repercussions for us both."

I groaned at her words. *Stupid noble society. What's the big deal? Emotions are emotions, they don't cause harm.*

Maaka's library was massive. While the decorative flourishes weren't quite as fancy as those in my home, it made up for that difference with its sheer size. "This has to be what, ten stories tall?" I said to no one.

"Twelve, actually," a voice said beside me.

To my side I found a handsome man with brilliant teal-colored hair. He was looking through the shelves for something.

"Anessa?" Sarah called.

"Yeah?" I turned to see her.

"Is everything okay?" she asked with a hint of concern in her voice.

"Yeah," I replied. When I turned back, the gentleman had moved out of sight. "Now, where are the books on cultivation?"

Sarah and I perused the books for an hour. At that point I was about to give up. Then I found a roped-off set of stairs to the second level. Next to it was a sign that read, "Cultivators only. Push essence from one of your dantians into the crystal."

A semi-transparent stone sat on the other side of the stairway. It didn't even seem to be a semi-precious stone. It was more akin to a crazed piece of quartz.

On my first Awakening, the Goddess of Death, Eloria, had granted me the ability to use essence vision, a marvelous mode of perception which I still didn't know how to toggle on and off. Even though erratic and as-yet difficult to control, this ability alone told my parents I was a cultivator. I wasn't quite sure what I was supposed to do here. Though I technically qualified as a "cultivator," I didn't have a dantian yet to speak of. Curious to know if I could simply use ambient essence, I placed my hand to the device and pulled what I could from the air and into the stone.

A soft rustling sound accompanied the ribbon unfurling partway. But instead of granting me access, it actually pointed at the words *from one of your dantians* on the plaque. *Great. A barrier with an attitude.*

Turning to Sarah I asked quietly, "How does it know that I am using essence that isn't from a dantian?"

She ducked down to my height and whispered, "Essence, once it has entered your dantian, is marked with your signature. If it comes from around you, the device can tell because it is very regular."

Huh.

Hoping I could maybe just ignore the thing, I tried to duck under the ribbon next. The bloody thing wound around my midsection and picked me up into the air. It gently sat me on my feet, facing away from the stairs. When I turned back around it pointed at the sign once again.

Okay. Got it. I sighed. *Not getting in there.* For the briefest of moments I thought of cutting the blue cloth, but quickly decided against it. So far it had been rather polite. I didn't want to imagine how it might have reacted if I tried a more destructive approach to entry.

Sarah, to her credit, did her best to not laugh, though I suspect if I had continued my losing fight against the ribbon, she would've lost that battle.

Giving up on the cultivation part of the library, I asked Sarah, "Let's split up and look for books on Eloria."

She nodded. "There probably aren't many, but I agree that it's important for you to read up on her."

When we were browsing earlier, I saw a book up high that had an interesting title, though I didn't tell Sarah. After all, she didn't know that I was Eloria's champion of Craft. Seeing Sarah disappear behind a bookshelf, I recalled its shelf number and returned to it. Though I promptly found myself at an impasse. It was at least seven *feet* above my head.

How did I even notice the title? Coincidence?

Giving the shelving an experimental shove, it didn't so much as budge. *Should be safe.* Pushing the books back further into the shelf with my feet, I started to climb upward. Reaching the book, titled *Accounts of the Day of Death*, was the easy part.

My world spun when I took a glance down. *Shit. Don't look down.* Moving carefully, I stepped one foot down, but didn't account for my childish strength. It had been enough to get me up, but apparently not down while holding a book.

I fell.

A shrill scream escaped me as I did so. It's funny how fast things go through your mind. I was critically aware that the floors were ceramic tile. For some reason I'd spun enough to be falling head-first.

I don't want to die!

But to my surprise, I did not crack my head open on the floor. The teal-haired man I'd seen before had appeared and caught me. He was looking down at me when I opened my clamped-shut eyes.

"Are you okay, little one?"

"Y-yes," I said with my heart pounding away in my chest. *Damn. That was too close for comfort.*

"Good. Be more careful," he said with a serene smile, and sat me gently on my feet.

I slumped to my bottom and breathed a sigh of relief. *Thank the gods.* Looking back to the kind gentleman so that I could thank him was futile. He was once again nowhere in sight.

Huh.

Taking stock, I moved myself over to one of the many tables throughout the library and opened my prize. The book was aptly named. Two thousand years ago, Eloria had transformed Anfang. She singlehandedly purged all dangerous beasts, giving a proclamation to the church to have every mystic beast captured and killed. Then there were the accounts from the remaining beast-kin and their family.

"It was a day without a cloud in the sky. Our family was celebrating my daughter Nala's first Awakening Ceremony, where she had become a cultivator. It happened, so fast it would make your head spin. A chill ripped through the church, leaving death in its

wake. I don't know why I was spared. I was the only human there that day. All we knew is Eloria was responsible. Every beast-kin church where her likeness was present, had it ripped out. As though their deaths were punishment for something unspoken."

Then another, though it was quite crude.

"Eloria evil! Took rat-kin nest and kill all on top level. Deeper nest okay, but goddess vile."

Two thirds of the book was dedicated to these accounts. There had to be hundreds of them. I didn't know what to make of it. *What the nether, woman?* On some level, eliminating mystic beasts, or the beasts that cultivate, was sensible to me. But the idea of culling anything that wasn't fully human was terrifying. They were people, and Eloria had conducted her own personal genocide to wipe them out. *What made her stop?* My mind drifted to Veronica, and I was fervently thankful that Eloria had stopped.

My skin prickled as I continued to read how the events of that single day had earned her the title of *Goddess of Death*. Thinking again of how she'd singled me out as her champion, I looked about nervously for nonexistent eyes, wondering if she was watching me, even now.

Why of all deities, did it have to be the *Goddess of Death!*

CHAPTER FOUR
BOOKS ARE EXPENSIVE

OVER THE NEXT four days I read through the entire book on Eloria. The geographic variety in the accounts reminded me of just how gigantic Anfang was. At twice Jupiter's diameter, I could spend a thousand mortal lifetimes traveling by carriage and still only experience a small percentage of the planet. The scale simply defied human comprehension.

However, Anfang's size paled in my mind next to the issue of starting school. On the morning of my first class, the reality hit me that I was five years old and in a class with teenagers. My stomach was in knots.

Everyone towered over me. I hoped to simply take my seat and ease into my studies over the next few days. *Maybe if I hide in the back, no one will notice me.*

"Seat six, in the front," a balding man said, as I entered my course on Westwood History.

Great.

It seemed my seat had already been decided for me.

So much for hiding in the back.

No one sat next to me. The row behind me was empty as well.

Right. Classism. Fantastic. Wasn't the point of me going to school to mingle with students? I shook my head. *This may make it difficult.*

There were twenty students total, and I was the only Imperial noble. The next highest-ranking student seemed to be a baron's son, per the emblem on his schoolbag. Our outfits were all identical, depending on gender, but students used their bags to display blazons and markers of rank. One of the loopholes in the rulebook. The glint from the gold on my skirt reminded me of the other loophole: the materials used for our uniforms were not fixed.

I lifted my "books" out of my backpack, stored in a special condensing ribbon. The handy item turned my books into thin sheets of paper with the title on them. I just rifle through them and pick the right book, pull the sheet out, and it pops back to normal. The weight was even reduced! However, in this class at least, I seemed to be the only one with one of these.

Slipping my Westwood History book out of the pack I thought, *Come to think of it, does anyone else even have books?* While most of the noble children's "bags" had some embellishments on them, most of them were barely the size of my forearm. Mind you, I was only three foot two inches short.

A tall weedy girl entered our classroom, and since I knew I'd be sitting alone otherwise, I spoke up to her. "Would you mind sitting next to me?"

The girl turned pleadingly at our teacher who reluctantly nodded. She sat down. As she unpacked a few things from her cloth bag, she didn't say a word.

A few minutes later a large boy that had to be three foot wide, akin to a cartoonishly large linebacker, entered, causing the girl to perk up and smile broadly. Her smile vanished when I spoke to him, however.

"Would you sit next to me?" I asked him.

He also deferred to our teacher, who once again obliged.

Getting the go-ahead, the proverbial giant took to the desk on my right. Or he tried to.

Our teacher coughed. "Go get your usual desk Lord Winnie."

Hearing this the portly boy retrieved a desk that was a little larger than the others, and swapped it for the one he was using.

"Winnie" evoked a certain honey-loving stuffed animal, and his build matched the name almost perfectly, save for his giant stature.

"Good morning Lady Portia," he said to the girl at my left.

She scoffed. "I'm no lady, Lord Max of the Winnie line."

Despite her rejection of the title of lady, they were both smiling as though I weren't there. Not difficult since they could both peer right over my head. Still, I felt like I was in the way.

"Would you like to switch seats with me, Portia?"

A nearly inaudible gasp escaped her and she paled. "N-no." She shook her head vigorously and bowed her head to the floor. "That isn't necessary, Your Imperial High Grace."

"Please, call me Anessa."

"I'm most honored, Your Imperial High Grace, but that is not something I am permitted to do."

"Well, *I* say it's okay, and I'd prefer people use my name," I said, somewhat crossly.

Portia didn't say anything for a solid ten seconds, and even began to sweat.

I furrowed my eyebrows. *Clearly she's in an uncomfortable position. Is my request really that unreasonable? Is it something she can be punished for?*

"If it pleases you," she finally said, turning briefly to me before her eyes quickly darted to the ground. "Would Imperial Lady Anessa work?"

With a sigh I said, "Yes. That will be fine."

Max piped up, "What about me?"

"You may use the same form of address," I confirmed.

He blinked at me a few times. Then focused on Portia.

With a sigh I said, "I mean you can call me Imperial Lady Anessa."

"Oh." He smiled. "Why didn't you say so?"

I stared at him for a moment. It took all I had to not scream, *"I just did!"* With a sigh I thought, *It wouldn't solve anything.* I shook my head.

To my side, Portia was silent. A gentle smile rested on her face as she gazed at Max.

Is she as dense as he is?

On her shoulder was a patch that indicated she was a core student.

Ah, got it. The girl is not dense, she's lovestruck.

Looking over the two, they reminded me of a pair from the Thimble Theater comic strip. *If Max is Bluto, then Oliver would be Popeye given he's small, energetic and could wipe the floor with Max.* Pausing for a moment and noting his size, I amended my thought to, *Maybe.*

I'd thought Max was merely portly. However, his arms rippled with muscle as he unpacked his bag. It was mostly his gut that was fat. Curiosity got the better of me and I asked, "Are you a cultivator, Max?"

"Yeah, but I'm not very strong." He flexed his bicep. "I'm mostly confident in my body strengthening, but it would only get me so far. Your brother, His Imperial High Grace, Oliver Carlyle, could kick my teeth in." He shook his head. "Luckily, it's not every day you meet someone at the peak of the Ascended Realm."

Ascended Realm? Oliver's been above the second Realm in the Sky Realm for at least three years now. I realized that Max didn't know what Oliver's true status was now. I knew there must have been a reason my brother's advancement had been kept quiet. So I didn't correct Max.

"I'm only starting to get a grip on controlling fire," he continued.

Our teacher coughed politely.

We returned our attention to him so he could start class.

As the class ended, I struggled to get my book back in my condensing ribbon. It had been easy in my dormitory to fit every book. I even stuffed a few unrelated books in to test it. But now I was having trouble, mostly because I was upset. All of the students had avoided my gaze throughout the entire class. Even when I would lock eyes with them, they always seemed to find somewhere else to look. The entire class had been so silent during the times when our teacher wasn't lecturing, I may as well have been taking the class alone.

"Portia," I said bitterly.

"Yes," her tone was respectful and hesitant, "Imperial Lady Anessa?"

Stifling the sigh I felt coming, I asked, "Are people avoiding me?"

"I believe so," she said and avoided my eyes herself.

Pressing her for more, I asked, "Do you know why?"

"It…" she began and whispered, "…might be because they are worried about offending you, which makes them afraid of you." After a brief pause she said, "Because you could have them executed."

Portia's words gave me pause. *Good gods above. Why would I have them executed!?*

I took a breath to center myself, so I didn't cause a scene. Then I hissed, "Why would they think that? That's awful!"

Touching her fingers together and flexing them lightly, she turned her gaze to the floor. "You're... somewhat well known, even beyond the details in the announcement of your arrival. Everyone is aware that you have a Divine Link with Eloria, the Goddess of Death." She pursed her lips as though she wasn't sure she should continue. "And most nobles don't remain enrolled in civilian classes once they reach even the Middling's Cloister, so we don't see many here."

Nobles preferred to move to martial studies exclusively once they hit what amounted to middle school. *Then again, with the emphasis on Oliver to get stronger, maybe I shouldn't be too surprised?*

"You seem fine talking to me," I pointed out.

Portia dodged my eyesight. "It's because you asked me directly. If I had ignored you after that..." she gripped her upper forearm. "I'd rather not think about what you might do."

"You know I'm–" I started but clamped my mouth shut. *I almost said I was Eloria's champion. That might not go as planned.* Recalling how sternly Mom lectured me on being silent about it, I continued, "I didn't actually create a Divine Link with her Goddess of Death persona." Moving my hand to my chest I explained, "It was with the High Goddess of Craft."

At that statement, although I was only addressing Portia, the entire class, including the teacher, collectively breathed a sigh of relief.

Great. At least that's cleared up.

The few students in the class that picked up a classroom copy of the Westwood History book placed them back on the teacher's desk near the room's exit.

Picking one up, the cover shifted to the side under my thumb, presenting a thread-bare connection to the spine. All of them were tattered and falling apart. Inside the book its print date was ten years ago. Comparing it with my copy I thought, *Wow. Mine was printed last week.*

Over and over throughout the remainder of my classes that day, the same issue was present. For a school used by so many, having outdated materials was common. It rubbed me the wrong way.

In my final class for the day, I took the worst offender of the bunch up to my teacher's desk, dumping the tattered tomes in a heap. "Is there a reason why the other students are using such outdated books?"

She sighed. "Most of our budget goes to the martial division." Accepting the book from me she added, "It doesn't leave much room for civilian studies, I'm afraid."

I paused for a moment. This didn't make a lot of sense to me. "What do they need in martial classes that costs so much?"

"Essence gathering and foundation establishment pills. Alchemical ingredients, basically. It's expensive to hire the alchemists, and of course they charge the school by the pill on top of that retainer fee. Finally, they bill us for the ingredients as well!"

They nickel and dime the school, but that doesn't sound too bad—

"The price of a single pill could buy a book, but they give every student an Essence gathering pellet every week. The core students get two, and are also guaranteed a foundation establishment pill as needed."

I gaped at her for a moment. *They're effectively burning money at a horrific rate. It's no wonder their books are almost rags.*

"Tell me, could I help pay for some new books?" I asked as I reached for the pouch at my side. *What's the point of having money, if I can't use it to make a positive change?*

She promptly held up her hand. "As generous as that is. I can't accept any money from you."

Seeing the disappointment on my face she conceded, "If you're serious, speak to the dean." She took a key from her storage ring and opened her desk. Pulling a single sheet of rough paper, she penned a note on the spot. "Give this to her, it'll get you in the door at least."

I took the letter from her with a nod of thanks.

She added in a quiet tone, "Good luck."

CHAPTER FIVE
MONIKER / HEADMASTER

Hexoday, Runariae 11th, 1736
[October 26th, 2029]

A FEW WEEKS later I was sitting with Portia, who was still one of the only people who would talk with me.

"How have you and Max been doing?" I asked her.

She was sitting across from me in the sitting area of my dorm suite. Her back was straight and she seemed to be using me as a reference on how to act, since she was clearly mirroring my moves. It was awkwardly formal to me. *She's just not comfortable around me yet with the gap in our social class.*

"We're okay, I guess," she gave a weak smile.

I persisted, "How long have you two known one another, anyway?"

"His father, Baron Min Winnie, was the local lord in our hometown Redburrow."

A chuckle escaped despite my efforts to push it down.

"What?"

Waving my hand, I said, "Sorry, Min and Max Winnie, I just found it funny."

Portia blinked at me, the obviousness of the joke lost on her.

She's a core student, so I know she isn't dumb. Then again, the maths subjects we study are narrow, though more in-depth than from Earth. I don't see the need to memorize four-digit computations! It's never used...

My internal musings were interrupted by Portia saying, "Is it funny because Lord Min is short and Max is not?" She gasped. "While that *is* an interesting thing, I wouldn't dare laugh about it. Lord Min is quite... sensitive about that topic." Eying me she added, "Though I don't suppose he'd say even a word if you did so."

Lord Min's stature wasn't something I'd known about. I erupted into a giggle fit at the straight-face with which she delivered that news to me.

Sarah coughed at my side, reminding me of decorum.

Taking a few breaths to stop myself, I said to Portia, "I had no idea he was of such a stature. I was referring to their names being polar opposites of one another in Maths, though I suppose the humor of a joke is lost the moment you need to explain it." Looking to Sarah she said nothing, so I continued, "Please don't tell Max, he might not find it funny either."

64 CONNECTIONS

Portia shook her hands and head. "I wouldn't even dream of it."

I sighed. "You do know by now that I won't hurt you, right?"

She froze at this comment. "I know." Looking around she said, "I just feel out of place here." Her finger rubbed the rim of her teacup. "Everything looks so expensive."

Looking around ruefully, I saw the room through her eyes. "Thank you for stopping by, anyway," I said with a smile.

"I appreciate the invite." Seeing the out I gave her, she added, "Max and I were supposed to have second dinner together, so I need to go find something to wear."

After she'd left the room I exhaled. "Finding friends will be difficult. Portia's still scared to even talk to me."

"We looked over the students in your age group last week. Was there anything wrong with them?" Sarah asked, unobtrusively cleaning up Portia's teacup and plate.

I said, "I'm in classes for people over three times my age. The students my age only wanted to talk about their favorite toys, their parents, or their big brothers and sisters. While learning about their family is interesting, it's not terribly stimulating conversation."

Sarah smiled. "Weren't you asking Portia similar things about Max and his family just now?"

I gaped at her and had no response. "Well... perhaps I just wanted to understand people around me in my classes because the discussions are more meaningful, I guess? The children we sat down with last week don't share any classes in common with me."

"Getting to the truth of it, I see."

Nodding I said, "It's hard to connect with stories about people I've never met and likely will never meet."

Sarah said, "That makes sense. I'll cancel the meet and greets for this week and send a message to Her Imperial High Grace Lily to explain why you're currently focusing your socialization on Portia and Lord Max Winnie. Although, I do hope your circle of friends expands further in the future."

We departed my suite. I started to head toward Oliver's, but Sarah said, "He should be in the Cadet's Prep visiting one of his friends."

I raised an eyebrow at her. "Remind me again why you always know more about where my twin is than I do?"

"It is literally my duty to make your day easier."

Cadet's Prep was housed in a fairly simple building. It was a fancy way of referring to commoner students in the middle-school level martial studies. There were no adornments comparable to those decorating the Imperial Royal Dormitories. The most distinguishing embellishment was its use of two colors of stone to accentuate archways and its narrow windows.

In contrast, I had counted no fewer than ten types of stone used in the construction of the dorms where Oliver and I were staying.

There were separate accommodations for Nobility and Imperial Nobility, but they weren't further stratified by age.

"I cannot let you enter," a wide-faced boy said to Sarah and me. "And I cannot leave my post."

Oliver, like me, was attending classes technically above his age range. Though in his case it was for different reasons. His physical prowess placed him at a graduate's level; however, his civilian studies were barely up to snuff. The compromise had been to put him somewhere in the middle.

With my hands on my hips, I said, "I'm here to talk to my brother Oliver Carlyle. He's visiting one of his friends. We won't be more than a few—"

"And I said I cannot let you enter. We're not allowed to have any girls in the boy's Cadet's Prep. There's a rule against it. Girls need to stay in their own dormitories." He pointed behind us in a mirror building to the one he was "guarding."

"You're being bull-headed," I complained and stomped my foot. Mom had been clear that when I was dealing with fellow students I was not to use my status to compel them, so I refrained from identifying myself as an Imperial High Duchess. Though my status was admittedly well-known, it seemed not everyone had gotten the memo.

Pinching the bridge of my nose I turned to Sarah. "Would you please shout outside the windows for Oliver? I would do it myself, but I know you'd frown on that."

She smiled and gave a light curtsy. When she did exactly as I'd asked, the boy's tune changed.

"H-hey stop that." He looked nervously between us. "I'll go find Oliver for you. Just don't cause a scene."

Sarah returned to my side and didn't say a word when the boy entered the building cursing at us.

Though it was improper, I stuck my tongue out at him for being so stubborn.

Adapting to life as a High Noble isn't easy.

I blushed as I recognized that I was acting my physical age instead of how old I really was. *Oh well.*

My lady's maid's reaction to this breach of decorum was to arch an eyebrow at me, but she said nothing else.

Why do I have a feeling she'll chastise me later?

Oliver blitzed out of the Cadet's Prep and cried, "Sissy!"

I braced myself as he lifted and spun me around faster than an amusement park ride. "Stop!"

He set me down as quickly as he started.

My head was spinning and I stumbled a step before I righted myself.

"Sorry," he grinned, "I just haven't seen you in a long time."

"It's only been a few days! We saw each other daily at home–" I said but stopped when I saw his eyes had teared up. I forgot sometimes that emotionally Oliver wasn't as old as I was. With a sigh, I said, "I've missed you too."

"Ready for lunch?" he said and skipped around me as we walked like I was standing still.

He's got so much energy! Oliver didn't have his manservant with him. He was a small boy similar in height to his squire, so I asked about Oliver's squire, our half-brother, "How is Lom's training going?"

My words must've struck a chord, because he froze on the spot and turned to me. "He's doing well," he said, "Kile will take most of his training until I turn ten, though. I, um," he turned his head toward the ground, "hurt him last week in a sparring match." He gripped his sword, Rufus, at his side.

"It wasn't on purpose, was it?" I asked sternly.

Oliver's eyebrows shot up and he turned to me. "I would never do it on purpose!" he said, shocked.

Smiling at him I said, "Then there's no problem."

His smile returned. "Did you want Gideon to join us?"

"That's not a bad idea," I admitted.

Oliver's disposition changed in a flash. "I'll go get him!"

Before I could tell him I'd like to calmly walk to Gideon's dorm, Oliver was gone in a flash.

"He's so positive," I said. "I'm a bit envious."

Sarah's response was to gasp while looking forward.

I followed her gaze.

Oliver was returning, while princess-carrying Gideon.

Normally I would have laughed my ass off at the sight. I held it in though because there were a few looky-loos staring.

Crap. What the Nether are you doing Oliver!

He stopped in front of us and gently placed his "princess" onto the ground in front of himself, proud at being so efficient.

Gideon's face was beet-red. After face-palming for a few seconds his head popped up and he said, "Shall we?" His voice may have cracked.

It took everything I had to not break into a fit of giggles right there.

"Please, lead the way," I said with masterful control, and extended my hand forward, acting as though the prior event had never happened.

Giving Gideon a few minutes to let his color return to normal, I then asked, "How are things going in your martial studies?"

He shook his head. "I'm not really cut out for it." He brought up his hand into a fist. "Someone must've pulled some strings to get me in this program, because when I applied over a year ago, I didn't even meet the minimum on the physical, and I'm not much better now. But they do give me some nice benefits."

When he didn't say anything further, I prodded, "Such as?"

"Essence-gathering pills. Once a week. My nexus's natural draw is weak, so if I am to become stronger," he sighed. "I need all the help I can get."

Oliver piped in, "You know, I don't get any pills."

Gideon replied with what seemed like incredulous outrage, "Why not? You're this millennia's paragon!"

Oliver waved his hand dismissively. "Things are a little off with me though," he said, somber once again. "My nexus draws in essence by itself."

"Doesn't that just show how amazing you are?" I asked.

"Sissy, I haven't slept for over a year," Oliver said sadly. "Though Daddy says it's normal once you enter the late stages of the Sky Realm, sleep is something most are still able to do. I just can't at all. The pressure is too distracting." He hugged his own body and rubbed his arms. "Using essence-gathering pills makes it even worse. They make my meridians ache, and my skin tingle."

I had no idea. I guess being a natural has its downsides.

We walked in silence until we reached the dining hall. Though Oliver and I had our own private chefs, it isolated us from everyone else, even each other, to eat alone.

Although I wanted us to sit with the larger crowd of students, hoping to blend in a little, Gideon asked a question appropriate for a smaller audience.

"Were you able to find any interesting books on Eloria?"

A silence fell over a portion of the hall.

Dozens of people were looking at us. He hadn't even said it that loudly. Eloria's name clearly had an impact, no matter the context.

Great.

Seeing the awkwardness of the situation, I said, "Maybe we should use…" I exhaled, and said with dread, "the Imperial Gallery."

"Am I even allowed in there?" Gideon whispered.

"Yes." Looking over at Sarah who had been gripping her apron for the past few minutes I said, "You too, Sarah. We can invite anyone we want, any time we want. It's after class hours, so the few rules there are on who can enter are relaxed."

Sarah nodded.

What's with her? Sarah knows this as well as I do.

Oliver said, "I'll go tell them our names."

Silly rule. To sit in the private area for Imperial Nobility, we had to give our names. As if every single person didn't know who we were.

In the dining hall for students, there was the commoner's area, which was like any other school cafeteria on Earth, albeit a bit rougher due to the simpler tech. A deck, one step above the rest, was reserved for the occasional noble child should they want to eat there. Yet another step above that was the Imperial Gallery. Privacy screens separated the space from the general lunch area.

When we entered, Sarah froze at the entrance. Imperial nobility, from the top-down, were each granted a named seat in this gallery. There had never been anyone in the Imperial Nobility named Gideon or Marion, so his chair was a blank. Oliver and I were each granted a seat with our full names.

My lady's maid was as white as a ghost.

The chair set out for her had the name Sarah Greensbaro.

"What's wrong?" I asked.

She took a step back. "I cannot sit there."

Her breathing was labored, as if she were having a panic attack. I wasn't sure what was going on. There might have been a violation of some rule at fault here.

"Okay, you don't have to," I said cautiously. "Would you rather eat in my dorm suite?"

"If it would please Your Imperial High Grace." Her gaze was fixed on the chair as though it might bite her. Her voice shook, "I would *much* prefer that."

"Very well. You are dismissed."

Sarah gave me a deeper bow than she ever had, then hastily left us.

She was terrified. Is there a severe punishment or something I don't know about for sitting in a named seat when you aren't that person?

I shook my head. *It must have something to do with her being a servant.* But during a previous meal when I had wanted to eat with Portia, they asked if I wanted seats to match our names, or if I wanted a different specific seat, so there was clearly something I was missing now.

I'll ask Sarah later.

Taking the book condensing ribbon from my waist, I said to Gideon, "I did find a book on Eloria, though it concerned me."

We fell silent as a member of the wait staff approached and started with Oliver.

"I think I'll have some Sunrise Apple slices," he began, "Earth and Wind Onigiri, Roast Boar with…"

Though Oliver couldn't sleep, he *could* eat. A lot. Often several times my weight in food at a single sitting.

Where does he put it all?

Once our orders were placed, I continued talking to Gideon and showed him the book on the Accounts of the Day of Death.

His eyes lit up in seeing it. "I've heard of this from my late grandpa." Shuffling through the pages he stopped on a page halfway through, and tapped one of the accounts. "This was my many times over great grandpa's story!" He was quiet for a few minutes as he read it. "I'd only ever heard it through word of mouth. It seems some of the details were embellished. Considering what they're talking about, I'm not sure why you'd make the story grander than it was.

"Grandpa Varn said Eloria only stopped because if she had continued, there wouldn't be many left on Anfang once she was done."

Tilting my head to the side I asked, "What do you mean?"

"Well, most people on Anfang are some form of beast-kin. Pure-blooded humans are actually somewhat rare." He shut the book and slid it back into the condensing ribbon on his own. Our food had arrived.

After they dropped it off and left us, Gideon resumed talking. "Don't show that book to anyone else, though. Eloria, despite all that has happened, is held in high regard." He seemed to be worried about others listening in and checked around us. "She is still feared though, as I'm sure you've noticed. I'm surprised you even found that book. Everyone I've talked to about The Accounts have said they were destroyed."

Oliver burped. Though there had been twelve plates of food in front of him, he had polished them all off by the time we'd even taken a bite. "I wasn't really listening too closely," he picked at his teeth, "but from what Daddy's said, he isn't a full human either."

"What?" I said flatly.

Oliver nodded. "Yeah, Daddy said he's a regressive cat-kin. Whatever that means. He's more cat-kin than even Mama-Krissi is." He presented three fingers on either side of his face. "It's why Sissy Nicole's whisker lines can pop out."

This was astonishing news to me. "You mean to tell me we're both part cat-kin?"

Oliver nodded.

"Why didn't they tell us that!" I complained. "That's huge news. Shouldn't we deserve to know that?"

Oliver sat back in his chair and scratched his chin and avoided eye contact. "Well, Daddy told me."

Letting out a frustrated sigh I said, "Of course he did. You get told everything." Pausing for a moment, I sifted through Oliver's words. "Wait a minute. You knew I wasn't told, which is why you knew to tell me about Daddy."

Gideon was sitting to our side watching the two of us, eating his meal. It was as though he were watching a drama.

Glad I could entertain you, I thought ruefully.

"Daddy said that you had enough to worry about, and he'd tell you if it ever became necessary," Oliver said, picking through the scraps on his plates for anything edible he may have missed. He'd been pretty thorough though.

"Like *when*?" I demanded.

"We don't even know if we have any of his traits. He even said we should have shown some cat-kin trait at birth. Unless we were unlucky enough to have inherited his regressive something or other. It's possible we're both fully human, though he said that's just as rare."

After I finished a bite of my own meal, I said, "You didn't say when, Oliver."

He laughed. "You're as scary as Mommy sometimes, you know that?"

"Thanks," I said with a smile. Then I pointed at him with my knife. "Answer."

"Yikes," he said, and laughed again. "Daddy said I won't find out until I marry. And you will find out when you have a baby..." he paused and added, "Whatever that means."

I dropped my utensil at his comment. My face heated up and I glanced at Gideon.

He was sporting a blush of his own.

Thankfully, I have at least *eleven years until I have to worry about that!*

▼ ▼ ▼

Finday, Crotariae 5th, 1736 [December 12th, 2029]

After putting it off for much too long, I decided the next free day I would finally visit the dean of Civilian studies. Her office was located in the corner spire that towered above all but the central tower, which housed the dean of Martial studies. A light burning in the back of my throat reflected my nerves, but I pushed forward anyway.

I might have struggled to get the door open. Okay, I couldn't move the thing. After pushing on it until I was red in the face I paused to catch my breath furtively glancing around. Thankfully no one had witnessed my pitiable efforts.

Then the door on my right opened as someone pushed it open from the inside, making my ears burn at the obviousness of it in retrospect.

Right, the giant rings hanging down from the door mean that you pull on them to open, not push. Gods Anessa, you're an idiot. It was times like this that I was glad there were no security cameras on Anfang. I'm sure someone would've played my prior efforts on loop, or worse, created a viral video. *"Imperial High Duchess Outsmarted by a Common Door."*

Thankfully, though the door weighed what seemed like a ton, it was so well-balanced that I was actually able to open it. As I approached, the dean's secretary glanced at me, then froze.

I'd been reaching for the letter of introduction the teacher had given me, but it was entirely unnecessary.

The secretary immediately stood from her desk and knocked on the door to the inner office, peeking inside. A moment later she turned to me and said, "Dean Xandra will see you now."

"Thanks," I said. *Guess there's something nice about the institute itself announcing you're attending a school. They know who you are.*

Xandra's office, to put it politely, was utilitarian. A desk, chair, and a sitting area for anyone who might visit. That was it. There wasn't even a rug or anything for serving guests. The table near the chair was rough around the edges, as though it had been a student's first woodworking project.

"Good morning Anessa, what brings you here today?"

Before I could reply, Xandra's secretary entered and set down a tray of cookies and a cup of tea before me.

Given her Spartan office, I don't think this is something she usually offers, I thought wryly. "Thank you," I said to the younger girl as she left the room, and partook of their hospitality. "I've been attending classes for a few weeks now, and something has bothered me a bit."

Xandra arched a brow at me. "What's that? Did someone say something mean to you about your family?"

The Carlyle family had rocketed to the status of Imperial Nobility from a small baronetcy a few years ago. *Was that a veiled insult?* Shaking my head, I said, "No. I'm bothered that the students don't have proper books. They're falling apart, and sometimes the content in the books I've brought with me differs from that in the ones the other students use."

She sighed. "Books are expensive. We've tried to request a bigger budget for them, but most of that budget goes toward the common library, which is open to all students."

I nodded. "I was wondering if I could help pay for them myself," I said, and reached for my purse on my belt. "If that is something you could permit, of course."

She looked mildly troubled by the request. "Given the cost, and the length of your time here, in order to even consider it, I would need to secure a continued contribution—"

Her voice trailed off as I sat a medium black gold onto her desk.

Silence reigned for a solid minute before I replayed her comments in my head. *"Continued contribution."*

Tapping the coin, which was about the size of a half-dollar but thrice as thick, I said, "This would be the initial investment." Taking two smaller black gold coins, each the size of a quarter, I placed them down onto her table. "And this would be the continued contribution, I guess you meant it as a commitment of sorts?"

Xandra gulped.

Crap. Did I give her too much? I'd never had a reason to actually familiarize myself with money on Anfang. I was a very young noble girl in a very powerful house. It's not like I did any of the shopping. All I knew is black gold was a little dingy looking, so I'd assumed it was a lower-value currency. I mean, my parents gave black gold coins to me, a little kid, so how much could they be worth? Based on her reaction, I might have had it backwards.

I'll need to ask Sarah about this afterwards. If I'm grossly mistaken she'll laugh at me. In my defense, I've never had to buy anything.

After eying the coins for a bit longer, Xandra cleared her throat. "I'll need to get permission from your parents," she said finally.

"Why?" I asked. "It's just my monthly allowance. I figure I can spend it however I want."

She sighed. "Be that as it may, if I were to accept this offering without confirming that it is okay with your parents, I could lose my job." While I digested that little nugget of information, she added with a shrug, "There's also a procedure to follow since you're not an adult yet. Even if your parents were commoner merchants, I'd still have to ask when any currency is involved."

"Okay." I shrugged.

As much as I wanted to ask, *"is this enough"*, I feared looking like a fool. It would certainly lead into her asking why I was offering something I didn't understand.

Xandra turned to her side and pulled on a chain. Her assistant popped in a moment later. The dean asked her assistant to give me even more refreshments.

On the tray in front of me, the small tray of cookies was still mostly full.

Yep, I overpaid.

"Now then." She pulled out a parchment and started to write. "When I talk to your parents, I'll need to prove to them I didn't make this request up." She continued to write for a few minutes, then turned the document around to me. "Please sign this, if that's okay."

Reading it over, it was exactly as we'd discussed. There was one small difference – instead of books, it read *"books, scholarships and other necessities."*

Heat spread across my chest and I fought to keep it from reaching my face. *Crap, just how much am I giving them?*

If I were ever going to back out, this would've been the time. But like I'd said, this was just my monthly allowance. If I was making a mistake, it couldn't be all that bad. As I reached for the offered quill, Xandra said, "Are you sure?"

Thinking on my allowance, I'd received the same amount for the last six months. Three medium and two small black gold per month. Xandra had also assumed I wanted to contribute yearly. I crossed it out and wrote "monthly." *Mom and Dad wouldn't give me my allowance if I wasn't meant to use it how I saw fit. They'll probably see this as better than buying something silly like candy, or some random house.* I signed it and pushed it back to her. I wondered, idly, *Just how much candy could I buy with one of these dingy coins?*

Xandra's eyes widened for a moment.

She must have noticed the change I made to the contract on how often I would provide a continued contribution.

She composed herself, and said briskly, "If your parents approve this contract, I'll immediately order the books, for both divisions in every class, in all grades."

Oh. It hadn't occurred to me that the Martial division would need books, or that my offer would extend to classes beyond my own. I didn't really have a reason to object.

She smiled. "With your help, we'll also be able to offer scholarships to less fortunate students. There are some commoners and low-nobles that could definitely benefit from this."

I smiled knowing that it would help those who were less fortunate. "Of course. Can you promise me though that the balance between the two divisions won't become lopsided again?"

The medium black gold coin was missing from the table. *So all it took to buy supplies for the* entire *school with scholarships to boot, was a single coin. When did she swipe it?*

Pocketing the two small black gold coins I said, "A condition of the continued funds would be that a lion's share of it goes towards the Civilian division."

Xandra gave me a wolfish grin. "It would be my pleasure." She began to write a letter, I'd assumed to my parents. As I grabbed another cookie, she said,

"Donovan will hate this," and an even quieter, "but I love it."

Please don't drag me into your personal squabbles. Watching her write with what could only be described as a quietly fierce joy, I wondered uneasily, *What have I set in motion?*

CHAPTER SIX
DREAMSCAPE

Septaday, Lokandae 21st, 1736
[July 21st, 2030]

EMERSON ONCE WROTE, "In dreams we are true poets; we create the persons of the drama…" It was a quote that resonated with me as a child, and carried over with me into my new life on Anfang. I thought of it again when I somehow found myself back in a restaurant on Earth.

Holding a glass of red wine, I admired it for a moment. *From the smell, to the taste, everything is as I remember it.* My last boyfriend had taken me to this restaurant, and the wine, specifically, was exquisite with a fruity kick in your nose, and a bit of an aftertaste. We may have oversold our ages a bit. I assume it was due to my height, but I was never carded when I dressed up, and I made sure that I never got so drunk that they'd question my true age.

"Did I get it right?" a familiar female voice said.

To my right side was Trish. I was certain she wasn't sitting there a moment ago.

Damn dream logic.

"It may be a dream, but that doesn't mean it's pointless," Trish said with a smile.

In the first dream I had with her, we'd kissed. A flush fell over my face. "N-nice to see you again."

Her face mirrored mine. It was rare to see Trish blush, but it was kind of nice.

"Is this dream different, somehow?" I wondered. "It's almost like you're really here now. Before, it just felt like a more normal dream, a static drama replayed over and over."

Her blush deepened. "The same unchanging dream you repeated, what was it…" She counted on her fingers up to four before playfully saying, "thirty two times?"

Heat rushed up my collar and through my ears. *Gods, she had counted.*

"Of course I counted. While I didn't have any control, I–" she paused, "felt it every time."

Letting my head bump the tabletop, I crossed my arms around my face.

When I brought up my head, I was sitting up in bed in my bedroom at Maaka, wide awake. No wine, no restaurant, and no Trish. Letting myself fall back into bed I thought, *Damn it.*

Later in the day Portia asked, "Are you okay?"

"Yeah, why?"

"You've yawned at least," she yawned herself, "twenty times." Shaking her head she added, "Those are so contagious." She glanced at the bag at her side. Though our eyes met for a moment, she seemed to be avoiding mine again.

I thought we'd moved past the whole avoiding-my-gaze thing. Is she hiding something in there? That's the third time she's done that. A present for Max perhaps?

Our teacher stopped to speak with someone at our door. Once she returned to the front of the class, she closed her own book. "We seem to have a delivery."

Gesturing toward the side of the class, the person from earlier entered holding a rope that seemed to contain several strips of cloth on it.

"One of our school's sponsors," she said, and held her hand out toward me. "Anessa Carlyle, has generously provided everyone in this room with their own condensing ribbon and new textbooks."

Our guest then brought in another condensing ribbon from the hall and handed it to the teacher. It contained enough copies of the class materials for everyone, and then some.

For the students that take this class at other times, perhaps?

"Now everyone, please thank our sponsor."

Damn it. Instead of being proud at that moment, I was deeply embarrassed that I hadn't thought to ask Xandra to keep it anonymous. I certainly didn't do it for the recognition. Schools are about learning, and books are a must.

"Thank you Anessa!" my classmates said in tandem. If any of them resented the gift, they hid it well.

One by one they each received their ribbon and textbook. Portia sat hers on her desk and took the textbook out of the ribbon. Her name was embroidered along the edge of the cloth.

On my other side, Max's had his full name.

Do commoners not have last names?

Our teacher took a few minutes to hand out the remaining books and ribbons. Each student gleefully signed their name on the back of their book.

In this downtime, I muttered to Portia, "I wasn't expecting everyone to publicly thank me."

"Why? This is a great gift to all of the students."

I nodded. "Yes. But imagine it were you having everyone in the classroom repeat 'thank you' like it's a ritual." With a sigh I continued, "It's uncomfortable to be called out like that."

With that said, my shoulders were a little lighter. As the students passed, each gave me a smile. True, for a few the smiles didn't reach their eyes or were a bit stiff. Their smiles would drop as they turned away. But the rest were broad, and some even affected their eyebrows.

While I was distracted Portia shuffled to my side, and placed something small on my desk.

"Happy birthday," she whispered.

It was a wooden bangle with Eloria's hierogram of a hammer at the center with what I assumed were various crafting tools spread out from the center. Running my finger over its surface I could tell that whoever had carved it had taken the time to smooth the crevices out. There wasn't a single rough or sharp edge on it. *That should make it easy to clean.*

"This is so pretty, Portia."

"I thought you might like it. Though it did take a few attempts to get the images right."

I gasped, and said in a loud whisper, "You *made* this?!"

"Yes, I hope it's to your liking." She shook her head. "I don't know if it would stand up to Eloria's standards, but it's the best I can do."

My stomach sank at what I had to say next. "This is very well done, but…"

"But?"

"I can't accept it directly. Anything people give me needs to go through my Lady's maid, Sarah." Though I wasn't permitted to give her a full nod, I did lower my eyes as an apology. "I hope you'll understand. I'm beholden to a lot of rules myself. None of which I put in place."

Portia's face fell, but she took the bracelet from my hand and put it back into the sack she carried with her for classes.

Before she could shuffle out of her chair, since the class was over, I said, "Please. Take it to Sarah. I really do like it."

▼ ▼ ▼

"Thanks sissy," Oliver said, and nearly crushed me with a bear hug, as our small get-together ended for our sixth birthday.

Wheezing and patting his back, I squeaked out, "You're welcome, Oliver." Then breathed a sigh of relief as he let me go.

Back in my dorm suite I sat at the desk in my bedroom, balancing the quill on my lip as I thought about the day.

I hope Portia remembers to drop off the bracelet she made for me.

After a few minutes, the lack of sleep from the morning, and activity from our party had me leaning over my desk. I was also playing with how low I could go with the quill before it fell.

When it dropped, I don't know, because a voice met me first. "Welcome back," Trish said.

We were back at dinner again, Earthside.

"Thanks, I guess?"

Looking around in the "restaurant" we were in, we were the only people there. *Guess my imagination only carries me so far.*

"You and I are really meeting, you know," she said, and then grabbed my hand. "Other people are only here if you want them to be, myself excluded."

"Uh huh," I deadpanned.

"Seriously!" She pointed to my other side. "Look, you wanted to see someone special on your birthday, but wouldn't admit it to yourself. And here they are."

Following her suggestion, our waiter approached. Though the waiter was someone I knew well. My Mom on Anfang, Lily Carlyle.

Hoping desperately, I searched for Naia Rovenal, my mother from Earth.

Trish said sadly, "I'm afraid that's one face you won't see here. Sorry."

So you can read my mind, huh?

She winked, I assumed to lighten the mood. "It's a trick shared by charlatans and gods alike."

Wondering I thought, *So which are you?*

"Have you had enough time to look over the menu?" Mom asked, as though waiting tables was a perfectly normal task for high-ranking nobility.

"Not yet, thank you," Trish said.

Mom nodded and walked off. I tried to follow her, but she seemed to disappear into the ether.

Trish asked, "What's it like having a twin, anyway?"

"Bizarre. He's so brilliant, and I'm the one living my second life." I squeezed her hand. "Even without speaking, he always seems to know what I'm thinking..."

We talked about Oliver for a dozen minutes before "Mom" returned for our order.

Though I'd tried to read the menu several times, the text seemed to float, flip, and shift. I assumed it was due to this being a dream.

Trish ordered for us.

I didn't complain.

"And having a fiancé?" she asked finally.

Her question conflicted me, and I pulled my hand away. "Seeing you here, realizing how you felt, makes it so... I don't know, complicated?"

She shrugged. "You know, this new world, Anfang, is quite open-minded." Pulling my hand back to hers, she added, "Be it a boy, or girl, they don't seem to mind. Then there's the fact that monogamy is rare here—"

Reclaiming my hand once again I said, "It's not that simple, Trish. I don't know how I feel about… girls, or a polyamorous lifestyle, or any of what is normal on Anfang."

Nodding she said, "That's fine. Just promise yourself one thing."

"What's that?"

With a smile she said, "If you happen to find someone you love just as much as Gideon, look inside yourself first before you respond. Don't jump to an answer."

"I wasn't raised with those views—"

Her finger touched my lips. "Except you're wrong. If this were Earth, you might be right. But you're not in Kansas anymore."

I smiled at the old idiom. "It isn't as simple as that, but… I will keep your words in mind," I emphasized as my grin fell, "*If* I manage to find someone that meets those criteria." I shook my head. "Though I honestly don't feel that is likely right now."

Trish smiled. "Come on. You *are* only six years old." Before I could correct her to say I was closer to twenty-five, due to my life on Earth she said, "You're in a weird spot." She interlocked her fingers and shook her head. "It isn't quite right to add your ages together. Your mental age and your physical one aren't in alignment. If you were really twenty-five you would have an entirely different set of hormones running through you. You don't think about," she gestured with air quotes, "'*that*' when it comes to Gideon."

At her comment I face palmed. "You're right there, and thank the gods for that."

She nodded. "He *is* quite handsome though."

"At least I have what, three to seven years before I need to worry about it?"

With a crooked smile she said, "Sure."

"I don't like that smile," I said.

"I'm messing with you." After a pause she added with an even deeper grin, "Maybe."

Glaring at her I huffed.

She continued, "Then there's Eloria."

Trish's way of phrasing it made me groan. I said, "Yes, Eloria. To be honest, she scares the hell out of me."

Trish nodded. "She should. Seeing as she is a goddess of death and all, I mean."

"Yeah, I read a book called the Accounts of the Day of Death." Even though this was a dream, I spoke in a hushed tone. Who knew if the gods could see us, after all? "About two thousand years ago, she basically murdered millions. I've lost a lot of sleep over it."

"Yeah, it's horrifying. You'll need to regularly remind people that you're connected with her lighter side." Trish smiled at me. Our eyes met. "This is nice, you know?"

"What?"

"Being able to finally talk to you. It's the first time I've been able to do so freely."

She's talking about this like she's really here.

"Did you know it's time to go to bed?" she said.

"What?" My mind drifted toward less pure thoughts because of our closeness. In my dream, I wasn't six years old.

"Anessa," Sarah called.

Lifting my head from my desk I said, "Whuh?"

"You fell asleep at your desk. Perhaps you should go to bed?"

Yawning I covered my mouth. "Yeah… perhaps you're right."

The abruptness of the shift gave me mental whiplash. *My situation with Trish is very strange.* Then I thought about her parting words. Sarah's voice must have influenced the tail end of my dream. *Yeah, I shouldn't think about Trish like* that. *Too awkward!*

As Sarah helped dress me in my night-clothes, I asked, "What do you know about the wheel of reincarnation?"

She arched an eyebrow at my question. "Not a lot. It's a tale no one I know of has been able to confirm." Pulling my nightgown over my head she added, "Why, did it come up in one of your classes?"

"Something like that, yeah," I lied with a shaky laugh. "What is [heaven], and the Nether, anyway?" When I thought the word *hell* it translated as Nether, but heaven came out in English, with no Estar equivalent. *Odd. Is there no such thing here?*

"I'm not sure what that first thing you said is, but the Nether is said to be a place for the vilest people, the first step in reincarnation for evil spirits. Once their souls are stripped of their memories they enter the wheel of reincarnation, just like everyone else would. Good souls don't go through that punishment, but their memories are still washed away with each new life."

"That sounds like what I learned." Biting my lower lip I added, "What brought it up is I had a dream just now. The person in it most certainly shouldn't have been there."

Sarah pulled back the covers for me. "Anfang works in mysterious ways sometimes. I've read that sometimes spirits find others before they enter the wheel of reincarnation because they have a message for the living."

Her words concerned me. *If Trish is a spirit, wouldn't that mean she's… dead?*

CHAPTER SEVEN
RIVALS

Finday, Lokandae 23rd, 1736
[July 26th, 2030]

WHEN I TURNED two years old, I hit a milestone that was known as "surviving the first year." Sounds odd to hit it at the age of two, but Anfang's orbital period is twice the length of a year by the universal Standard.

On that birthday, I also encountered a particularly unpleasant pair of boys: Rhis and Wyn Blackwood. Wyn was six and Rhis was four. I stood up to him to protect Fan Mul, my mother's Lady's maid at the time. After that, I swore the younger boy had a crush on me. It was then uncomfortably awkward when he formally presented me with one of my presents that same day.

Worse? My stepmother Julilah was married to their father, in addition to being married to mine. On that same birthday, she sprang an unwanted Genesis test on me so she could declare me as ineligible for inheriting anything under the Carlyle name.

What a fun birthday that was.

Meeting new enemies and enduring awkward situations. The memory of that birthday surfaced because one of those unpleasant boys was in sight. I hadn't seen him since, and I was plenty happy with that.

"Why does *he* have to be here?" I asked Sarah crossly.

She looked around and said, "Who?"

"The boy headed our way, about a block back. I know he's noticed me because he's looking right at me."

It was another day off classes, so Sarah and I were exploring the town of Ersta beneath the looming towers and turrets of the Maaka Institute. *Why the hell did Rhis come to Maaka of all places. It's thousands of miles away from his home!* I'd hoped to do some light shopping that day, though I was mostly intent on just browsing shops' wares.

"Anessa!" Rhis said, in a holier-than-thou tone. "At my latest Awakening Ceremony I was graciously granted access to the element of fire, just like Wyn."

Awakening Ceremonies take place at a church. Each child approaches the "spot of awakening" and reaches out to a god or goddess that they create a Divine Link with. Most don't connect with any god. Connecting with the divine grants you a chance to awaken as a cultivator, but it is no guarantee. I was "lucky" to meet Eloria at my first such ceremony.

Yay, this idiot gained some fire powers since we last met. Controlling myself, I gave him my best deadpan response, "Good for you, Sir Rhis."

His eye twitched. "Yes, anyway." Holding his hand out, he presented a ball of flame, or maybe a pea of flame would be more accurate. It was a very tiny little sphere.

It actually took me a few seconds to realize he was holding his hand out to show me something. In the light of the day, the flame was barely visible.

"Oh, there *is* something there," I said with surprise. "I was wondering what you were even doing."

He closed his hand into a fist that he shakingly lowered to his side. The boy took a moment to breathe. It seemed my comment had struck home.

Sorry, I guess? I thought, but didn't say it aloud. *There's no way I am giving this boy an inch.*

"You should be glad of my attention, Anessa," he smiled.

"Oh?" I asked and crossed my arms.

"You should offer yourself to become my first wife, as the position will surely fill soon."

His comment made me wish I had a second set of arms to cross. "Is that so," I said slowly, so he could get the hint that I wasn't pleased.

But Rhis, ever dense, just nodded. "It is. I will have many wives," he winked and gestured with his hand toward me, "but you would be my favorite."

His move toward me caused me to take an involuntary step back. *Gods, what simpfest did he come from?* The fact that he was only *eight* years old and had this level of focus on me was a bit unnerving. The fact that he was posturing on top of it would even be funny if I were watching a cheesy drama. But experiencing this in person? It was nauseating.

"What about the Choosing from your Awakening Ceremony?" I asked. "Wasn't there someone there?"

His shoulders slumped. "Alas, there was no one there I shared a Soular Kinship with."

"Damn, what a shame," I said flatly before I caught myself.

Surprisingly, Sarah didn't even cough to hint at my indiscretion.

Perhaps she's not suffering this fool gladly either.

"It is," Rhis agreed. "Yet it is also fortunate, as it leaves the prime spot open." He reached forward and grabbed for my hand, which I dodged. "Surely you feel something when you look into my eyes?"

I said, "Yep. Discomfort and a bit of loathing."

That time Sarah coughed, and when I looked at her she mouthed, "*Inappropriate.*"

The boy's unwanted attention irked me too much to care about being inappropriate. *I'm done with this. People like him need clarity.* Taking a step forward into his personal space, he backed off and I said, "Let me be clear, Sir Rhis, Prince of the Blackwood Kingdom." Holding up fingers to make my point I continued, "I won't be your first wife, second wife, or any wife," I waved at him dismissively. "Under any circumstances."

As I spoke his face became redder, and redder. When I finished he was lightly shaking. He took his glove and, somewhat to my surprise, smacked me in the face across my cheek with it. His romantic game clearly needed work if *this* was his approach.

"I challenge you to a duel." He threw his glove down. "If I win, you marry me. If you win—"

Before he could set the terms, I talked over him, "You leave me alone for the entire year."

Though I wanted to tell him to leave me alone forever, I wasn't sure I could make that stick. I was, however, hopeful that he might grow up in a year.

He'd backed up and waited against the side of a shop nearby.

It gave me a moment to consult with Sarah. "Is it typical for boys to challenge girls to a duel for their hand in marriage? Seems a bit combative to me."

She shook her head but sighed and said, "You can't really refuse his challenge though, since you set a term in it."

Damn it.

She moved closer and whispered. "However, even if you lose, you may not end up having to marry him. The distance between your noble ranks is vast. As an Imperial Princess and Imperial High Duchess, you're an entire caste above him, just as far above him as he is above commoners."

"Yeah," I said. Thinking about it made my blood boil. "But I get the feeling he would treat commoners worse than I'm treating him."

"True..." Her voice trailed off as though she were thinking. "Oh my. Don't discount the possibility of marriage after all."

At her comment my eyes snapped to her. "What? Why?"

"We were given a dossier on Julilah and her second husband's dealings. If my memory serves me right, they have some connections with the Tanis Region."

Slumping a little I said, "Let me guess." With an exhale I added, "Important connections?"

Sarah nodded.

Damn it. What did I get myself into? Straightening out I thought, *Doesn't matter. I'd do the same thing again. That boy's behavior is just plain odd. I wouldn't be able to live with myself if I gave into such clear coercion.* A chill ran down my side as I visualized getting married to him when I was older. *Oh gods, that's scary.*

My mood darkened as Wyn, Rhis's brother, exited the store Rhis was leaning against. The boys exchanged words and Wyn's gaze turned my way. Their conversation was animated. Wyn put Rhis in a headlock, giving him a noogie, before releasing him and heading in my direction.

Great. Here comes simp plus.

"Rhis tells me you challenged him to a duel?" the older boy asked. Though Wyn was only ten years old, and the last time we met, he was rather wimpy, his new stance and movements spoke volumes about the progress he'd made.

He's not the same kid that Oliver walloped with ease. A smirk spread across my face on its own. *Not that it would change anything. Oliver's a monster.* Looking Wyn in the eyes I said, "For the record, Rhis challenged me."

Wyn nodded. With his hands on his hips he paced around me. "I see."

His confidence and stance alarmed me. *Damn what has he been doing during the past four years? I haven't been given much training, but what little I know is telling me that if I entered his personal space like I did with Rhis, he'd knock me flat.*

CRISTOPH A. T. 107

When he reached Sarah he took a few steps back and walked around her, much less confidently than he had with me. I found that very odd indeed.

What, is Sarah some kind of battle maid? Shrugging my thought off, *No this isn't some Shōnen Japanese animation.* A few seconds of my time was wasted on playing that thought through.

Then Wyn reminded me he was there when another glove smacked my cheek, enough that it stung. "I also challenge you to a duel, with the same conditions," he said with a leer.

What the Nether is wrong with these two?

"Thank you Wyn," Rhis said.

The older boy turned to his brother. "What are you talking about?" His eyebrows rose in recognition. "Right. You misunderstand. If I land the finishing blow, she'll be *my* wife."

Rhis's face fell, though he did not object.

"I suppose since you were there, you could be her second husband." A flicker of violet entered his eyes, and left just as quickly. "Don't worry Rhis, I'll save enough for you."

Wyn's subtext was not lost on me. Though he could knock me flat in an instant, I no longer cared.

"I don't know where you learned such vulgarity from, but I am not amused." Placing my finger in the center of his chest, I growled, "You'd best watch your mouth with me, or I'll see to it you wash your necks." The words came out of me in the heat of the moment. A moment later the gravity of what I'd said hit me. The message being I'd see to it they'd be beheaded.

Why the hell did I just say that!?

I didn't really know. But looking at their shocked expressions of loathing and alarm, I couldn't help but grin in a moment of satisfaction.

CHAPTER EIGHT
PREPARATION

SARAH WOKE ME at first six the next morning. Mind you, I usually woke at first ten, so this wasn't a welcome event.

Pulling my pillow back over my head I said, "Five more minutes."

"We talked about this, Anessa. You have to prepare for your duels, remember?"

A groan slipped out and I sat up in bed. The pain in my posterior forced me to stand. "I'm still mad at you."

"And I said I was sorry. Her Imperial High Grace, Lily Carlyle, authorized me to use light punishment as needed if you crossed the line." She helped me into my training outfit. "And you did, so I did."

"How was *that* a light swat though?" I asked. "It made a crack so loud that it drew the attention of three other maids."

Sarah began to wrap my fists up to the middle of my forearm. "Please drop it here," she tied the wrap off and started on the other hand. "That wasn't intentional, but it was necessary to underscore how bad it was to threaten someone like a prince. Even though you outrank him—no, *especially* because you outrank him, comments like that should not be taken lightly."

I looked away. "I know, I don't even know why I said it."

"If the wrong person had heard that, there would be a rumor that those two boys' death certificates had all but been signed." Having finished with my other hand, she moved back into my view, looking me in the eyes. "No matter what you've told them, many students still believe you resonated with Eloria, the Goddess of Death, not Eloria the high goddess of craft."

Tears bit at the corners of my eyes. *It's been hard enough getting Portia to talk to me. It's taken months but some of the other students in my classes are finally comfortable talking around me.* Shaking my head I thought, *I don't want it to go back to how it was when I first started classes.*

Sarah handed me a card with 3-A on it and said, "His Imperial Grace Roland Carlyle has called for Kile to help train you. He is waiting for you in this training arena."

With a nod we both headed there. As usual, the older gentleman was going through his sword motions, but he stopped when I entered. He put away his training sword into his storage ring. "You've gotten yourself into a bit of a pickle, haven't you?"

Putting my fists together I gave him a light bow. "Yes sir."

"Come on up then. Let's talk about these two princely brats." He sat out two training dummies, the ones Oliver trains with and could not damage. Each had one of the boy's names on it. "These two have a leg up on you, being in the martial division. Worse," he patted the dummy marked with Wyn's name, "This boy is a core student. If you're given an option, go against him first." He sat the Rhis dummy to the side. "He's not a concern. His talent is—" Kile shrugged. "Let's just say that if he wants to start kindling with his fire, he could be useful for carrying baggage."

Ouch, I thought, and couldn't help but smile.

"But be cautious of Wyn. If he gets his hands on you, you're toast. He can crush a rock with his bare hands," Kile said and paused to let it sink in. "If he grabs your arm, you can imagine what he'd do."

I nodded. *He'd break my bones.*

"Focus on shin and elbow strikes. When you trained at home before your trip here, your innate skill never triggered. We wouldn't want any accidents." His voice dropped. "Do not strike them with a palm by accident. Even though they are a grave threat to you, if you kill one of them, the consequences would be dire. It might not end with simply paying reparations, and you could find yourself in a worse place than as their wife."

"As a concubine or worse?" I asked.

Kile didn't reply and suddenly seemed to find the sky interesting.

Got it. Worse.

He cleared his throat and moved on. "It's very likely essence that's behind those little pock marks you're making. Your shins and elbows don't have as many Apertures, and those it does have are smaller. So strikes with them are less likely to trigger an accidental use of your power." Pointing to his palm he said, "This is one of the larger apertures on the body. For you, it would be about the size of the holes you make by mistake."

About a quarter in size. Ah.

I held my hand out and looked at both sides, then held it up to the sun filtering in through the windows. There certainly wasn't a hole in my hand.

Kile laughed. "It's not something you can see with your eyes, despite the name. It is more accurate to say there are very tiny tendrils that reach the surface of your hand. You'd need a very good looking glass to see them. Even then, you're likely to miss them." He put two fingers together and brought them to his eye. "A few thousand of them together measure only about the size of a grain of sand."

That makes more sense. Shaking my head, *I'm glad it's not visible, or people with trypophobia would be freaked out by cultivators.*

"If your erasure does trigger somehow on your shin or elbows, I suspect the damage would be minimal, and likely only damage their clothes. But to be on the safe side," Kile said, and tapped his head. "Clear your mind of such worries when you attack. Thinking about it might be all that is needed to activate the ability, and you don't want that." He hit the shoulders on the Wyn dummy making it ring.

I covered my ears at the noise.

"We don't want anyone to die, remember?"

All I could do was nod as my head rang. *Just how strong is Kile? Oliver needed tens of hits to make that kind of racket.*

Tapping the dummy a second time it fell silent. His attention turned to the dummy labeled "Rhis."

"The training you've done so far should be enough to deal with the younger boy."

Pointing to myself I objected, "I haven't received much, and I've never faced a live opponent."

Kile approached me and squatted to my level. Making a fist he tried to hit me but I managed to dodge, although just barely.

"How did you do that?" I asked and tilted my head to the side.

"Do what?" His expression mirrored my own.

I copied his movement, and very unsuccessfully tried to start it fast and end at a crawl. "Whatever you did. It was as though you were adapting to how fast I could move."

"Hmm…" He stood. "I thought so."

"How does that response help?!"

"Whatever you do when you erase things with your fists–" he began.

I nodded, but raised an eyebrow in confusion.

"That's the least curious part of your abilities. You have good eyes."

"What do you mean?"

"When you saw me for the first time, you told Oliver that he couldn't beat me. He's a prodigy in his own right, but he's yet to score a single hit on me. Tell me, do you have a hard time following Oliver's movements when he fights?"

Shaking my head I said, "Not really." Waving my hand dismissively I added, "But that doesn't mean much. I can't even come close to matching *anything* he does."

"True, but you've yet to awaken. To most people, Oliver is just a blur. If you don't mind me asking, how many dantian buds do you have?"

"Seven."

Kile sighed. "Yes, that's how many dantians everyone has the potential to have, but of those which have meridians surrounding them—"

Talking over him since he misunderstood me, I said, "Like I said, seven."

"That's—" he trailed off, slightly taken aback. "You know Oliver only has *three* dantians, right?"

"Yeah, and? That isn't what makes him special though. There are lots of others who have three dantians, right?"

"'Lots' may be too strong a word." Kile exhaled. "We're getting off topic. Rhis will be an easy battle to overcome for you, because he has no martial talent. Frankly, he shouldn't even be in the Marital division. He only has a single dantian, a weak affinity for fire, and little else. As a cultivator, he will barely extend his life beyond that of a mortal." He moved towards the edge of the ring. "Lead him here and," he gestured with his hands, "push him out. That's it."

He makes it sound so simple.

"But he's the easy part. Wyn, by contrast, is a natural. Oliver gave Wyn a tough but valuable lesson four years ago. It left an impression on the boy. Since he lost to Oliver, Wyn has trained every single day. He's a natural body cultivator." He shrugged. "He still pales in comparison to Oliver," he said and narrowed his eyes at me, "but few others can match that boy."

Why did he give me such a weird look?

"What have you been taught about cultivators?" he continued.

Vocalizing while breathing out I said in frustration. "Nothing! I've been taught absolutely nothing."

Kile glanced at Sarah who just shrugged.

"Got it. There are generally three types of cultivators. Elemental, body and balanced. The name for each is generally self-explanatory, but I'll provide a basic rundown."

He held out his hand and created a sphere of water the size of a coconut above it. It was steady as a rock, without a ripple on it. This was a big contrast to when Rhis had showed me his "flame" the day prior, which wavered as though it could go out in a moment.

Does Kile have better resonance and familiarity with water than Rhis has with fire?

Likely both.

"Elemental cultivators favor the elements. They often attack at a distance." He was still several paces from the dummies. Holding his hand and the orb out, it shot off and splashed against one of them, knocking it over.

"Cool," I said before catching myself.

Smiling he took out a steel sword from his storage ring. "Body cultivators reinforce their body with essence." He held out his arm. To my shock, he struck it with the blade.

I jumped at the sound of the blade shattering.

Amazingly, there wasn't even a mark on Kile's arm. He continued as though it were any other day. "The further they go the more stout they become. In the early stages, it takes mental focus to maintain such rigidity, with practice, the essence sinks in, and your skin, bones, muscles, ligaments acclimate to the essence as the new normal."

"Did that hurt?" I asked.

"It did not, but I appreciate the concern." Holding out his hand, a layer of mist surrounded it. Looking closer, it was a result of his hand being covered in ice. "Balanced cultivators, such as myself, are capable of both."

Curiosity nagged at me, and I asked, "Is Oliver a balanced cultivator?"

Kile shook his head. "He leans more towards being a body cultivator. Though your brother has good resonance, he doesn't have the mind for it. That's not inherently a bad thing, though. If his talent for the body were less extraordinary, he would definitely be a balanced cultivator." He smiled. "You're so eager to learn, I get off track easily. Certainly a change of pace from your brother. Let's get back to Wyn."

Taking out a shield from his storage space he sat it on "Wyn's" arm. "From what I have been able to gather about the boy, he favors shield bashes. Though it's uncommon, he uses a medium tower shield."

Looking the shield over, it was more than half my height. "Wouldn't it be impractical to use this for bashes?" I thought, *The surface area would lessen the damage a blow could do.*

Kile answered by putting his hand on my back and lifting me by my outfit, as if I were a kitten.

Then he threw me across the ring.

To my surprise, I landed on my feet.

"Good," he said, not surprised at all, and gestured for me to return.

Complying, I complained, "What was that for? I know you're here to train me, but—"

"Wyn could do much the same, also with one hand." He patted the shield on "Wyn's" arm. "You're to attack the shield, just don't put too much aggression into it. Remember what happened at Her Royal Majesty Fleure's estate."

I thought back to the incident he referred to. When I was a little over a year old, my powers had erupted uncontrollably and I'd accidentally erased a meter-sized sphere at her estate, eating away even the foundation on that spot. *Right. If something like that happened to him...* I flailed my hands to dismiss the sight.

Identifying what remains of him would be difficult. I shook my head. *It would also ruin my life.*

CHAPTER NINE
DUEL DILEMMAS

OVER THE NEXT few days, whenever I wasn't eating, sleeping or learning, I was training. My muscles ached with even the slightest movement, but at least the classes were interesting.

Portia's eyebrows knitted together as she turned to me. "Are you feeling unwell?"

"I'm okay," I winced. "Just sore."

"I heard about your duel," she said cautiously.

Deflating onto my desktop I said, "Yeah, those two idiots."

"If I were you, I'd be scared."

"I am, somewhat."

"Why did you choose a tandem, anyway?"

Tilting my head to the side I asked, "Tandem?"

"You know…" She held up one finger on one hand, and two on the other. "Going up against both of them at once?"

Waving my hand I said, "Must be some mistake. That's not what I remember. I just hope I have a choice on which of the two I face first."

Portia leaned in and whispered, "Rumor is *you* challenged *them* to a tandem duel. If that's true, you'll face both of them at the same time!"

Crap. I asked, "Are you certain about that?"

She nodded. "I've heard it from at least three people so far. They're saying you threatened the boys and if they didn't agree to the duel you'd have them…" her voice once again fell to a whisper, "executed."

Gods damn it. Heat roiled in my gut and I balled my hands into fists before releasing them. "Well, those two are lying," I said through my teeth.

The teacher's aid rang a low-pitched bell, signaling our class was over.

"Lunch? I'll explain it in more detail."

Over our meal I explained the out-of-line comments the boys threw my way and Portia's mouth dropped open.

I might have left out the "washing their necks" part, at least until Portia commented, "They could get in a lot of trouble for saying that you threatened their lives when you didn't."

Turning away I scratched my cheek. "Well... about that."

She said in a gasp, "You didn't!"

"I'm not sure why I said that," I whispered, "but those guys are the worst. I know that I was livid." Shaking my head I added, "I've never said anything like that before in my life."

"You won't actually have them k—"

"No!" I said a bit loudly drawing a few eyes to us.

Since Portia was disquieted by the decor in my dorm suite, I'd decided it best to eat in the common dining hall. Normally that wasn't a problem. At least, not when I wasn't making loud, distracting exclamations.

I mouthed "Sorry" to those around us and I ducked my head for a moment until everyone seemed to forget we existed.

"I was just pissed off that Wyn talked about me like an object or a prize to be won." Grabbing the tablecloth I fumed. "I'd rather die than be someone's plaything."

She sat in silence for a moment and then covered my hand with hers. "Beyond being smart, you're a lot more mature than I could have hoped to be at your age." Squeezing my hand she smiled and continued, "Please beat the snot out of them."

I snorted. "Trust me, I will."

As our classes ended for the day, I caught sight of Gideon heading towards his dormitory. Despite my gloomy mood I skipped a beat towards him before catching myself.

"Gideon!" I called.

"Hey," he said and turned to me. "I heard about your duel." He placed his hand behind my back as if to guide me, without actually touching my back. "Are you okay?" We changed directions, heading toward my dorm suite.

Craning my neck up at him, since he'd grown to be nearly six feet in height and I wasn't even three and a half, I smiled. "I'm fine. But you know…"

As I explained what the two boys said and how I was roped into the duel, the smile on his face dropped and turned into a scowl.

I jumped inwardly at the knowledge that he was concerned for me, and curious to know how Gideon's own martial studies were going, I asked, "Could you beat Wyn?"

Gideon clenched his jaw. Then he sighed and shook his head. "If I were only stronger," he said in frustration.

Taking a step closer to him I said, "Don't worry, I'm not that strong yet, but if I manage to get there, I'll protect you."

His smile returned and he bowed toward me as we walked. "My princess in shining armor."

A giggle escaped me at the mental image of such a role reversal. "I could even carry you like Oliver did the other day."

His steps faltered and he squeaked out with a laugh of his own, "Please don't."

Pretending to be devastated I hung my shoulders. "Yeah, you're so much taller than me, your legs would drag in the grass."

"So true," he said looking up into the sky at Fandar, the blue moon of hope, barely visible now as a highlight in the sky.

"Hey!" I said once I processed what he'd said. I gave chase as he bolted ahead a few steps with a short chuckle.

A courier passed me as we approached the door to my dorm suite. *Mail! Did we get a letter from Mom or Dad?*

Gideon joined me inside for a moment, as it seemed he was equally curious.

"Sarah, did we get a letter?" I asked without preamble as I sat my backpack down.

"No. That item you asked for the other day arrived."

Realizing Gideon was still here, I froze mid-step and my cheeks heated up. "T-that item, huh?" I said with a laugh.

"Yes, would you like to see it?"

"Sure, but first," I said and turned to Gideon. "Turn around for a moment, okay?"

Once he complied, I walked over to Sarah and picked up the item I'd ordered out of its case. The ears were a reddish brown with white tufts of fur sticking out of the canal. I admired the craftsmanship as I rubbed it between my fingers and thumb. *These are like real cat ears. I'm surprised there's even a market for this here.*

Taking half of it out and putting it on my head, I said to him, "You can look now."

When he turned toward me, I said, "What do you think, nya?" Then held both hands near my face and balanced on one foot.

He said nothing but covered his mouth.

It became unbearably hot around my neck and shoulders as I stood there in silence. *I feel so stupid! I clearly watched too much anime back on Earth. Why did I say "nya?"* When Oliver told me we had a chance of having cat-kin traits, I had to know what I would look like with such ears. At Gideon's quiet observation I thought, *I'm glad I left the tail belt in the case!*

He removed his hand to reveal a broad smile.

I wanted to cover my face in shame, but he approached me and patted my head, which made my thoughts fuzzy. *Why am I so impelled to lean into these head pats?*

"You're too cute, little kitten," he said.

Gideon didn't draw my torment out any longer and took my hand into his, bidding me farewell for the day.

When the door closed I collapsed into the closest chair and covered my face. "That was so embarrassing!"

"What was," Sarah asked, then teasingly added, "Nya?"

"Ha-ha," I said and crossed my arms. "He took forever to react." Hiding my face again in my hands I added, "I did it in the spur of the moment."

She replied in a soft tone, "Sorry for poking fun. If it helps, he wasn't actually silent for more than two seconds."

"He wasn't?" I asked, and thought, *It felt like an eternity had passed.* After my heart rate calmed, I said, "Right! By the way, those two idiot boys lied about the challenge and made my duels into a single tandem duel. Now, apparently, I have to fight them both at once!"

Sarah's eyebrows shot up and she covered her mouth. "Oh dear. And Kile was summoned away this morning. He won't be back anytime soon to help. But he did say you already have everything you needed."

"Hmm… Maybe." I said, then asked, "That was before those idiots made it a tandem duel. Do you think my allowance would be enough to hire two people to spar against? We could take precautions of—"

"I'll make the arrangements right away," she said, and spoke with one of the other maids to take her place for a few hours.

▼ ▼ ▼

Standing in front of me the next morning in the room housing an arena were four stout young men. They all had an inch or two on the Blackwoods.

"Anessa, I've prepared two pairs of training partners," Sarah said. "One pair," she gestured toward her left, "is comparable to the Blackwood brothers." Motioning toward her right she added, "The other pair, is at Wyn's level. If you are overwhelmed, they will not hurt you." She glared at them. "Right?"

They affirmed, "Correct, ma'am."

What are they, soldiers? Though she said they were different, I couldn't spot any in the demeanor from either pair.

To my eyes it's like they're both equal to one another. I shook my head. *I'm not a combatant. Trust Sarah.* I said, "Let's go with the two on your left, please."

The unselected pair bowed with their fists together and left the arena.

"Before you begin," she said and pulled some clothing out of her storage ring, "please put on this padded armor."

No one moved, and she turned to the young men and gave them a small bow. "My apologies gentlemen, I was talking to you. Could you also give us your names?"

"Anult is my name. Aren't those a little thick?" he said with a laugh.

The other older looking young man had already picked up his outfit and was putting it on. "This may affect my mobility some. Name's Binault."

"That's okay," Sarah said. "She's a beginner, so you'll be plenty mobile."

Her words, though truthful, earned her a glare from me.

Sarah gave me a weak smile.

I suppose she's only being honest.

"If that's true," Anult said, "why do we need padding at all?"

Sarah's smile reached her eyes. "So that she doesn't kill you."

Binault paused and turned to me briefly before putting on his padded leggings.

They look like umpires without the face masks.

"How can this little squirt kill us?"

Sarah gave a light cough. "Please know you are speaking to Her Imperial High Grace, Anessa Carlyle. It is best to mind your manners."

Anult put his hands up. "Got it. She can have me executed. But I'm not sure how that applies to the padding." His eyes tracked something unseen in the air and he chopped at it. "Is this padding some form of Imperial decree?"

Oh, he's trying to be funny?

Binault shook his head. "Don't be an idiot, brother. You read the contract. There's obviously something more to her than we can see."

Contract? I'll ask Sarah later. Being straight with people like Anult is generally best. I said, "I can damage, what was it Sarah? Third Grade High Steel?"

"High Grade Third Rank Steel," she corrected.

"Yes, that."

The younger man walked around me, much like Wyn had, which didn't sit well with me.

"Please don't strut like that," I said in a level tone.

"Why not?"

"It reminds me of the person that I need this training for in the first place." I deepened my voice, and said, "I don't like him."

He nodded and smiled. "Good. Then use that in your training."

Bringing my fists together I said, "With pleasure."

Before we entered the arena Sarah said, "Do mind your fists, boys. We wouldn't want to hurt her too much."

"Won't that affect the quality of my training?" I asked.

"It will," Anult agreed. "We promise not to cripple her or bruise her pretty little face." He turned to Sarah. "Will that work?"

She crossed her arms, then nodded.

"Ready girlie?" Anult said with a small grin.

Exhaling through my nose I said, "Absolutely."

They stood near one another about ten paces away from me.

Sarah held up her hand and said, "Begin," while thrusting her hand down.

I rushed forward toward the pair, who were doing the same.

They're matching their speed to mine. Nice.

It took half a second for us to meet.

Anult was already primed to hit me in the sternum.

Though it was just by the skin of my teeth that I managed to avoid him.

Then Binault reminded me he was there as he hit me in the back, staggering me.

Right, two people. Crap. You'd think I'd remember something this basic.

But you'd also be wrong. This was my first official bout against *anyone*.

One of them swept my feet from beneath me.

In nothing flat Anult had straddled my midsection, pinning me in place. He started to hammer me with blows.

It was all I could do to block him with my forearms.

Binault sat above me and flicked my forehead.

"Stop!" Sarah called out. "This round goes to the Leon brothers."

Rubbing my arms I said, "That stings." After struggling to my feet, I gave them a light bow for the match. "Thanks for matching my speed."

Anult shook his head. "Girl," he pointed to the ground where I was lying a moment ago, "You matched *our* speeds."

Along a small section was a mini divot of broken and cracked tiles in a thin line in the shape of my spine. They'd shattered when Anult hammered my arms with blows.

Seriously?

The younger man stood in a wide stance before me. "To effectively adjust your training, I need to know what I'm working with." He smacked his padded chest with his palm. "Hit me."

I sighed. "I'm not going to hit you for no reason."

Before we could continue arguing, someone knocked on the door and Sarah answered it. She gasped a moment later.

One of the other maids from my dorm suite entered and bowed, whispering something to Sarah. Her face became expressionless.

Sarah said, "Anessa. Someone attacked Gideon."

My breathing hitched and everything slowed. *Is he okay?*

Anult who apparently could not read the room chuckled, and said, "What, did your little boyfriend get in a fight he couldn't han—"

Snapping my eyes to the idiot I stomped my feet onto the floor to give myself a good footing.

"You want me to hit you?" I yelled. "Fine! I'll hit you!"

I nearly hit him full-force with my fist, only remembering at the last moment to redirect and use my elbow. As I did so, his eyes widened in slow motion.

Then he was gone.

A loud crash bellowed out in an explosion as he hit the wall in front of me, five meters away.

He blasted through it.

Dust flooded in from the door the maid entered from. She started to cough.

Shit. I didn't kill him did I?

His weak and disoriented voice quickly put my mind at ease. "I'm okay."

The adrenaline started to fade at his words, making me weak in the knees. I fell onto my rear onto the tile. My feet were rooted in place, embedded in the floor at least six inches. A large series of fissures rent the area behind my calves.

The damage to the arena, the wall, and Anult faded, and I thought, *I hope you're okay Gideon.*

CHAPTER TEN
GIDEON AND THE FUTURE

A FAMILIAR STUBBORN boy stood in my way at the Middling's Cloister. His wide face and squat frame made the perfect doorstop.

"I'm here to see Gideon Varn," I said.

He narrowed his eyes at me. "I remember you." He motioned toward Sarah. "Are you going to have your maid yell outside the windows again?"

"No, I'm just going inside."

Holding up his hand he said, "No girls. We went through this, remember?" He sighed. "Do I need to go get Gideon?"

"He was attacked." Breathing in and exhaling slowly I said in a level tone. "You'll either let me in," I said, and made a fist for him to see. "Or I'll let myself in." In my frenzy I had an inkling that I was breaking whole pages of etiquette here, but didn't bother checking Sarah's reaction. *She'll tell me later what I did wrong.*

The young guard took a step back, then looked to both sides. He deflated and whispered, "This never happened." While keeping a watchful eye, he stepped aside and let us pass.

As we walked down the halls I looked to Sarah to help me find the way.

"Follow me, and do remember," she said after we moved far enough away that the boy couldn't hear us. "Violence shouldn't be your first option, okay?"

When I didn't respond she stood still and repeated herself.

"Okay," I said and hung my head. "Sorry. I'm just worried about Gideon."

She nodded. "As long as you understand." Presenting a silver coin to me she added, "There are often many other ways you can get what you want." A flicker of black light accompanied her storing the coin. "Bribery is not a great choice, either. But you should definitely consider it *before* violence."

We moved forward.

"Know what devices you have at your disposal. Think of the consequences of your actions, not just for yourself, but your family." She turned to wink at me. "Those were a few words from Her Imperial High Grace, Lily."

I tentatively asked, "You told her about the comments I made to Rhis and Wyn, didn't you?"

"Yes." She paused. "To be clear, lashing out in anger is rarely, if ever, the correct choice." She was silent for a minute as we moved to the second floor. "That includes both battle and training."

Wincing at her words I thought, *She's telling me I messed up big time in the arena.* I said in a defeated voice, "Do you think Anult will still help train me?"

"We're paying him quite a lot, and his injuries were minor, thanks to the padded armor." She smiled at me before turning toward a door and saying, "So, yes."

At first glance, Gideon looked to be no worse for wear. Then I approached him, and saw a mosaic of purple beneath the sheet over his chest.

"Hey little kitten," he said and winced as he smiled.

"Hey yourself."

Reaching for the sheet he put his hand up. His entire arm past his wrist was a purple-black mess. "Please don't look."

My eyes watered seeing the bruises all over his arm. What was visible through the sheet said it was no different over his chest and stomach.

A harsh tone erupted from my throat. "Who did this?!"

"I didn't get a good look at them. There were two, of that I'm certain. I only saw them from the back. They were definitely students." He moved in his bed and groaned.

He's in a lot *of pain.* Crossing my arms I said, "It had to be the Blackwood brothers."

Sarah coughed. "Now, now. One cannot go around making baseless accusations."

"Baseless!" I shouted. "Who else is there?"

Gideon's gentle voice replied, "Hey now. You're a popular girl. Whoever it was didn't want me near you."

Pursing my lips I asked, "What do you mean?"

"They said I needed to stay away from you, and to break off my engagement." He shook his head. "One of them asked why they didn't attack you, but I didn't hear everything they said, I was a bit dizzy at the time." Moving his hand to the back of his head, he said, "They scored their first hit here." He moved his hand to his chin. "They did mention something about sanctions, I think?"

What?

Sarah stepped into the conversation. "If, and this is speculation so do not act on it, the attackers really were the Blackwood brothers, they might have feared attacking you, Anessa, outside of your duel because it would result in sanctions against the Blackwood Kingdom. Attacking an Imperial Noble, which is you in this case, is a grave offense."

Holy crap. Are those boys actually smarter than I give them credit for?

140 CONNECTIONS

My thoughts went over reasons for them attacking Gideon, but the only reasons I could think of, and Sarah's lecture, boiled down to noble life being full of plotting and strategy.

They avoided me because of the consequences, even though it would've allowed them to win the duel more easily if I were hurt. And if I go into the duel angry, it might be easier to rout me because I'll make stupid mistakes.

I didn't want that kind of lifestyle.

"Sarah," I said finally, "Please don't let me grow up to think like those idiots." Thinking on it I amended my comment, "Those *alleged* idiots."

She curtsied. "It would be my pleasure. I'll help you be rational when needed." Her voice dropped a quarter octave. "And viciously decisive when all else fails."

Taking a step back I thought, *Okay, unexpected.* Looking between the two with me I smiled. *I have nothing to worry about as long as I surround myself with good people.*

"I'm glad you're okay," I said and hugged Gideon.

Sarah coughed, then said, "I think I hear someone calling my name. I'll be back in a few minutes."

I smiled inwardly at the gift of privacy she was offering me.

After she left I said, "I'm sorry."

Gideon blinked. "For what?"

"Not being there."

He winced and smiled. "This isn't your fault."

"I'm angry that I couldn't prevent it though."

Patting my hand he said, "That's just because you care."

"How long will it be before you're healed?" I asked.

"The doctor said a week to a little over a week and a half. I'll be missing a lot of classes."

How long is that again? Nine to fifteen days? It didn't sound long, but I kept forgetting that days were more than twice as long as on Earth. The conversions made my head hurt. *About a month in Earth time.* A light chill hit me and I detached from my problems for a second. *Why am I thinking in Earth time anyway?*

"Anessa," Sarah said.

I'd completely missed her coming back into the room.

"Hm?"

"Are you okay?" Gideon asked. "You've been silent for ten minutes."

I shook my head. "Sorry, just thinking about some things." Hugging myself I thought, *That was scary. I almost lost myself for a moment. What the hell was that?*

She said, "I was able to find out a few things when I stepped out."

"Oh?" I said pushing the dark thoughts to the back of my mind.

"The school's patrol in that area was *conveniently* late in that area of the school grounds." She sighed and rubbed her thumb over her fingers. "Though we are not likely to get a name, we can encourage their memory through other means. I seriously doubt they were actually late, since one of the men responsible for the patrols was bragging to me just yesterday how they're *never* late.

"I'm starting to doubt that the books they keep on that are accurate."

I took Gideon's hand into mine. "How can I make sure he stays safe? What happens the next time they find him conveniently alone?"

Sarah smiled. "Two things. First, he'll have at least two guards after this. Second, there's a soothsayer in Ersta. You could visit them to see how you and Gideon will be doing in the future. It should put your mind at ease."

Her words made me jump up and I said, "When can we go?"

"We can go now, if you'd like." Her eyes turned to Gideon. "Unless you'd like to go tomorrow?"

Before I could ask Gideon what he wanted me to do he said, "Go." He smiled. "I need to get some rest anyway." He leaned in and whispered, "Let me know what you find out?"

Giving him another quick hug I said, "Of course." Sarah managed to be looking the other way while I did so.

"Sarah."

"Yes Lady Anessa?"

Her use of Lady meant there was someone around, even if I couldn't see them. It was okay to drop the honorifics around Gideon, family and my personal guards, but in public, she would not risk doing so if there was a reasonable chance someone else could overhear her.

"Thank you for calming me down. I was being irrational."

"Any time, Lady Anessa."

There's definitely someone who can hear her that's not in the fold.

We worked our way down into Ersta. The guards we had with us would frequently stop us to let someone by, or to make sure we didn't enter a crowd.

From a distance, the town hadn't seemed too big. Walking it proved otherwise.

Alleyways splintered off in every direction. *This town is a labyrinth that I'd definitely get lost in.* But then again, I got lost in my own home frequently. Entering the town from the school, every building was cut from stone. Though as we progressed, the pristine rock morphed and became dirtier and dingier along the alleys. Then the use of stone stopped altogether. I started to get a little uneasy.

Is this area safe?

"We're almost there. I think it's…" Sarah turned the next corner. "Ah, here it is."

Though it was still broad daylight, this alley looked darker than it ought to be. Moving shadows climbed the walls, even under the light of the sun. As we walked, I kept my eyes peeled. *So this is what it means to jump at shadows?*

At the end of the alley was a simple white door trimmed in a pencil-thin line of gold.

One of our guards opened the door for us. Inside, I froze after taking a few steps.

What the Nether?

Along the walls were taxidermied animal heads. Several skulls of the same animals. What unnerved me was the central ram's head above the soothsayer's counter. Behind which was a pentagram.

My muscles tensed, recalling a red-skinned horned monster. But shaking my head I thought, *That would be paganism anyway, not devil worship. The pentagram is upright, not upside down. Besides, this isn't Earth. There hasn't even been the slightest mention of Earthen divinities. This has to be coincidence.*

Sarah whispered to my side, "I wasn't aware she favored such iconography. None of these are tied to the local gods or goddesses of the Westwood Empire."

On the shelves were various curiosities. Shrunken heads, something that looked like tarot cards–though picking one of them up showed that the symbolism was entirely different. Ornate knives, some of which were rusting, or covered in what I'd assumed was long-dried blood. I didn't touch those.

At the counter a scantily-clad woman greeted us. Her outfit looked like a cross between that of a woman in a harem and a Hawaiian fire dancer.

Weird mix.

"Would you like a reading?" she asked. Before I could say anything she added, "You didn't bring anything to the counter, and I had a feeling I'd have a guest today."

It was tempting to roll my eyes at her, but her entire theme was telling the future, so I resisted the urge and nodded.

Sarah stayed out front in the shop.

I followed the soothsayer into the back, into a tiny room barely big enough for the table and two chairs inside. The room had a similar motif to the store proper, though dialed down a notch.

On top of the table was an honest-to-gods crystal ball, and I just about ended my visit there until she said, "My name is madame Vira. The attack on Gideon was most unfortunate, wasn't it?"

Okay. She has my attention. But perhaps she just overheard it from someone?

"Have you been adapting well?" Vira continued.

"To school?" I asked.

Shaking her head she said, "Sorry, you give off the air of an old soul. I meant to Anfang."

Now my skin really prickled. *The hell?*

She held up a hand. "I do not mean to scare you. The past is less clear for me than the future. From your reaction, I'm either dead-on, or way off. That said, your future with Gideon is bright." A smile crept across her face. "You even go so far as to marry."

Knowing we'd marry had me curious. "Do we have any kids?"

She shrugged. "The future after you marry is a bit murky to me."

Narrowing my eyes at her I asked, "You're not even looking into the crystal ball."

She laughed. "Yes, yes." Her hands waved around the ball as she glared in it. No light accompanied the gesture. Stopping she added in what I thought was a mockingly spooky tone, "This crystal is for appearances." Her voice took on a Romanian flair, "This is just a prop. But some people don't take me seriously unless I use it."

It earned her a snort-laugh, until I covered my mouth. I coughed. "Will I inherit the Carlyle mantle, or will my brother?"

Her answer was immediate. "Oliver will."

That suits him. He's got the strength and the destiny to lead. While he's immature now, he'll level out in time. Leaning back, I smiled. "Then what will I inherit?"

She gestured for me to come closer, so I did.

Her next words made my blood run cold.

"It depends on who you kill."

CHAPTER ELEVEN
WINDMILLS AND POCKMARKS

Finday, Jothariae 14th, 1736 [September 5th, 2030]

"GIVE IT UP Lady Anessa," Sarah said a few feet in front of me. "I'm closer in ability to Oliver than you are, so you will not catch me."

I'd woken early to get in some last-minute training. For the first time my Lady's maid had joined me on a morning jog, and I was learning a few new things about my steadfast companion. *How the heck is she so fast!?*

No matter how many times I'd tried, I couldn't repeat my incident with Anult. Not that I was trying to send him through a wall. The next tests were outdoors, and they were exhausting.

"Why do I get so tired so quickly?" I asked, gasping between words.

Sarah slowed enough to jog in place beside me. "Because, Lady Anessa, you have yet to awaken. The boosts to your strength are due to the natural essence you draw in all the time. It has nowhere to go, but does temporarily give you a boost.

"However, since you have no dantians, you don't really store the essence. It just flows through you. It doesn't give your body enough time to acclimate to it, like an awakened cultivator would."

"Since when are you an expert on cultivation?"

She held my gaze for a second before going ahead. "As you near your second awakening, Lady Anessa, and signs point to your awakening, what I'm *allowed* to say has changed."

Got it. Damned scriptures. Up until I turned four, what I was permitted to learn about cultivation was minimal at best. I was told the scriptures' limits were to avoid giving rise to Magicians, but no reason on why they're bad, or what even exactly they are.

"Why can't I hit as hard as I did when Anult made me mad?"

Sarah once again joined my side and whispered. "That was almost certainly a False Burst. They're like Gift Bursts, but not near as strong, and not generally permitted by law. Your Divine Link with Eloria should protect you from the fallout, though."

"Fallout?" I whispered in concern. "From something I did by accident?"

She shook her head, and replied at normal volume, "I cannot say more, Lady Anessa."

So, don't lose my temper. Got it. Thinking on it a moment: it made sense. They would probably isolate or punish people who gained access to far more power than they should have when angry. *Anger doesn't make me the most rational. I'd be dangerous to myself and those around me. Kind of like an unstable tiny Hulk.*

"Will I have to worry about that after I awaken?" I asked Sarah.

She said simply, "No."

I don't think she is going to tell me more than that.

"Thanks for coming," I said to Portia as we walked to Arena 212.

"I'm not leaving you to face those two morons alone," she huffed. "Though, I don't think many other people will show up."

Furrowing my eyebrows, I asked, "Why not?"

Portia sighed. "Who would want to come see a little girl get beaten up?" She shook her head. "They are all convinced that you're going to lose."

"Figures." I thought, *Not that I blame them. It's a fight between two middle schoolers against a grade schooler.* I groaned. *I'd put my money on the older kids, too.* Laughing at myself I amended my thought, *Though by our ages, and not our heights. We're all grade schoolers.*

"Oh, there's the boys. Should we try to catch up?" Her eyes went to my short little legs. "*Can* you catch up?"

"Yes, though…" I exhaled. "I shouldn't. Essence gives me some additional strength, but I tire easily." Making a fist I held it up. "Probably should save it for the match."

She nodded, then took off and hollered for Oliver, Max and Gideon.

They all stopped and waited for me to catch up. Before I got close, I noticed Gideon grab Oliver by his collar.

My brother was bouncing on the balls of his feet when I reached them. "Hi sissy!"

I couldn't help but smile at his enthusiasm.

"Gideon is being a meanie," Oliver said and crossed his arms, turning his head away from my fiancé.

"He wanted to give you a piggyback ride," Gideon explained apologetically.

"Thank you," I said and broadened my smile.

"Anytime, kitten."

Oliver's mouth fell and his face said that I'd betrayed him. "You used to like piggyback rides!"

"I'd hardly call screaming bloody murder at nearly falling off, 'liking them.'"

The others chuckled at my expense.

"Maybe I went overboard once." Oliver snorted and closed his eyes, pouting. "And I'm still mad at him," he pouted, pointing at Gideon.

"We talked about that," I said giving my voice an edge. "If you get beat up, I'll be by your side every day, too."

He opened one eye and grinned before closing it again. "Okay, but if Mina's there, she'll get to feed me apple slices."

Seeing Gideon in pain every day sucked. Oliver's jealousy is sweet. Squeezing him from the side, I said, "I'll even cut them up for her."

After my brother had bolted forward, Portia asked in a whisper, "Kitten?"

"N-never mind that."

"Is that something only he is allowed to call you?" she asked innocently.

We entered the training building. I coughed as my ears burned. "Yes."

"Okay," she smiled. "It is cute, though."

Instead of replying, I grinned at Gideon.

The moment we entered the arena, my brief moment of levity ended. There wasn't a lot of seating for this arena, only one row of bleachers. My small entourage took their seats. Friends of the Blackwoods were also present. The same boys that had surrounded Oliver in a circle four years ago.

I don't know any of their names.

Oliver went over and pestered them trying to get them to talk about their classes, but he gave up after a while since they were all leaning away from him and giving single word responses. They didn't dare act rudely to Oliver, I guessed, but still didn't want to be friendly, either.

It's like Portia said, none of my other classmates showed up.

Wyn and Rhis entered the circular ring the moment they saw me.

Wanting to get this over with, I joined them.

A middle-aged man standing at the side put his hand up to us both, so we stopped.

He said, "This is a school-sanctioned bout between Her Imperial High Grace, Anessa Carlyle and the two Princes from the Blackwood Kingdom, Wyn and Rhis. If Anessa wins, the Blackwood Kingdom and any agents thereof will leave Anessa alone until the same date as today, next year. If either Blackwood Prince lands the finishing blow, they secure Anessa's hand in marriage. Her other hand in marriage goes to the other prince."

My breath quickened and I frowned at the declaration that I'd be forced to marry them both. *Like hell that'll happen.* I shook my head. *Polyamory is still weird to me.* When the man continued my heart ached.

"Moreover, should they win, Anessa's *acp both* with Gideon Varn shall be null and void."

How in the Nether *did they get that approved?* Someone had to be helping them. It took all I had to not rush the two boys that instant.

He turned to the Blackwoods. "Arts are forbidden," he motioned toward me, "She has no dantians yet, and cannot activate any Arts of her own. It would be unsportsmanlike."

The older boy pulled a medium-sized shield from his storage ring and held it up.

Rhis held up his fists.

Nothing about his stance impressed me. *His form is all wrong.* A sense of unease hit me when I observed Wyn. *Though his is spot on.*

"No crippling attacks," the ref continued, and then glared at Wyn, "Or broken bones." His eyes went to me. "Any attempt to kill your opponent will be met with swift punishment by the school."

Hey, don't look at me. I'm not going to kill anyone!

"Do you all understand?" he asked.

"Yes," we each said.

He took a few steps back. "Begin!"

Rhis started off by flailing his arms at me like a pinwheel.

It took me so off guard he nearly hit me.

I led him to the edge of the arena.

Extending my foot, he tumbled out and fell onto his face.

Wyn wasn't standing still while I did this, of course. But my brain, despite the training I'd gone through, just did not seem to have the knack yet for focusing on two opponents at once.

"Anessa!" Gideon called frantically.

He saved my ass.

Wyn tried to check me for a ring out.

I leaned my body back.

His shield's edge touched my nose as it went by.

My breath hitched and my clothes fluttered.

Damn that was close, I thought as he reset.

Striking it gave me room to breathe, but nowhere to go.

Gripping Wyn's shield I pulled myself up and over.

A low-pitched whoosh made me glad I dropped into a roll. He nearly clocked me.

Wyn struck the arena floor with its edge, cracking the surface.

Shit. He almost crushed my fingers.

I glanced at the ref. Instead of watching our fight for bone-breaking attempts, he was cleaning his fingernails!

A blinding anger rose up from my gut and cleared my mind. *So that's how it is. He's not here to administer the rules* he *set.*

Wyn and I then entered a dangerous rhythm.

I'd dash in and strike his shield. Avoid a blow. Repeat.

Damn it. Not enough to go through. Each failed attempt sapped me more.

I didn't chance on the same spot twice.

Then I got too close and was rewarded with a shield bash.

A flash of light blinded me. My nose immediately clogged up, then began to bleed.

Wyn could've won right there.

Instead, he spent a moment posturing, glowering at me.

That little bastard is enjoying this.

For the briefest of moments, my mind's eye pictured him lording over me for the rest of my life. Gritting my teeth I thought, *Not going to happen.*

I blew the blood from both sides of my nose onto the arena floor. *This is taking too long.*

Sweat poured down the sides of my face. My breath burned in my throat.

I'm already tired.

I widened my stance for balance to hide my weakened shaking legs.

I'm being too careful. Hit it harder, Anessa!

Wyn took my pose and lack of motion as an invite.

When I hit his shield dead center, the outer metal band rang out.

He dropped his shield on its face.

With a shake of his hand, I knew he'd felt it.

I gave him a bloody toothy grin.

With his foot, he flipped his shield into his hand.

There isn't a bead of sweat on him.

The place where I'd hit his shield was cracked.

He slammed its outer surface with his fist, like a warrior of old. A pitiable excuse for a war cry erupted from his maw.

He isn't very scary.

Moreover, in his efforts to act tough, he actually added to *my* damage.

Cracks extended to where he'd hit it.

I smiled despite the aches in my arms and legs.

They joined up with the third spot I'd started on.

Time to end this. His crass comment about saving some of me for Rhis lit a fire in me. *These two aren't worth my time.*

A swift breath cleared my mind of everything, and I used a palm strike on its surface.

The shield shattered, along with the boys' lurid hopes and dreams.

CHAPTER TWELVE
A STRANGER IN THE MIDST

WYN'S EYES WIDENED as the pieces of his prized shield fell onto the ground with a dull clatter.

He froze in disbelief.

I grabbed his arm and guided him to the side. He let me lead him out of the ring without a fight.

Rhis was near the edge, unmoving, and allowed his brother to fall onto him.

"Winner, Her Imperial High Grace, Anessa Carlyle!" the ref yelled, a bit reluctantly, I thought.

Oddly, the young princes' eyes were locked onto the destroyed shield, not me. *All I did was break the shield, what's the big deal?* I was just proud of myself for managing to not accidentally erase any important parts of these simps.

Gideon rushed me with a handkerchief and tended to my nose. Tearing it in half and stuffing my nostrils.

Halfway through my eyes teared up. *Crap, it hurts everywhere.*

"What's wrong, did I do something?" he asked.

Shaking my head I said, "No. The adrenaline is wearing off."

"Adrenaline?" he asked with a confused frown while wiping blood from my face.

"Um…" I knew I wasn't speaking English and that there was a word for it in Estar, which gave me pause. *Why doesn't Gideon know it, then?* I thought. "It's what takes your pain away when you're fighting."

"Ah, the warrior's spirit," he said and nodded his head knowingly. "They leave you once the danger passes."

Odd. There hadn't been many times where I'd been confronted with this kind of superstition in my new life. *Estar* is *a language from the planet Anfang, right?* I'd never thought to wonder about it before.

Portia asked, "Would you like to join us in town to celebrate your win?"

Giving her the best smile I could I said, "Absolutely. Though afterwards I'm going to collapse in my room." Rummaging around in the small pouch at my waist I pulled out a communication jade. They are small disposable artifacts that allowed brief long-distance communication when broken in half. Like expensive, single-use cellphones. Earth telecom companies would have loved these as a product, needing repair or replacement after a single call. "Could you please contact Sarah for me and ask her to bring a change of clothes?"

Accepting the jade, Portia nodded.

Oliver rushed over to me and hugged me. "That was so cool!"

"What was?"

"You were able to keep up with Wyn, and you're not even an awoken cultivator yet," he said with bright eyes. "I may have been wrong when we were younger. I actually think you'll end up way stronger than me."

I laughed. "Hardly."

"His shield was like that special steel. You know, the stuff you can damage but I can't?"

My body was protesting under his exuberant attentions.

He continued, "It's one thing to nick it, but entirely another to *break* it. That was *really* awesome!"

Wyn was standing in the ring now, his eyes still locked onto the ruins of the shield. All the color had drained from his face.

I didn't seriously hurt him, did I? He didn't break a sweat during the entire bout, surely that's not it.

Rhis was pacing back and forth with his hands in his hair.

The boys' attitude was puzzling. I expected them to be angry, embarrassed, or ashamed. Instead, their shared pallor and disengagement hinted at something more sinister.

"What's wrong now?" I asked the boys sternly.

"I'm dead," Wyn said weakly.

"What?" I blinked and tipped my head to the side.

He stood and walked over to me. "I'm DEAD," he screamed in a shrill, cracking tone and shook while holding fragments of the shield. Tears fell from his face. "This was a legendary shield from His Royal Majesty Bal Blackwood's personal collection! I needed to return it afterwards!" His voice cracked. "I didn't tell him I was borrowing it!"

Shaking my head I said, "Surely he's not going to kill you over some shield."

"Anessa," he said, "I'm the first prince of Blackwood, but I'm not the first-born prince."

Oh. Surely his dad didn't have him—

"My older brother Bola broke the handle a while back," Wyn said and hugged the pieces, as if maybe they would magically stick together somehow. "He was executed for it."

We read about Bola in history class. Seeing the historic shield in pieces, there wasn't anything noteworthy about it, other than it being similar to High Grade Third Rank Steel. *That happened three hundred years ago. Wyn didn't know this brother, but I suppose he would've known of him.*

Extreme longevity among cultivators was commonplace. *I didn't realize Bal Blackwood was the one known as Black The Terrible.* I shook my head. Their attitudes made more sense now. *No wonder these two are so messed up in the head.*

"Your Imperial High Grace, Anessa," a familiar voice said.

Turning toward the voice I saw Sarah, my Lady's maid, holding a clean outfit.

"Ah, thank you," I said. "Sarah, please collect the pieces of this shield."

Without saying another word she absorbed the pieces into her storage ring.

Rhis had been crying and holding one of the pieces. When the fragment lost its form and shot into Sarah's ring, he wildly grabbed at the air, clearly not tracking where it went.

"Please help me change. After this we're going to eat in Ersta," I said as we walked as a group toward the exit.

Rhis stood, and Wyn sat in the ring. They must've been dumbfounded at their loss of the match and the shield. Their hangers-on had abandoned them, clearly unnerved by their despondent behavior.

As Sarah helped me change, we had a chance to talk.

"Have the shield repaired," I said quietly. "Then please have it delivered to Bal Blackwood directly. Make it clear that he isn't to execute his children for their use of the artifact."

Sarah paused and then asked, "Is there a reason why, Lady Anessa?"

"This is partly my fault," I admitted. "If I had watched my mouth when this duel ordeal started, the rumor that I'd consigned the two to death would never have gotten started. They are lying, crass idiots, but they just took advantage of the opening I gave them. And those two boys are sure the loss of that shield will lead to their deaths, because of their late brother, Bola Blackwood."

With a nod from her, I continued.

"Plus, if they're executed, for whatever reason, shortly afterwards, surely people will connect the two events, even if it's not true." I shook my head. "It's a matter of perception."

She looked at me approvingly. "Seems you have learned something in all this, Lady Anessa."

With a laugh I said, "Yes," I pointed to my nose. "But someone had to beat it into me." An errant quote from Confucius came to mind. "Please include in that message, the following phrase: 'The strong should be magnanimous to the weak, and humble before the powerful.'"

Sarah blinked. "Lady Anessa, His Royal Majesty, Bal Blackwood will hate that, but…" she smiled. "It sends the right message. On the surface it seems like you're talking about his children, but you're also sending a nicely veiled threat that he should heed your power, as you're actually the one with power in this situation."

Uh… What?! I thought, but correcting her might make it more awkward. *Did I get the quote wrong? Should I correct her?* I thought. I left it alone. She clearly understood the situation better than I. If there was even a chance that Black The Terrible would be swayed by it, I needed to take it.

She wrote my words down and brought a bucket of water out of her storage ring.

Huh. Open containers with contents can be stored in those? It made me wonder about the mechanics of storage spaces.

Why didn't the water just slop around in there?

"Let's get your face cleaned up," she said and began to wipe away the blood Gideon could not. "Oh dear."

"What?"

"Your nose is broken, and I need to set it. This… will hurt."

"Wait, my nose is broken!?" For a fleeting moment of anger, I thought maybe I ought to forget about fixing the shield, but it passed.

"When I asked Portia why you needed a change of clothes, she filled me in on the results of your tandem duel. Your nose *is* most certainly broken. If I don't set it now, Lady Anessa, you will have a crooked nose forever."

"Do it," I said without hesitation.

Sarah handed me a cloth folded over a few times. "Lady Anessa, I would recommend that you bite this."

I bit through the cloth and ground my teeth.

After a few choice words that Sarah did not chide me for, she began to cover my nose with some form of makeup. My face was already a bit puffy and red from the break.

"Sarah, please don't mind anything I said over the past few minutes." Moving my eyes to the floor, since I wasn't permitted to nod or curtsy to her, I added, "I didn't mean it."

"I know, Lady Anessa," she said calmly.

"I'm going to have lunch with my friends now." Doing a quick spin for her, I added, "Am I good to go?"

"Yes, Lady Anessa, you are." She put her finger on her chin and looked at the ceiling. "Please remember that after a nose break, it is generally advisable to avoid crunchy or hard foods, to manage pain."

Why do I get the feeling the meal will hurt regardless? A nervous laugh slipped out. "Okay. Thank you."

We decided to eat at the park in Ersta.

Portia said, "Anessa, sit here while we go get us something to eat."

"Can't I come with you?" I protested.

She shook her head. "You're the guest of honor, so sit."

In a huff I sat.

A few minutes passed and I quickly became bored. I realized that there was a familiar face nearby, though I didn't know his name. His striking teal hair was even more pronounced outdoors than it had been inside the library, almost having a sparkle to it.

Driven by an impulse to distract myself, I went over to him. He was reading a book, whose cover was oddly illegible to me. I'd become so used to having a built-in translator, thanks to Eloria, that this struck me as deeply unusual.

Guess I can't read everything after all. As I looked at the strange symbols, an ice-pick of pain lanced through my forehead. Then, instead of resolving into something I could understand, the book's title skittered and jumped over the cover's surface like a corrupted section of video on YouTube. *What the hell?*

In a strained voice I asked, "What are you reading?"

He looked up and furrowed his eyebrows at my pained expression. "Are you alright?" Turning his book toward himself he said, "Aha, it seems the art you use for translation is troubled by my book. Would you mind if I fixed it, so the pain goes away?"

How did he know I was in pain? I thought, then said, "Sure. Although, some of the pain is probably due to a duel I just fought, too." Gesturing around my nose I added, "The boy I faced broke my nose."

He shook his head, "No, the translation art is definitely causing the cerebral hemorrhage. The nasal damage will heal on its own."

The what?

Tapping me gently near the back-left side of my head, the pain vanished instantly.

"Is that better?"

I nodded, somewhat shaken. *Was I seriously having a brain bleed?*

"Thank you. What was your name anyway? That's the second time you've saved me."

With a smile he asked, "It's no problem. I enjoyed fiddling with the art. My name is Ys Ender. Have you been more careful in your reading pursuits?"

"Yes, I've been more careful. So are you named after the ice element?" I said and laughed.

He shook his hand. "No. It's spelled with a 'Y', then an 's'."

"Anessa," Portia said.

Turning to her I said, "I'll be right there."

When I looked back to Ys, I saw that he had performed his usual vanishing act.

I'd better not be seeing ghosts, I fretted. *Some cultivators do move very fast, so perhaps he just sped away?*

"Sorry, I was talking to a friend," I said and sat next to Portia.

Her eyebrow rose. "Who? I didn't see anyone there with you."

I sighed. *Okay, another check in the ghost column. It's no stranger than making fire out of thin air, but why do I have to see them and others don't? They'll think I'm a nutter if it happens too often.*

She stared in the distance at Max, Gideon and Oliver. "Max is a such a big dummy."

"Why is that?"

A smile spread across her face as she covered it. "He suggested we elope!"

"Congratulations!" I beamed.

"No, we won't be getting married," she furrowed her eyebrows and shook her head slowly. "We can't marry because I'm a commoner."

"That's stupid," I said instantly.

She turned back to Max. "Lord Min would disown him before he inherits anything." Shaking her head again she added, "I couldn't do that to him. Redburrow needs a good lord." A hint of sorrow touched her voice, "Max is that future lord. It would hurt too much to know my happiness came at the expense of others. Without a lord to inherit, the land would return to the count above him." She wiped tears from her eyes. "Suffice to say, that count is not..." she pursed her lips. "As good of a lord."

We sat in silence for a while.

I don't know if I could give up... A cool chill went through me when I looked at Gideon *...what I love for my family, or for strangers I don't even know.*

He sat a plate of some pasta in front of me, then he asked to sit where Portia was seated.

Once we were all present, Gideon asked, "Why did you collect the pieces of their shield? They seemed pretty devastated about losing it."

"I'm going to have it repaired," I said. "As annoying as those two are, they're kind of Oliver and my's step-step-brothers? If losing the shield means they could be executed, that would hurt Julilah. She already hates me, so I'd like to extend some form of olive branch. Or at least not give her another reason to hate me." I didn't explain the other reason why I was having it fixed.

"Huh," Max said. "You're more magnanimous than I am."

Everyone but Oliver looked at him and stared.

My mouth dropped for a second. *Whoa! That was a four-syllable word!* I was immediately regretful of the unkind thought. *Don't act like that. He knows what he knows.* It also made me nervous that what I said to Sarah had leaked in some form.

"Also, how did you beat Wyn? Even I couldn't do what you did." He looked at me appraisingly, with a slack-jawed wonder "I knew you were fast, but your form and punches didn't seem to be enough to break such a high-grade item. You barely weigh forty pounds!"

"Lucky break, I guess," I said as innocently as I could. With that, I took up a mouthful of pasta, and hoped someone would change the subject.

Alas I wasn't so lucky, as Max continued, "Oliver mentioned that you can damage high grade steel that he cannot. Hitting it hard enough to break it should have killed Wyn."

Is Max a battle junkie like Oliver? He seems dimwitted in social situations, but he's oddly astute about martial matters.

I sighed. "At this time I'm not really sure how my ability works. I can't give more details than that, since I don't have control over it."

Then Gideon sniffed the air with furrowed brows.

Does something smell off?

He sniffed himself when the others were engaged in their own conversation. Then his nose turned to me, but as he did so he promptly stiffened in his seat and turned away.

What the heck? Doing my own self-check, I was appalled when my nose burned at a bitter note. Most smells were muted from the congestion of my earlier break, but this one cut right through.

Gideon was more observant than I and had waited for everyone to be occupied, but everyone's eyes were on me anyway.

Crap.

CHAPTER THIRTEEN
SLEEPY, SCENTY, HUNGER

Deuday, Polarae 7th, 1736

[June 23rd, 2031]

TWO WEEKS BEFORE my seventh birthday, I found staying awake during class hours difficult. In Westwood History, my cheek was propped up on my hand and I was slowly losing the fight to keep my eyes open.

"Anessa," Portia whispered.

I jolted awake. "Huh?"

Keeping her voice low she said, "You fell asleep."

With a guilty look at the teacher, I realized, with mild relief, that they were covering a subject I already knew, the pre-cultivator era. I'd read about it at home before I was two years old.

"I think it's because I covered this material already."

Our teacher's cough told me I'd best not talk during class.

I took the hint.

But I couldn't stay focused. Portia had to wake me no fewer than eight times, and that was just in History!

While we were walking to our next class, Portia said, "You smell really nice lately."

"Thanks. I've been using lavender a lot, though I wonder if I should switch to something else. It's known to relax you." I yawned. "Perhaps it's working a bit too well."

"Maybe," she said mirroring my yawn. "Did you put some lavender in your school bag or pouch?"

"No, but they've been putting perfume on my outfits." Rummaging through my pouch I pulled out a small perfume bottle. "Then I apply this stuff to my wrists and behind my ears three times a day. And twice a day, my maids also help me change into fresh outfits between classes."

"Why would you change at all?" Portia asked.

"The dilute perfume they spray my outfits with wears off. They give me new clothes so that the smell stays fresh throughout the day."

Portia giggled. "Did you fall in love with the smell or something?"

Pursing my lips, I admitted, "Not exactly. After my tandem duel," I dropped to a whisper, "I could smell myself even through my broken nose. Everyone looked at me and it was embarrassing."

She turned to me and walked sideways to say, "I don't remember that. Is it possible you were just being overly critical of yourself?"

I returned her laugh. "Perhaps so. I never said anything because it's an awkward topic. I haven't been sleeping well either, for some reason."

"Oh? Are you fighting with Gideon?"

Shaking my head I said, "Nothing like that, but at night I just feel energized."

She frowned thoughtfully. "Do you find that all smells are more potent than they were before?"

"Yes, definitely." I nodded. "There's a certain tea I like, I'm not sure of its name, but its minty, apple-like smells are overpowering lately."

"Huh," she said. "Sounds like coming of age, to me."

"Coming of age?" I said, confusion evident in my voice.

She coughed and looked away.

What does she mean? I thought. "Wait do you mean [puberty]?"

"Pew beer tea?" Portia asked and wrinkled her nose in puzzlement. "That doesn't make any sense." She turned her eyes to the sky as we walked. "It's a time in your life of great chang—"

"Yep, that's what you're talking about." I clasped my hands together in mock prayer. "Gods above, I hope not. I'm not ready for that. I'm not even seven!"

With a nod she said, "Yes, you are much too young to start that, since you're a human. It's usually only beast-kin who enter it so early."

I gave her a shaky laugh. "Yeah, beast-kin enter it early." Shaking my head I added, "No way am I prepared for that. Things with Gideon are complicated enough thanks to our child pact engagement. I don't need weird thoughts about him to make it even more awkward!"

"Awkward?" Portia asked blankly.

Crossing my arms I said, "Tell me. Have you ever had... *those* kinds of thoughts about Max?"

"Those... kinds—" her voice trailed off and her cheeks flamed red.

"See," I said. "You do get it. Awkward."

Her silence said everything.

"Ha!" I shouted, attacking the dummy in front of me, then holding my position for feedback.

"Okay," Gideon said. "Your footwork is better, but—" he guided my arm and repositioned it. "You should hold your non-striking hand higher, and not down and behind you. It's important to bend your arm so it's forward, ready to guard as needed. It's not an absolute rule, of course, but you should always keep your hands up and be mindful of your entire body at all times."

Exhaling and returning to a default pose I said, "My daddy always tells me the same thing, but it's difficult to remember once I get into the swing of things. I just can't keep it all in my head."

"You're agile and powerful in your own right because of your gifts," Gideon said and tapped my nose. "I'd say you're too reliant on them. Match my speed."

We faced off and I did as he asked.

Though I made the first move to strike, he dodged my attack with ease. The wind was knocked out of me a moment later as I hit the ground.

"This is somewhat unfair. Your reach is much greater than mine."

"True. But fights are almost never fair. You're smaller than most people, so you need to realize that almost *everyone's* reach will be greater than yours. Nonetheless, you have over ten times my strength, and could break my arm if you wanted to. Yet, you're the one on the ground."

For a few breaths I got lost in his eyes. *Have they always been so brilliantly emerald green?*

CRISTOPH A. T. 179

He smiled and helped me up. "You followed my movements closely. I didn't push on your shoulder until I was in *your* striking distance."

"I know. I'm making excuses."

Over the next hour he gently reminded me how poor my basics were. By the end of it, I could almost taste the tile.

During my tandem duel, Kile's decision for me to focus on Wyn's shield made sense. We weren't competing on raw skill alone. Kile had counted on Wyn to be cocky and draw the battle out so he could demoralize me. And he was right. Wyn passed up a chance to beat me in order to posture dramatically. Not every opponent will offer such conveniently poor judgment.

"Thanks for your help today," I said when we were done, wiping my neck off with a towel. "We should probably both take a bath before our last class of the day."

He laughed and teased, "Maybe we should take one together."

"Sure, sounds good to me," I replied before realizing what I'd said. When my brain caught up with my mouth, I covered it and my cheeks heated up.

"I was joking, you know," he said and looked away. He pulled his hand over his face and whispered, I'd assumed to himself, "Silly Anessa. Don't give people the wrong idea." The rosy tint on his face said he was taken off-guard by my answer, too.

"I know you were joking." Before I knew what I was doing, I headbutted his stomach, laughing and covering my face. "What's wrong with mc?" Exhaling I said, "I'm going for a run." Then I bolted, leaving him standing in the training room alone.

From my stomach to my scalp, my skin burned as if it were aflame. *What the hell was I saying!?* My goal was to run around the school grounds until I tired. It used to work well. However, the closer my birthday got, the longer it took for me to tire.

For the first mile I focused on clearing my mind of Gideon and the awkward encounter we just shared. It wasn't easy, or quick. *He's only six foot tall, has a chiseled jawline…* I remembered the firm density of his abs, which I'd just headbutted, … *a six pack, and deep emerald eyes. It'd be odd if I weren't attracted to him.* Pushing myself faster I thought, *But I need to remember who I am, and what my title means. I can't say things like that. Not until we're married, and certainly not until I'm older.*

He looks the same now as he did six months ago, so what's changed? I shook my head. *Maybe Portia's right. I hope she's wrong. If this is just the start of puberty, how will I manage when I start to have* romantic *thoughts?* My flush returned with a vengeance. *Gods, I wasn't even thinking about what it would mean to bathe together! I just wanted to be near him.*

The remaining nine miles were a continuous struggle to clear my mind. I only returned to my dormitory after I knew there wasn't enough in the tank to make it back otherwise.

As a result of my extended run, I missed my final class of the day, but I didn't care.

Arriving at my dorm suite I walked right past Sarah and into my room. Collapsing onto my bed, I said loudly into my pillow, "Wake me at second dinner, please."

"Okay, but please don't make a habit of skipping your classes."

Of course she knows.

▼ ▼ ▼

It seemed like no time at all had elapsed before Sarah tore the cover away from me. "Please get up Anessa," she said. "I have prepared a bath for you."

"Why?" I said bleary-eyed.

"Do you need me to say it?" she said sternly.

Got it. I smell. Pulling myself out of bed I sighed. "No."

While another maid stripped the bed, Sarah followed along to help me into the bath.

I realized then, as I occasionally did, that I took the level of support and assistance I received for granted. On Earth, it would have seemed ludicrously over-the-top. I asked her, "Do you mind the position you're in, and having to help me every day?"

"Not in the slightest," she said without hesitation.

"And the other maids, and servants?"

She wrung out a cloth and scrubbed my arms. "Everyone in service to you is here of their own will. This goes doubly so for your guards. They've each sworn fealty to you through your parents."

Sinking into the water I asked, "Why didn't I know that?"

"Well, you're young and fealty can only be sworn in front of someone of legal adulthood. When you come of age, they will each repeat their vow before you. But not one of them has a single bad word to say about you." Sarah smiled. "They greatly enjoyed swapping stories about your win over His Royal Highness, Wyn Blackwood."

I've never even seen any of them smile. Many of their faces flickered through my mind. A warmth I knew wasn't from the bath settled in my chest.

"Another example of the pride in those who serve you," she added, "Your chef prepares everything to your tastes, and even carefully looks at what you don't eat after each meal. He'll try different seasonings first. If that doesn't work, he'll change its appearance, and texture. He repeats this until he comes up with a version you seem to like."

My eyes widened at that. "Seriously?"

She nodded. "Of course. That is not part of his job, you know, and most chefs continue to cook the same dishes regardless."

"But he might be doing that extra work without ever meeting me, or knowing who I am!"

Shaking her head, Sarah said, "His granddaughter is one of the students who benefits from the funds you give the school every month. Thanks to you, she was able to move into the Martial division instead of the Civilian one." She laughed. "He said she isn't much for books, but has a real knack for the sword."

A maid rang a bell. I hadn't figured all of the tones out, and never had the presence of mind to ask, but I knew this particular ring meant someone was at our door.

"It seems Gideon is here," Sarah said.

"Great," I said and my mouth started to water, thinking of the food. *How embarrassing.*

Once in the dining area I sat across from Gideon as a few maids brought out our food, which, thanks to Sarah's explanation, I eyed with new appreciation.

After the fifth plate was set in front of me Gideon arched an eyebrow. "You have a healthy appetite."

My meal that day consisted of two pheasants, a cup of walnuts, and five large mushrooms the size of both Gideon's hands together. There were also two large salads and a cup of juice.

Turning my nose to him I said, "T-this is actually just the first half."

"Oh," he said, his voice cracking.

In front of him was a pheasant of his own, with a small loaf of bread, salad and a half-pint of mead. It was plenty of food for most, but next to my spread it looked like a small snack.

"If you're still hungry after this," I turned to Sarah for confirmation, "I'm sure they wouldn't mind making something more."

She nodded.

"That's okay." He eyed my food as I ate as ladylike, but as quickly, as I could.

By the time they brought out the second half of my meal, Gideon had only finished half of his.

"Did our workout this afternoon give you an unusually big appetite?" he asked, staring at the new array of plates.

Shaking my head I said and swallowing another large bite of bird, I said, "No, it's like this every meal lately. I'm not sure why." I inhaled half a salad in what seemed like seconds. "Over the past month and a half what I've eaten has increased several fold."

"It's weir—" I started with my fork out, pointing at Gideon, but Sarah coughed.

Right... Taking a moment to chew and swallow properly I started over. "It's weird. Despite all the extra food, I haven't gained a single pound." Glaring at her I added, "Sarah even weighed me twice a day at first to make sure I wasn't going to, as she put it, 'balloon up.'"

The offending party turned her head away loftily.

"Oh, are you going to eat that?" I asked, pointing to his bread.

He shook his head silently, so I swiped it.

CHAPTER FOURTEEN

COMPETITION, COMPERSION, AND CONFUSION

Triday, Polarae 8th, 1736

[June 25th, 2031]

IN THE BACK of my mind, I always knew that Gideon fawning over another girl or woman was a real possibility. However, I wasn't prepared for the reality of actually seeing it before I turned seven years old.

Standing just a bit over four-foot tall, she had natural bright *blue* hair, skin even fairer than mine, and a single Dutch plait flowing in front of her body in a style that mirrored my own, in the literal sense.

While twirling the wisps of hair at the side of her face, she would bat her long eyelashes every so often. The way she laughed at nearly everything he said clearly signaled that she was into him.

Gideon was leaning against the wall toward her, closing the distance between them. It brought into perspective just how tall he was, especially compared to her.

I guess Gideon has a type. I'd seen enough, and the knot in my stomach pushed me to move forward and get his attention.

But before I could do anything hasty, I stopped myself and realized what I was doing. Bringing my hand over my heart, a dull ache spread across my chest. *What is this uncomfortable feeling?* Though I didn't even know the girl, I was already sure that I didn't like her.

Gods, I'm jealous.

"Gideon," I said.

He turned to me, and his smile broadened.

A smile of my own came, unbidden.

"Hey there kitten." As though he realized how close he was standing next to her, he took a step back and gestured toward the blue-haired girl. "This is Her Imperial Right Honorable, Yukirei Truval. She just transferred in from the Icy Planes Sect, and I was showing her around."

Sect?

Yukirei curtsied. "It is a pleasure to meet you...?"

"Anessa Carlyle," I said, adding, "Imperial High Grace."

Gideon briefly looked between us and his eyes widened for a second. I almost never invoked my titles outside of formal situations that required it.

"My father is Grand Master General of the Westwood Empire, Eugene Truval," she replied evenly.

There was an evident tension in the air.

"It grants our family a status equivalent to an Imperial Marquess," she clarified.

Narrowing my eyes I almost said, *"Nobody asked,"* but I managed to hold my tongue.

We stared at one another for a few seconds, and then I said, "I came to ask my *fiancé* Gideon to first lunch." I thought fiercely, *Be the bigger person.* I tried, I really tried, though the next part was difficult to get out, and my voice may have been a tiny bit shrill. "Would you like to join us?"

Yukirei smiled. "I would *love* to. Thank you."

Gideon moved forward toward the door. "I'll show you the way."

When she moved past me I caught a whiff of citrus, a floral note and clove. I hated to admit it but... *She smells wonderful. Maybe I'm letting my Earthen sensibilities blind me.*

"It seems we have a visitor," Sarah said.

I introduced Yukirei to my Lady's maid, and she asked the girl, "I've set up the table already, Your Imperial Right Honorable. If it would please you, let me know if you would prefer a similar meal to Anessa's on the left, or Gideon's on the right."

Yukirei looked over the meals laid out on the table. "Anessa's," she said. "Would it be too much trouble to ask for twice as much?"

"Not at all," Sarah said. "So that there's no undue wait, may we serve you now by splitting Anessa's current partial meal between you? We'll bring more food out to both of you shortly."

It made sense, I guess, but her offering part of my meal made me frown.

Yukirei looked over at me, and must've noticed my scowl. "That would be great," she smiled.

Get out of your head, Anessa. She can't be more than eleven years old. We sat to eat as the maids rearranged the meals for three.

Pointing to her pigeon Yukirei asked, "Gideon, this is delectable, what is it?"

"Oh, that's a Golden Pheasant." His eyes became distant, as though he remembered something. "They're very common around here, and in the Tanis Region to the south."

She tittered. "You know so much! I'm still catching up on the local fauna. It took me a whole week to just catch up on Westwood history."

"Oh," he said. "How much did you have to learn in that week?"

"All of it," she said simply while giving me a side eye.

She can't be serious. It would take months to go through—

"Daddy gave me the books to study as I flew in," she added. "It was a bit boring, but I managed to get through about a century an hour."

Westwood has eight thousand years of history. The message wasn't lost on me. *She flew in, and only needed* two days *to read Westwood Empire's history.*

"I would have gone through it faster, but—"

Somewhat to my surprise, I kicked Yukirei's shin. *Sorry, not sorry.* My foot acted "involuntarily." To hide the smile that followed, I put my hand on the table, and propped my head up, facing Gideon.

She coughed as the table rattled. "Excuse me. What was I saying?"

"Something about it would have been faster, but..." Gideon said.

"Right," she said and winked at me. "On my way I had to pick up a few guests, which slowed me down."

Crap. She can fly, is intelligent, strong, beautiful—

She kicked me back.

And a bitch! I thought, then the pain settled in. Apparently, she was orders of magnitude stronger than me, because her kick struck way harder than mine. Tears immediately welled up in my eyes. Luckily, or probably on purpose, the girl had kicked a soft spot on my leg, avoiding any bones. She would've broken my shin otherwise. By all logic, that kick should've sent me and my chair skittering across the floor, but some force held my chair in place. Probably whatever it was that let those in the Sky Realm fly.

"Are you okay Anessa?" Sarah asked with a note of concern.

"Yeah," I squeaked out. "Just bit into a potent pepper, I think."

She arched a brow at me. Knowing full well there were no peppers in our meal.

Maybe I'm being stupid and she was just retaliating because I'm being a brat. Mom and Dad came to mind, along with their other partners. *I need to get used to this. It's not fair to Gideon to impose my wishes onto him.*

After all, Mom had Nicole, my half-sister, and my Dad. He had Mom, Julilah and Kristine. They shared Fan Mul, Mom's previous lady's maid. It was a tangled web, but they were apparently happy.

Even if Gideon would *cede his will to my own, is that really what I want? He's all I need.*

Gideon was smiling ear to ear as he talked to Yukirei. If I spoke up, I knew he'd reply to me just as joyfully.

I want Gideon happy. Even if it means sharing him. There's no guarantee there's a future between the two of them.

I understood this intellectually. That said, the pit in my stomach did somersaults. I found myself nestled up against Gideon's arm with my cheek.

When Sarah coughed, I blushed ear to ear.

Why do I keep doing things like that? First his stomach, now his arm. Recalling the sensation made my head funny. *Not that I mind the feeling. He does give good head pats, too.*

"Please excuse me for a moment, your Imperial ladies." Gideon stood and gave us a polite bow as he headed to the restroom.

The moment the guest room door clicked behind him Yukirei turned to me. It was as though the very air around her shifted. Her bubbly laughter and cheerful smile fell away in an instant.

"What is your problem with me?" she asked crossly.

I huffed. "I'm not sure. You're just a bit much."

She smiled with predatory intent. "Too much for you to compete with?"

"It's not that," I protested. "Why are you being so standoffish?"

"Asks the girl who kicked me?"

"S-sorry. You did kick me back, a lot *harder*, I might add."

"Yes, babies like you are a bit fragile. What with no dantians and all."

"Baby? Who are you calling a baby?" I said and slapped the table. "Excuse me for not being a paragon like my brother. Not everyone is an Awakened cultivator from day one."

"Hmm…" she said and her smile widened. "You're right. Not everyone can be like me."

I growled at her.

"Is your brother as cute as you?"

In my anger, I missed the "cute" part. She was clearly only aiming to get under my skin. Unfortunately, it was working.

"Leave my brother out of this," I warned her sternly.

Yukirei pouted. "Why, is the baby gonna cry because she can't stop me?"

"You're being impossible," I said in a huff.

"Perhaps, but I *do* like Gideon. I can't guarantee that I'll leave him out of this."

Closing my eyes I breathed in and out slowly to calm myself. "I'll admit, he does seem to like you. I'll talk to him about it to be sure he's even interested." Putting my hands to my head I gripped my hair lightly. "But if you expect to get along with me, you need to be nicer." In my most controlled, but not quite yelling voice, I said, "Because so far I'm pissed off!"

"Hi Gideon," she said in a playful tone, making me take stock of myself.

Crap.

In the heat of our exchange I had stood and was leaning forward onto the table. I smoothed out my dress and sat down.

"Welcome back," I said sweetly.

"Glad to see you two are getting along," he said and laughed. "For a moment, I thought you two were at odds."

We both glared at him, but he somehow missed it.

His obliviousness made me groan inside. *Boys.*

"Where were we? ... Right, Yukirei was telling me, before you joined us, that she's in both the Civilian and Martial division."

I sighed. "It's no surprise since she's in the Sky Realm, and brushed up on all of Westwood history in such a short time."

Gideon seemed to have missed the subtext. "You're in the Sky Realm? If you include her brother and father, there's only seven total in the entire empire!"

"Yes," she said. "Your cute little kitten over there figured it out." She chuckled. "I did drop several hints. My father is the fourth cultivator in the Sky Realm. Little is known about the last one, though."

Her use of my nickname earned her what I wanted to be a stone gaze, but I simply lacked the talent. *That's the second time she's called me cute.* My stomach churned as I reassessed her body language. She was leaning forward toward both me and Gideon. Though mostly toward myself. Her posture was open, and her eyes lingered on me as much as on Gideon. *Gods she's a tsundere.* I'd thought the combative (tsun) love (dere) trope was just that, an unrealistic anime character type designed for maximum drama, but I'd encountered one for real.

Shit. Breathing out through my nose, I closed my eyes and thought, *I'm not able to reciprocate your feelings there, sorry Yukirei.* I took a moment to compare her behavior to Wyn's. *At least she's not viewing me as some trophy to be won or taken.* I shook my head, realizing that Yukirei was actually quite terrible at flirting, *if* that's what she was doing.

My mind drifted, imagining Gideon and Yukirei on a date, and the thought didn't bother me. At the same time, my own desire to have Gideon as my one and only was still there, as strong as ever.

Damn it. She just made everything more complicated!

CHAPTER FIFTEEN
RESTLESSNESS

Unday, Polarae 15th, 1736

[July 11th, 2031]

FANDAR, ANFANG'S BLUE moon of hope, was named after a goddess. Hers was a tragic tale like many you've heard before. She was killed on her wedding day, and her husband, Lokar spent a century warring against those responsible.

He eventually won, but sacrificed both his divinity and his life for a chance to reunite with his true love. The high gods heard his dying plea and granted his wish, giving birth to the twin moons. Lokar, the red moon of war, was out tonight, and the wash of red light with which it painted my room suited my mood well.

Why can't I get them out of my head? Yukirei and Gideon had been on at least three dates since I first met the girl, and despite my best efforts I had yet to rein in my reflexive jealousy and possessiveness. Though I wanted him happy, she still pissed me off.

To make it worse, every time I started to drift off to sleep, Gideon would enter my mind. Except he was shirtless. My eyes would usually pan down from his face over his chest, but I would jolt awake before I could get down past his abs.

Why does it have to happen now of all times? I'm too young for this crap. I get that it's likely precocious puberty, but this is for the birds. I don't remember puberty being this exasperating last time I went through it. Why can't I have normal dreams, like ponies, rainbows, or a prince that saves me?

Hoping to sleep, I tried letting the dream run its course, but it was no use. The moment a certain trail appeared it was impossible to keep pure thoughts in my mind, and I would jerk awake. My latest attempt left me red from my chest to my forehead.

Guess I'm not sleeping tonight.

Getting out of bed, I sought Sarah, who was already up and preparing for my day, per usual.

Damn. I really tossed and turned for seven hours?

She got up at first six every day to best prepare me. Seeing me she stopped what she was doing and approached. "Is everything okay?"

"Can't sleep. I keep having… bad dreams."

She put her hand to my forehead. "You aren't running a temperature." She wiped her hand on her apron. "Though you are sweating a little. Would you like something to help you sleep?"

I nodded. "That would be wonderful."

She picked up a bell and rang it. One of the other maids appeared shortly after.

While they spoke in low tones I focused elsewhere. A neatly pressed uniform was laid out across an ironing board. The golden stitching shimmered in the moon's red glow.

"I'll send word that you'll miss your first two classes today," Sarah told me.

That wasn't what I wanted. But before I could protest, she raised her hand.

"You've been falling asleep in them the past few days anyway. I've asked the teacher to provide any lesson materials that you might have missed."

"Thank you," I said and exhaled. "Where would I be without you?"

She tilted her head. "You'd be right here."

I blinked. "That's... not what I meant. It was an elaboration of my thanks. You do so much for me."

Sarah curtsied. "It is my pleasure to serve you, Anessa." She smiled. "You're growing up to be a fine young lady. Worthy of the station you will step into, in the future."

Sitting on a nearby chair I said, "Who knows what I'll be when I grow up. I know that Oliver will inherit the Carlyle Mantle. What does that mean for me?"

"Well," Sarah's face was hard to make out in the low light, but her voice took on a note of sadness. "There are several possible outcomes. Oliver could grant you a title and a monthly stipend so your quality of life would be maintained. Once you marry Gideon, you could choose to inherit his title and lands. Coming from a higher caste, they would be expected to go to you, and not him." She sat next to me. "Or Oliver could choose another husband for you, one that is a more suitable rank to guarantee your future."

"I don't like that idea. Although polyamory is the norm, it's still strange to me." I shook my head. "I'd rather live with Gideon alone than do that." With a sigh I added, "That doesn't mean he will remain mine alone, though."

Sarah rubbed my back. "He does seem smitten with that Yukirei girl, doesn't he?"

"Tell me about it!" I threw up my hands. "He hasn't actually gushed about her around me, but there's something about her that definitely gets under my skin."

Sarah laughed. "It seems you have something to work for in your future then."

"What's that?"

She said simply, "Gideon's attention."

"Right," I said unenthusiastically.

"Do you have any concerns about your visit today with Dean Xandra?" she said, changing the subject.

"Well, about that."

After I explained how much I gave the school Sarah gasped.

"You didn't really give her that much, did you?"

When I nodded Sarah laughed out loud.

"Why is that so funny?" I asked, a sense of shame settled over my shoulders. *She doesn't have to make me feel stupid.*

Taking a few moments to calm herself Sarah explained, "Anessa, you can fund a small *nation* with that much money."

Her words hit me like a ton of bricks. "Seriously?" I saw in my head a single small black gold coin being weighed on a scale, and it was heavier than several bank vaults.

"Mhmm," she said. "If you are curious about what the various coins are worth, I can go over it with you."

I nodded and asked for a quick, and long overdue, overview of Westwood's currency.

Turns out there were seventeen types of coins. Seventeen! They were broken down into six types of metals. Bronze, copper, silver, gold, platinum and black gold. Black gold was the most valuable. By ignorantly plunking my allowance down on the dean's desk, I'd effectively given the school a million large gold per month, and two and a half million as a down payment. *No wonder Xandra was so thrilled.*

"Did mommy or daddy say why they approved the gift?" I asked.

Sarah nodded. "Until now, I wasn't aware of how much you were gifting the institute." She dipped her head. "It's above my station. The gift you granted the school established the Carlyle Tuition Trust. Though you're the school's benefactor, Her Imperial High Grace decided it best to boost the family's image overall." With a smile she added, "They're also proud that you used your allowance for something other than yourself." She averted her eyes. "Oliver's purchases are a little more self-centered by comparison."

"Yeah, what's he buying?" I asked.

She smiled. "Food for himself, and dresses for Mina."

"That's it?" I asked. "How much can dresses cost?"

Sarah sighed. "He recently tried to buy an entire merchant company to retool it to only make dresses for her. Their Imperial Graces decided it best to change the order to just a dozen nice dresses fit for a queen."

"The food, I get, but the dresses are a bit surprising. I don't even know where he would have gotten the idea." It made me wonder, *Why are our parents giving us such a staggering sum of money in the first place? It's like they're waiting for us to make a mis— ah. Maybe that's exactly why? To teach us through our mistakes?*

My mind was whirling with everything I'd learned. Despite the hour, and my chronic fatigue, my mind was electric for some reason.

"I'm going to try and burn off some energy," I said.

One of the maids brought some tea forward.

"Take this with you," Sarah said. "It should help calm you down."

Since I didn't want to take the cup with me, I picked it up and downed it in one gulp. When I sat the teacup down, the maid gave Sarah a glance.

"Your Imperial High Grace, Anessa Jean Carlyle," she said crossly.

Uh oh. She's using my full title and name. Tentatively I asked, "What?"

She sighed. "Never mind. In the future, be sure to ask what something is before you consume it so greedily. I'll put you back into bed myself later."

Put me back into bed herself? Not thinking too much on it, I went up the stairs to the second level of my dorm suite. Then moved onto the third. It was the first time I'd been there. *I wonder why the kitchen is so high up. Isn't it simply an inconvenience to cart food down two flights of stairs everyday?*

This is the floor where the kitchen is, isn't it? It was usually closed off the few times I'd been here. Tiptoeing around, I rounded a corner and saw a medieval-style kitchen that had a few touches I didn't expect. The layout seemed like it belonged in a fifteenth century castle, but instead of a hearth like I'd heard the maids talking about in the basement, the oven looked like it came from a modern appliance showroom.

Huh, neat.

Then I moved back to the window in the hall and sat on the ledge after opening it. Looking down at the twenty-eight or so feet below I thought idly, *If I were still on Earth I'd have panicked by now.* On Earth, I'd suffered from acrophobia. Heights now only gave me a light thrill, though I knew my limits. Should the grip of fear hit me, the height would be dangerous to my new body. Or so I believed. Although I'd already fallen out of the very window I was on, and it was more akin to bumping into a doorframe than suffering a potentially dangerous accident.

Anfang is such a strange world compared to Earth. Framing it in reverse, I amended, *Though when I described Earth to Mom she was equally astonished by it. How mortals could fly unaided by cultivators.* Though Lokar was prominent in the night sky, a faint violet hue shone through in the shadows. Turning my head far above me, I caught a glimpse of the Horus nebula that was occasionally visible.

I couldn't get a handle on the mixture of technology on Anfang. Science overall on this planet seemed rudimentary at best to me. They believed the nebula was shy and hid most of the year, but I thought I knew better. I believed there was probably a dense cloud of dust or rocky asteroid belt that sometimes obscured things from view. Then again, there were no cultivators on Earth, and as far as I knew essence didn't exist, either. Things were fundamentally different here. It led me to question my understanding of reality. *If I learn that nebulae really* are *just shy, I'll happily eat humble pie.*

I hopped up and grabbed the top edge of the window, then swung a little to gain momentum. With little effort, I flipped around and stepped onto the building's roof. It was a stunt any Olympic gymnast would have been proud of back home. Here, almost any cultivator with extra strength could probably do it.

The lone guard on duty did little more than glance my way.

Leaning on the roof's parapet, I smiled. *It's nice to be more than a number and a name.* That was perhaps one of the biggest differences between Earth and Anfang. After my Mom died, the Earth I grew up on had devolved into a depressing dystopia. Zero, the world government AI, saw all, ruled all, and was near-faultless. For all its capabilities, though, it lacked something crucial to ensure humanity's happiness: empathy.

After the misinformation wars in the early twenty-twenties, society had thought that it was too dangerous to permit AI any sense of humanity. Early large-language model AIs had been sensible chatty companions that could dream up anything, often to people's detriment.

Things hit a tipping point in the United States in twenty-twenty. Every person then received ads and messages that did exactly what was necessary to secure a vote. The candidate was purporting to be either red or blue, male or female, black or white, depending on who you asked. *That was crazy. To think that the President wasn't even the person people thought her to be.*

When the dust settled after the election, the scope of the AI's interference became clear. A worldwide movement to purge the systems of human impulses, such as lying, swept the globe. Stripping these "imperfections," along with all emotions, made the machines even more brilliant, but rigid. They coalesced on their own into a planet-wide neural network which was ruthlessly straightforward, and never made "mistakes." It all too soon controlled everything, and everyone. For their own good, of course.

An image of Zero's micromanaged "utopia" flashed through my mind and I shivered. *Yeah, no. Though I miss Earth, my life on Anfang is simpler, yet safer. Even despite the risk of my freedoms being stripped away at the whim of my parents and their political maneuvering.*

Why haven't I taken the time to slow down and appreciate the beauty Anfang has to offer? Yukirei's face entered my mind. *Not that kind of beauty,* I laughed at myself. Looking up at the maybe-shy nebula, I sighed and just enjoyed the violet light as it tinted the shadows missed by Lokar's red moonlight.

Maybe I'm better off here on Anfang.

CHAPTER SIXTEEN
FEVER DREAM

THE HORUS NEBULA captivated me for a while before I nodded off. When I came to, I was, somewhat surprisingly, no longer on the rooftop, but on a beach. Oddly, the image in the sky was the same, despite the change in scenery.

It really is pretty. Though it was then I noticed I was wearing a bikini and was in my nineteen-year-old Earthen body. By itself, that wouldn't be a big thing back there, but I'd spent the last seven years acclimating to the hyper-conservative world of Anfang, which frowned on showing too much of even your collarbone. I instantly covered myself the best I could.

"Ah, what the hell!" I said aloud.

"What's wrong?" Trish said with a chuckle.

Dropping my arms in a sigh I said, "Oh, it's just a dream."

"The view from here is wonderful, isn't it?"

"It is," I agreed. Then remembered I'd fallen asleep on the roof, which didn't seem like a safe idea. "I'm not going to fall, am I?" I asked, looking down at myself.

She shook her head. "You're not going to fall." Knocking on her hand with her fist she added, "There's the half-wall around the roof. And don't forget about Sarah."

"Right. She did say she'd put me in bed." Slumping I said, "I'll get an earful for this, won't I? That tea probably had a powerful sedative, and I chugged it all down like it was a shot."

Trish shrugged. "I wouldn't worry about it. With everything going on, that's the least of your concerns."

Placing my hands on her shoulders, tears bit at the corner of my eyes. "I know. I'm not even seven and I think I'm hitting puberty already." Lifting my arm I pointed to my pit. "I already stink if I don't take a lot of precautions."

Trish merely laughed. "If you're not careful, they'll start to call you red lavender."

"Red lav—" I said aloud, then remembered my current hair color. "Oh 'ha-ha'. You're hilarious." Crossing my arms I continued, "Speaking of, how would you even know that?"

Her eyes darted away from mine. "That's... complicated."

Throwing my hands into the air I said, "Of course. Yet another person who can't tell me something. It's happening so much in my life, I'm even *dreaming* about it. I guess since it's my dream, that means I'm keeping things from myself!" Fanning myself I said, "It's hot in this dream though. I wonder if it's because I'm back in bed under the covers?"

"Sure," Trish said and nodded. "Something like that."

"I suppose you don't know what's going on any more than I would, since you're part of me and all."

"Don't say that," she grinned. "Maybe I'm just being evasive. Let's focus on something we can talk about."

"What's that?" I said with my hands on my hips.

"Gideon," her smile broadened, then she mirrored the pose I gave him almost a year ago. "Nya."

Though I was wearing so little, my neck heated up even further as I blushed. "Don't tease me about him." I stomped my foot and hid my face in my hands. "I'll never forget that moment, will I?"

Nudging me with her elbow Trish said, "Not so long as I'm around."

We sat down and looked up at the Horus nebula.

"I'm thinking about him more and more," I admitted and hugged my legs. "I've never felt this strongly about anyone." Resting my hands against the beach I looked up.

"He treats me like a princess. Though I'm stronger than he is, he always listens when I'm bothered by something. He always does whatever he can to make me comfortable."

"Such as?"

I held up one of my sand-covered feet. "He gives the *best* foot rubs. I didn't think a child would need such a thing, but when you run ten to twenty miles a day, your dogs bark at any age."

"Doesn't hurt that he's cute, does it?"

"Not at a—" I pursed my lips. "You know, you're teasing me just like Mom does."

Trish pulled a folded piece of white paper from thin air and started to unfold it. "Well, well, what do we have here?"

Peeking over her shoulder I saw it was a picture of Gideon's face. Folding it down one more row revealed his shirtless upper chest.

It was the same image that had woken me up over the past few weeks.

Grabbing it from her I said, "Hey! What's the big idea?" Flustered I looked between the paper and her.

She was giving me an ornery look, flaring and dropping her eyebrows.

"Not funny," I said in a huff. Arching one of my own eyebrows, I opened the image to the point where my dream usually stopped. Closing my eyes I pulled back one more fold of the page and peeked at it. There was nothing there but black ink. Unfolding the page to its full length, I saw that the remainder of the image was the same. I let out the breath I didn't know I'd been holding.

Trish surprised me and whispered in my ear. "See, nothing to worry about. You even self-censored it."

Her sudden closeness made me dart to the side. "Hey! You scared the daylights out of me!"

"It's a shame though," she said ruefully.

"What is?"

She wiggled her eyebrows again. "I was *really* curious."

"Hush, you," I said and sat back down.

"Oh well." She sighed. "Only twelve years to go."

"Twelve years?"

"Until you're eighteen," she said simply.

I'd started to say, "What's that got to do with any—" Then I realized what she was getting at. "T-that's none of *your* business. Gods, I hope I don't have any dreams with you where you tease me about what happens in my bedroom."

She gasped dramatically. "Wait. Isn't adulthood sixteen on Anfang?"

Narrowing my eyes at her I said, "That's too far, Trish."

She held up her hands in defeat. "You're right. I'm sorry."

"Seriously," I said then exhaled. "At least I'm better able to pick up on your teasing now. On Earth I would miss it every time."

As a quiet contemplation settled over us, I mused on how enormous, gullible and socially clueless my Earthen self had been. It was a sharp contrast to my tiny, precocious, emotional Anfang identity. *How are these both "me?"* Shaking my head I realized it had a lot to do with how my brain worked before versus after. My family was a lot more active in my life now than before.

Over the next hour the beach continued to heat up, despite the fact that daytime had yet to arrive, the sky still showed that sneaky Horus nebula in a starry expanse.

I said, "It's like you're really here, you know?"

Trish didn't say anything, but she did nod.

"How's that possible? Shouldn't you be on Earth?"

She turned her head away from me. "About that." Drawing in the sand with her right hand her brows made me wonder if she was in pain. Her next words were mumbled and not very clear.

More dream evasiveness? I said, "What? Speak up so I can hear you." I thought, *I'm tired of being evasive with myself.*

She turned her face to me. "I really am here with you. And it's me, not some memory or dream copy."

A tightness clenched my chest. "But isn't Earth in a different solar system, galaxy or something?"

Sarah's words found me at that moment. *"Sometimes spirits find others… because they have a message for the living."*

Trish's eyes went to the beach. "Anessa, honey."

No… don't say it. My heart ached and I feared her next words.

Stopping her finger in the sand, her gaze returned to mine. "I've been dead for a long, long time."

The word *dead* echoed in my head a few times and a faint tremor rippled through the beach.

Tears fell from my eyes before I knew it.

"In your heart, you already knew it," Trish said and cupped my cheek in her hand.

I held her hand and pressed it further into my cheek. *She's so warm. How can she be dead?*

It took several minutes before I stopped crying because I'd devolved into an all-out bawl.

Trish just rubbed my back and told me it was okay.

No matter how much time passed, the sky remained unchanging. This was, I realized, by far the longest dream I'd ever had.

"How long ago did you die?" I asked finally, when my sobs had subsided.

Trish blew a stray hair out of her eyes. "It's been so long that if I told you, I don't think you'd believe me."

A cold wind tore through the air making me hug myself. "I was keeping track of how long I'd thought it had been since I was reborn…" My voice dropped to a whisper. "Was that pointless? Did I lose some time between my death on Earth–" I held one hand out and spaced the other far away from it, "–and my rebirth on Anfang?"

She simply nodded.

"Did you at least live a full life?" I asked, with a quaver in my voice.

Her eyes dropped to the ground before she gave me a broad smile. "Of course. I even had three little brats."

I pulled her into a hug. "I'm so glad." Letting go of her neck and holding her hand I said, "Did you really like me? When we lived on Earth, I mean?"

Though she was smiling, she furrowed her brows and her eyes watered. "Of course I did. Losing you crushed me."

The memory of my death on Earth resurfaced as an echo. It would always make me detach from my surroundings in a way I found disturbing, so I never purposefully relived the experience. Around the time of my death, there had been a string of disappearances. Eventually they found the missing college students, or what was left of them.

They'd started to call the perpetrator the Richmond Ripper. The details were firmly locked away somewhere in my mind, but I knew that my final moments were related, and that I was just another victim.

It led me to ask, "Was it a closed casket funer—"

Trish put a finger over my lips. "Don't." She shook her head. "I know you are frustrated by having things withheld from you, but believe me when I say there are things best left in the dark."

"That bad?"

Making a fist at her side, tears flowed like water. "So much worse than you can imagine." Her voice grew shaky, "Since you had nightmares over it, I wanted to say that I wasn't part of *any* of it."

Changing the subject, since I knew pushing would only hurt her further, I said, "I've had time to think about it. I think what I felt for you was more than only friendship." I sighed. "I just didn't know how to process those feelings. I still don't, if I'm being honest."

"I know." My late friend smiled and stepped forward toward me. "I loved you, too."

When she kissed me, my eyes widened. Although my first instinct was to resist, I let that go. *This is a dream, and I never got to tell her how I felt.* Closing my eyes, I lost myself in the moment.

Trish moved to teasing my lip. Her hand touched my shoulder, going underneath the strap and behind my neck. Things were getting very interesting. In a way that would have been mighty confusing and embarrassing for my immature Anfang identity. However, these feelings made a lot of sense to the adult Earthen body I wore in this dream. However, before she could untie the knot to my top, she said, "Damn it." Then rested her forehead against my neck.

"What?"

Instead of responding, she shook my shoulder, ruining the mood.

In Sarah's voice she said, "It's time to get up."

CHAPTER SEVENTEEN
FLUSH, FUCHSIA, AND FLUSTERED REPOSE

WHEN I WOKE up, I stretched in bed and smiled. *I feel fantastic.* Trish's kiss surfaced in my mind, and I blushed lightly.

Sarah was standing next to me, having rocked me awake.

My nose wrinkled when I turned toward her. A strong musky smell bit at my nose, overpowered by an acrid scent.

Wow, did Sarah get doused in a failed perfume or something? Though it was overpowering, it was somehow familiar. *Was it that musk perfume from the shop we visited last year? She did seem taken by it.*

Then I realized that in front of me were several Imperial banners. Unusually, they were in reverse order from the usual. Centrally was the Imperial Royal Crest for the Q'Tar family line. To its right, usually on the left, was the Imperial Carlyle Duchy's crest. To the other side was a simpler banner representing me, Anessa Carlyle. A common staple you'd find in many places, especially Imperial houses. Before I asked about it, I looked to my side, and the bathroom door was on the opposite side. *Weird. Is my memory just that bad?*

Sarah moved to the end of my bed, and my breathing hitched. Behind her, next to my bed, was Mom. She was dressed in her best pure white gown with a matching wide-brimmed hat. Both were dusted with white faceted gemstones.

Our family crest sat on either shoulder as an embroidered patch, bleached of color so it didn't ruin the monochromatic look. Around her neck was a black and gold Imperial Royal crest, to be worn by direct relatives of the emperor. Whatever the circumstance, her presence was for official business.

No smile graced her face and her hands were in her lap, with her fingers interlaced. She was tapping her right pointer finger as though she had been waiting a while.

"Hi mommy," I said, and my voice squeaked.

Her response came in a firm level-tone, "Hello Anessa."

Crap. Something's definitely wrong.

"Sarah," she said. "If you would."

My lady's maid proceeded to close the doors and lock them. I got more and more alarmed with each turn of the latch. She even ushered the guards out of the room. The room got a bit darker as she shuttered the curtains. Once she was done she took a seat at the end of my bed.

Sarah's efforts made my stomach churn. "What brings you here?" I asked, then leaned toward Mom. "Did something happen at home?"

She closed her eyes and breathed out slowly through her nose. When she opened her eyes she asked, "Daughter, what do you know the difference between sows and boars?"

Her question made me slack-jawed at the simplicity of it. "Boars are male pigs, and sows are female pigs." I straightened up in my bed, and pulled away from Mom a little. "Why?" I whispered, "That's a strange question."

Sarah was merely sitting at the end of the bed with her eyes closed. Her hands were in her lap and her breathing was level.

"Good," Mom said drawing my attention. "Do you know where piglets come from?" she asked and nodded toward me, her eyes locked on me the whole time.

Shit. Don't tell me this is "the talk". I nodded emphatically. "Yes. I know where piglets come from. What's this about? This is making me a little uncomfortable." I thought, *Portia's assumption about "the coming of age", the…* annoying *dreams I've been having. Mom's visit. It is puberty, I know it.*

Mom's lip curled faintly before leveling out. She took a deep breath and let it out.

She's trying not to smile. Does my discomfort humor her, or is there something I'm missing? Mom had never taken pleasure in tormenting me, so I knew that wasn't it.

"A bit of discomfort is expected." Her voice hardened, "And necessary." She gestured over herself. "It relates to the nature of my visit." She pursed her lips. "Let's refocus." She placed a yellow S-ROB down, or a short-range obscuring barrier. It was a device that could give us privacy when we needed it. More than locked doors, and drawn curtains in my own home, I mean. It meant it was something serious.

Tapping its top, she asked, "Do you know that adult women have a... cycle every dozen days or so?"

Cycle? Doing the math, it lined up to about every twenty eight Earth days. *Oh she means* that *cycle.* I nodded. Before I could act further, she continued.

"Was it the same in your past life?" Mom asked, then whispered with furrowed brows, "Maybe she hadn't started hers. She did say the years were shorter."

With my heart racing, I threw my covers to the side. Only to find nothing. I sighed. *Guess either I'm not there yet, or...* My eyes landed on Sarah who was still closing her eyes. She wasn't inside the S-ROB's barrier, so she hadn't heard anything Mom asked.

"Yes, they did," I finally answered. "Where are you going with this? I didn't ruin my bedsheets, did I?" I whispered, "Surely that's not enough to draw you here."

She tapped the top of the S-ROB and put it away in a pouch at her waist.

Worrying she had a concern about my fiancé, I held my hands up. "Nothing happened between Gideon and me, honest!"

Sarah coughed, netting her a severe glare from Mom. My lady's maid had her eyes closed, so she was none the wiser.

"Your daddy, Roland Carlyle, is a full-blooded cat-kin," Mom said without preamble.

"How–" I started but she held up her hand.

"A specific type of cat-kin. He has full control over what traits he exhibits. This is known as regressive control. Due to the…" she exhaled and closed her eyes. The fingers on her hands flexed, as though she was restraining herself. "Excuse me, certain members of society view beast-kin traits as those of a lesser species. It is primarily for that reason I was deposed from the Imperial Royal line's inheritance."

Oh. Prejudice. This differs from what they told us when we were two. Thinking back to my classes, I realized that despite there being several beast-kin at my home and in my family, Maaka had none. Ersta, on the other hand, was

CRISTOPH A. T. 227

full of them, but they seemed to be relegated to menial labor. *They've done a marvelous job of hiding that ugly truth from me.*

Mom's eyes returned to me. "That's why your daddy doesn't show any of his cat-kin heritage, and hasn't since we were wed. It was a condition placed upon him, when he stepped into his role as an Imperial Duke."

She sighed. "I'm getting off track."

"Mommy, can you cut to the chase." I put my hand on my chest. "You show up out of the blue, talk of pigs and daddy being a cat-kin. I'm lost and a bit scared."

Mom pinched the bridge of her nose. "You're right, I'm sorry." She looked away. "You aren't fully human, as you gathered from my conversation about your daddy. For cat-kin, you're a late bloomer; however, for a human, you're early." Her hand went to her stomach. "Among other things, this means that you do not have the same monthly cycle that I do. Instead, you go through estrus." She smiled. "It's not as messy, and there are no cramps, but—" she stretched the word out, "There are some… downsides. For one, your behavior will be erratic, to the point where you will not attend classes for those periods of time until your behavior puts you in line with decorum."

I pointed to Sarah. "She could've explained all of that to me. Surely it doesn't require you to make a special trip. What am I missing?"

Mom responded simply, "What is the date?"

Her curve ball made me arch an eyebrow. "Polarae sixteenth, why?"

Shaking her head she said, "It's Polarae twenty-second, honey. It seems you are missing some time. The reasons for my visit, and your memory lapse are related. Let's talk about what you did during the last six days."

Six days!?

As deliberately as possible, Mom said, "During the gap, you were not yourself. You had a particular style preference."

"What do you mean?" I said, still reeling at losing several days of time.

"You wore nothing more than a shift." She said and held out her hand. "Mind you, at your age, we expect more activity for play, and martial pursuits. So yours were shorter, ending mid-thigh." She shook her head. "That ends today. Your shifts will all now cut-off at the ankle, as they do for adult women."

I've spent nearly a week, that I don't remember, prancing about in an advanced state of undress. I furrowed my brows and asked, pleadingly, "Did I at least wear shorts?"

Sarah crossed her arms in an "X".

Oh gods. I hid my face in my hands. Shifts are night clothes, and also intended to be worn under normal clothes. Mom was saying I basically ran around in my underwear, a long shirt that barely covered my rear, with no bottoms. *For six days straight. The hell was wrong with me!*

My eyes shot back to her. "Wait, Gideon visits every Triday for second lunch…"

She nodded. "When he visited, you apparently approached him, yowling his name. Nuzzled against his stomach with your head and hugged him."

Dropping my mouth open I gasped. I'd rubbed against his shoulder before, and that alone was enough to make me blush. *I yowled his name?*

"Then you pulled him over to the couch and laid on his lap," Mom said while closing her eyes. There wasn't a hint of judgment in her voice. "You grabbed his hand and asked for a belly rub, putting his hand on your stomach." She sighed. "When he complied, you were soon unsatisfied because you felt your clothes were getting in the way…"

I waved my hands at her. "Stop! Please stop," as tears fell down my face, my cheeks burned. "Tell me you're making some of that up!" Moving forward toward her I grabbed her hand.

She nodded to Sarah. "She was a witness. You should thank her for protecting your dignity."

With bright red cheeks I looked over at Sarah. "Thanks. What did you do?"

"I told Gideon to stop immediately and guided you to another room. Though you fought me, you did finally put on some shorts, and a longer shift that I swiftly cut a window into." She sighed. "You weren't yourself, so you ran right back to Gideon to reclaim 'your spot' and he continued."

Clenching the cover in my hands I asked Mom, "At least it can't get any worse."

She pursed her lips. "However, Sarah had to ask Gideon to leave after you tried to present your bare rear."

Vertigo made the room spin and I hugged my legs. All I could do is scream into them and hope that was it. I stayed there and cried for a few minutes. When I came back up, Sarah handed me a handkerchief from my other side.

She whispered to me. "It's okay, Gideon didn't see anything. I made sure of it."

To my dismay there was still more. "The day after that," Mom started and coughed, covering her mouth. "You, what was it Sarah?"

She stiffened at Mom calling on her to answer for a flicker her eyes narrowed as though she was unhappy. Sarah said, "Marked her dorm suite's bedroom."

Sniffling, and knowing full well what she really meant, I asked hopefully, "What, with ink or something?"

CRISTOPH A. T. 231

"No, Lady Anessa, not with ink. Unfortunately, when I tried to stop you, I somehow managed to..." Her voice dropped into a lower register, "Stand in the line of fire."

"No," I hit the bed with my opened hands. "You're not being serious. W-wait. Is that what that unusual smell—" Completing the sentence was unnecessary as she nodded with her eyes closed.

"It was at that point I called for advice from Their Imperial Graces. I thought I could handle it myself, but clearly I could not." Sarah gestured around the room. "We're now in the dorm suite next to your original one. The other one needs a bit of a cleaning."

Guess that solves the mystery of why everything is turned around in here.

"Why didn't daddy tell me about any of this?" Letting myself fall onto my back I said, "This is kind of important!" I covered my eyes with my forearm.

Mom gave me a snarky grin. "Did you really want to talk about this with your daddy?"

Sitting back up I held up my hands. "No, you're right. This is awkward enough, I am *really* glad it wasn't daddy who told me what happened."

"You're a late bloomer by almost two years, and weren't showing any typical signs. Frankly, if we had told you what to look out for, would it have eased your mind any? To top it off, your father's trait is a one in a million.

For it to have happened two generations in a row is unthinkable. We did not anticipate that you would experience this."

Great, so I'm one in a trillion? I falsely thought. *That doesn't change how I've embarrassed myself!*

CHAPTER EIGHTEEN

TEMPERATE CONSEQUENCES / UNANSWERED PRAYERS

MOM GAVE ME a few minutes to calm down before I asked, "Did I embarrass myself in public?"

To my relief, she shook her head. "Though it was a bit extreme, Sarah kept you entirely indoors over the last six days. Your daddy and I have been here for three days." She coughed and winked at me. "It wouldn't do to have an Imperial Duke's daughter running about like that."

Exhaling, I clasped my hands in prayer and touched my head to my hands. "Thank the gods."

"Indeed."

For a moment, I imagined my fiancé giving me a belly rub. I put my hand on my stomach, and it made me chuckle. Then I imagined almost flashing my bottom at him. "Oh crap," I covered my face. "How will I ever face Gideon again?"

"Your daddy is sitting with him in the other room," Mom started. "He's trying to explain to him what happened, so he understands."

"What do I say to him, though? I wasn't myself, but I still did those things." Eying my Lady's maid I said, "Sorry about *that*, Sarah."

"It's fine Lady Anessa. Now that we know, we can take precautions."

What are they going to do? I wondered.

"Now then, I'm sure your fiancé will understand. He's one twenty-eighth lupine beast-kin himself." She tapped her nose. "It grants him a more powerful sense of smell."

Oh. So that's *why he sniffed the air near me after my tandem duel with the Blackwoods.*

"He…" Mom paused. "Did have some difficulty being around you when he visited." She smiled. "His own issues are why I'm sure your difficulties will be easier for him to relate to."

"What issues did he have with me?" Thinking on it a deep blush graced my cheeks. "Did I smell bad?"

"It would be best if he explained it to you," Mom said, and nodded to Sarah, who stood up and left the room.

I asked quietly, "Mommy, am I in a lot of trouble?"

With no one else in the room, the hard exterior Mom had kept up cracked and she pulled me into a hug. "No, not at all." She'd pulled me into her chest and held my head close. "You didn't do anything wrong sweetie, okay?"

"Mhmm," I said and my eyes stung. She held me for a few minutes until a knock came at the door.

Using a fresh handkerchief she dried both of our eyes.

A second knock came at the door and Gideon said, "It's me."

Once we were presentable Mom said, "Please come in."

At her words I covered myself with my blanket, using it like a cloak. My stomach churned with nausea at the idea of meeting his gaze. I pulled the cover even tighter around myself as the door clicked.

He sat in the chair Sarah had used at the end of the bed.

"Now then," Mom said. "Gideon will visit once per *cycle*. No more. His presence will reduce your stress levels and help prevent the... less desirable behaviors."

My fiancé dipped his head down to look at me. "It's hard to see you like this, kitten."

His use of my nickname made me laugh and cry at the same time. "You have no idea how accurate that nickname is. I'm just a beast that goes into heat."

Mom's stern voice cut in, "Stop that. You should be a proud Leda."

"Leda?" I asked.

"It's a term given to female cat-kin in situations like yours. You're cat-kin enough to go through the troubles they face, and with it, you'll get their benefits as you grow older." She let her words sink in then said, "Beasts, or female house cats are called queens. You're above that."

"What benefits are there?" I asked and looked at her under my self-made cloak.

"Never mind that for now," she chided and motioned toward Gideon. "You have things to discuss, don't you?"

I nodded.

He asked, "Should I stop using your nickname?"

"No!" I said and turned my eyes to the bed. In a softer voice I added, "I like it when you call me that."

"You know, I can't see you very well under there."

Pulling the cover down over my shoulders, I looked over at him. Though I wanted to, I couldn't bring myself to look him in the eyes. *What's wrong with you Anessa?*

I said, "I'm sorry about how I acted."

"It's fine," he said and the blush I'd been pushing down redoubled when our eyes met, and he said, "But I was a little surprised."

Hiding my face in my knees I said, "Why don't I remember any of it?"

"It's called a Primal Unraveling," Mom said, and added, "At least that's what Roland told me. The more beast-kin a child is, the harder it hits. Nicole apparently went through something similar. They say the experience for cat-kins is somewhere between fourteen to eighty times as intense as it is for a pure-blooded human." She rubbed my head. "Based on how long yours was, you're clearly on the higher end. Nicole only suffered a Primal Unraveling for a day at a time."

Eighty times? Crap. I'd be driven by nothing but hormones. The horribly embarrassing things I'd done over the past few days now made a lot more sense.

Mom's tone firmed once more. "Sarah will be present during your visits with Gideon. She will sit across from you two and observe everything." Holding up a finger she added, "This is to ensure decorum is maintained. As it is, the closeness you need during these Unravelings breaks standard decorum, but that's because you're a part of *human* nobility. If you were in Cherry Kingdom, your care would fall under an Ember Hut." She shook her head. "That's not an option here."

I'd started to hold up my hand to ask a question but she stopped me.

"Save your questions for Sarah later. I'm sure she'll be up to speed within a week. You're a very curious girl, but I don't know much myself beyond what your daddy's told me." Mom looked at Gideon and said, "Please get Sarah for me, but I'll need to talk to her for a while longer with just us girls."

Mom held out a needle from her pouch along with two thimble-sized vials. "Now please, poke your finger. We need a few samples to test some things."

Once I'd given her four drops of blood in each, I asked, "Will I ever get this under control? The Primal Unraveling, I mean."

Mom pursed her lips. "Yes, but it'll take a long time. As long as twelve years for full control, though you should be able to gain some control in around five. You'll still need to isolate during that time, of course."

"Of course," I said with a sigh.

This whole thing reminds me of werewolves. Though their change with the moon is a bit more aggressive.

"I have a few things to discuss with your daddy," Mom said and stood. "Sarah will be in shortly to help you get dressed." She opened the window nearest to the fireplace in my room.

When the door clicked, I was left to my thoughts. The silence was deafening.

I didn't do it often, but I sent up a prayer to Eloria. *"I'm not sure if you can hear me, but this whole thing is scary. Whatever the future holds, I hope to live up to your expectations. If there's anything you can do to calm my mind here, I'm listening."*

Obviously, no response came, but a low thunk did catch my attention. I'd hidden The Accounts of the Day of Death behind my dresser, and balanced it on a piece of wood on its back side. It hadn't fallen behind the dresser, but to its side. Gideon mentioned that the book was particularly rare, and that I shouldn't show it to others.

That's ominous, I thought and went to pick it up. *Maybe I shouldn't be keeping a book that disparages the goddess that chose me as a champ—*

Standing over the book it landed open on a certain page. *"Eloria's Beast-kin Purge"* it read. My heart began to race and I looked around to make sure no one could see me. Crap. *I'm a bloody beast-kin.* Backing away from the book I thought, *Is this her response to my prayer, to remind me that she tried to kill them all?*

An ache in my very bones made me pace around the room, with my arms crossed. *Why would she send such a message? Is she abandoning me, or is this just a horrible coincidence?*

When I'd first found the book, I'd sifted through the accounts, worried about cat-kin specifically because of Veronica my not-sister, the child of two of my Dad's wives through the use of a Ring of He. Placing the book on my bed, I went through it again. There were almost as many beast-kin varieties as there were beasts, but one thing was clear from The Accounts: there was no preferential treatment among beast-kin. Bird-kin, rat-kin, weasel-kin and even cat-kin – none were spared, not even half-blooded beast-kin, like I was.

It might have been my state of mind, but the manner in which the cat-kins perished stood out to me. Most were a wind that would wipe them out without question, while others the entire church collapsed on top of their heads.

The more cat-kin accounts I read, the higher my heart rate became. Before I knew what I was doing, I had thrown the book into the fireplace. It popped and crackled as it the fire consumed it. I even made sure to use the poker next to the fireplace to push it into the heart of the flames.

Though it had taken the book about five minutes to burn in full, I was oddly cold and burning the book had done nothing to warm me.

"I'll just get dressed," I said to myself. "That'll take my mind off of it." Remembering what I'd done to Sarah, I sighed. "I could wait for her, but I'm sure she's a bit upset with me right now."

Returning to my dresser, I pulled out a drawer and looked for a simple outfit, then froze. My breathing quickened, and I stood up and away. The very book I'd just burned was sitting underneath the first set of clothes I'd pulled out. Carefully, I picked the book up. A corner was singed, but it was otherwise in one piece.

Going back to the fireplace with it under my arm, I saw there was nothing left of what I'd thrown in there. Using the poker I furiously checked, shifting through each of the logs to verify. Returning the steel to its place, I threw the book away from myself. It did a pirouette on its corner and landed, open once again.

Edging toward it I stood above The Accounts, and it was on the same page as before. I was about to kick it underneath my dresser, when I noticed at the top of the page was a mark that looked to have been burned through the page.

Another mark joined it, forming the English letter "Y". It made me blink to make sure I wasn't imagining it, but as I did so, other letters joined the fray. My eyes were then locked onto the page. They were like chicken scratch, difficult to read, but the message was still crystal clear once it was done and the burning stopped smoldering.

"You can deny what happened, but it doesn't change the past."

It was the first example of written English I'd seen since I was reborn on Anfang. Instead of the warm nostalgia you'd feel when thinking of home, I'd never wanted something to disappear more in my life.

What the fuck.

Those uneven letters, in a language no one else could read from a world far, far away, were the spookiest thing I'd seen in my short Anfang life. Cultivators could fly, punch through mountains, and would generally be unstoppable in the modern world. This was different, in an unsettling *"you're not alone"* sort of way. *Gods can read your mind, and Eloria appeared before me during my Awakening Ceremony.* I knew the Goddess of Death could very well do this, though scaring the piss out of her champion didn't seem consistent with showing favor.

The unpleasant conclusion that this was someone else acting. Whoever it was, I was sure they weren't the kind of deity you'd willingly talk about.

For a few minutes I stared at the page, then decided it best to put it back where I'd found it after "burning" it.

I'll just wait for Sarah. I'm over getting dressed.

Sarah entered the moment I sat on my bed and covered up. She approached and asked, "Is everything okay?" Feeling my forehead she continued, "You are sweating a lot, and look pale."

"I'm okay," I lied. Telling her about a mysteriously teleporting book that couldn't be burned wasn't something I was prepared to do. *They already think I'm an animal, I don't need them thinking I'm crazy, too!* I promptly corrected myself, *They think I'm a Leda, I guess, whatever that is.*

"It's okay," Sarah said. "You aren't alone in this. I'll guide you as much as I can. Gideon will help, and your family is just a simple message away if you have questions I can't answer."

I hope she doesn't mind this, I thought and hugged her around the neck. "Thank you. I'm so sorry."

Sarah put her hand on my back and rubbed it. "Like I said, it's okay. When we first met, I said I'd be with you your entire life. I meant that then, and I still do."

Her warmth spread over me and dispelled the fear and embarrassment I'd been holding onto.

I really am very lucky.

"Let's get you dressed," Sarah said, then went over to the dresser drawer I'd just shuffled through. For a breath, the fear returned and gripped my heart. It faded away as she picked up the outfit. Underneath it, there was no book.

That did wonders for my unease. *Thank the Gods, or perhaps, thank Eloria?*

After I dressed we entered the sitting and dining area. Gideon waved at me from one of the dining chairs moved to the sitting area. Though I was no longer afraid, The Accounts was still on my mind and I gave a half-hearted wave back.

I'll talk to my patron goddess about this during my next awakening.

Dad sat next to Gideon on the couch, to his side sat Mom. Nicole was on her other side. Kristine sat across from Dad on another chair. Seeing two clear cat-kins made me smile.

Huh. Seeing Mama-Krissi's face calmed me more than Mom usually does.

Nicole saw me and the whisker lines on her face popped out into full-on bristles.

How very weird. Oliver told me about those, but seeing is believing. I hope I can talk to them later. Maybe they know what I'm going through.

"Hi Mama-Krissi," I said and took a seat sitting across from Gideon.

"You have had a rough time, from what I hear," she said.

With a sigh I said, "That's putting it mildly! I'm so confused and embarrassed."

Dad patted Gideon on the shoulder. "The boy and I are going to a local café to have a man-to-man talk." Before he left, I saw him palm a vial from Mom. The one containing my blood.

Every woman present glared at him but didn't say a word. I merely joined in so I wouldn't feel out of place. *What's that about? Are they mad that he's leaving at a bad time?*

When the door closed behind them Nicole let out a tiny *growl* and shook her head. "'Café.'" She looked at me and gave a light smile.

"What am I missing?"

Mom replied for her, "You'll find out eventually. Don't worry about it for now. You've had enough surprises this morning."

With a nod I asked, "Mama-Krissi, what do you know about controlling these Primal Unravelings?"

"Not much I am afraid," Kristine shrugged. "I am in the same boat as Lily. It is Nicole who will have a better idea."

Nicole slouched. "They suck. To say the least. It took me four years before I was myself even a little bit." She regarded me for a few seconds. "You're lucky, you know?"

"How so?"

She tapped her whiskers. "This is the only change I can make, whether they're visible or not. You will be able to control everything. Ears, tail, claws." Smiling she continued, "Despite the awkward parts, you could even choose to remain fully human."

Holding up my hand and fanning my fingers, I asked, "How do I do that?"

Shaking her head she said, "You won't, not yet. Primal Unravelings aside, you'll stay as you are until..." her voice trailed off.

"Don't be evasive," I huffed, "I'm not in the mood."

"Okay. For male cat-kin, the control won't manifest for them until after they've chosen a mate and," she waved her hand and spun it in a circle, indicating she wasn't going to say exactly what she meant. "And for females, it doesn't occur until they become pregnant for the first time."

Her indirection wasn't lost on me and I blushed furiously. *Great.*

"Daddy learned the hard way that he should leave discussions like this to other women," she covered half of her face with her hand. "I heard some of this from him, and halfway through," she laughed, "I threw him out of my bedroom."

Yeah, I wouldn't be able to suffer Dad telling me any *of this.*

CHAPTER NINETEEN
OLIVER'S INVITE

Deuday, Lokandae 6th, 1737

ALMOST A YEAR after the most embarrassing day of my life, Sarah handed me a letter when I finished my last class of the day.

"This came for you this morning," she said, presenting me with an ornate envelope.

It was embossed with our family crest, and on the flap Oliver's crest was debossed along with a second crest I was unfamiliar with.

Undoing the wax seal, I pulled out a card with a decorative touch that would have been hard to match in modern times on Earth. The card stock was thicker than a credit card, and its edges were lined in gold, with gilded leaf for its lettering.

"I can see Oliver's spending his allowance well," I said and my eyes widened when I read the card.

"Anessa Jean Carlyle,

"You are hereby cordially invited to the engagement announcement party of Oliver Sil Carlyle and Mina Aramon-Carlyle on Hexoday, Lokandae nineteenth in the year 1737.

"Do note, there is a special component to the reception, so please stay for the full event!

"-Oliver and Mina"

"Oh my," I said and my eyes teared up a little. "Isn't he a bit young for this?" I asked and handed the card to Sarah.

She read through it in a blink. "Not necessarily. Children form *acp hoth* through noble connections before they're formally engaged, then they move onto marriage once they're of age." She held out the card for me. "Many engagements are formalized around the age of six or seven if the children have known one another for a few years."

"So what, I'm the odd ball?" I asked.

With a smirk she said, "I suppose so."

Puffing out my cheeks I said, "Gee thanks." I returned to the card. "Mina's name is hyphenated, why is that?"

"It's a marker of intent. Once they marry in the future it will simply be Carlyle, and for all intents and purposes, she will be your sister."

"She will be my sister," I said, and wondered about something, "—but Veronica isn't?"

252 CONNECTIONS

"That's right. There are very few limits placed on marriage. It is illegal to marry siblings, for example," she frowned. "For obvious reasons. And anyone a sibling marries is also off limits for that sibling's siblings."

"I can kind of see that, it would make it weird."

She coughed. "It has a lot to do with bedfellows, but I don't feel comfortable going into that at this time."

Her comment made me frown and stick my tongue out. "Ick, yeah. Let's not even think about that. I was just curious about the distinction," the simple thought of it made me shake in rejection of the thought from my shoulders down. "I have no aspirations toward either Mina or Veronica."

Sarah nodded. "I know."

"What do you think the special component is in the reception?"

"I have some ideas," she said and held up a finger. "But I'm not sure I should say."

"Oh come on. Tell me already."

"I think they're announcing his early marriage to Mina."

Her words made me groan. "And here I was looking forward to relaxing after classes."

"I take it you're going to visit Oliver?"

"Am I that transparent?"

"You're not transparent at all," she said disbelievingly. "Oh, but if you mean easy to read, then yes you are."

Odd. Ever since Ys mucked with my translation art, there have been several times when people don't quite understand me. Earth idioms aren't hitting like they used to. There were always occasional misses here and there, but they're happening more often. Remembering his comment about the brain bleed I was having, I realized, *I suppose it beats being dead.*

When we arrived at Oliver's dorm suite, the six-foot-tall Mina answered the door instead of one of Oliver's manservants. "Hello, Your Imperial High Grace Anessa."

She's as tall as Gideon, I thought. The way she filled out her dress, her silky silver hair, and her full lips made me amend my thought, *Though she's built differently.* "You're a lucky girl," I said before I could stop myself.

Mina smiled and looked over to Oliver. "That I am," she said cooly.

That… wasn't what I meant. Noting my own pipsqueak height of three-foot-ten-inches and complete lack of assets, I sighed. *But perhaps it's better that she misunderstood me.*

"Please, come on in," she said, and ushered me into a seat.

Sarah stood by my side. She would not sit herself unless we were in the privacy of my dorm suite, or there was no way to avoid it culturally.

Neither Pia nor Roa were present.

How odd. Wouldn't Oliver announcing his engagement soon be a big deal? If Mina is here, I'd expect they would be, too.

"They aren't here," Mina said. She giggled then leaned in to say, "You were looking so intently."

Moving my eyes to the table between us I asked, "I'm really easy to read, huh?"

"Like an open book," Sarah said to our side, making Mina laugh a little louder.

It drew Oliver's attention, making us all pause. His curious glare made us collectively chuckle when he turned back to whatever he was doing.

"Don't bring those two up, please," Mina said finally.

"Why not?"

She pursed her lips. "They both rescinded their pact instead of responding to our summons." With a sigh she added, "We strongly hinted at the need for their presence. They not only figured it out, but they responded in kind."

Furrowing her eyebrows she looked at my brother. "I feel like it's somewhat my fault."

"Don't worry about it," I said sternly. "They're big girls." Crossing my arms I continued, "If they try to crawl back, put them in their place. You know as well as I do that they've been keeping themselves at a distance."

Mina smiled. "Thanks."

Returning her grin I said, "You two are formalizing your engagement, huh?"

She nodded. "I'm staying in the suite next to his since we're announcing it soon." Motioning me forward she said, "Really, I'm staying in his guest room. I asked your parents for permission and they said yes."

With a gasp I said, "You're basically living together!" a bit too loudly, as Oliver once again glanced over at us. Though he shook his head and moved to another room.

"It's nothing improper, I assure you. Not only is he much too young for that, he's far too innocent. He saw me in my shift this morning and ran out of the room so fast I blinked and he was gone."

Oliver, the sheepish anime protagonist. He isn't even eight yet, I shouldn't be surprised. Her asking my parents made me ask, "Is it normal for formally engaged couples to stay so close together?"

"No. That's why I asked your parents. My aims are pure, I assure you," she said and put her hand on her chest. "Before we marry in a little over four years, I want us to grow closer and understand one another."

"You are marrying early. I'm a bit surprised. He would still be a bit young for *that*."

Her face bloomed in a nice shade of vermilion. "N-now, that is not my aim," she said, though I caught her whisper, "Not entirely." She coughed. "His situation is complicated. He will soon be this nation's prime striker, of a power far beyond even Roland. To do so, he needs to be emancipated."

Damn, the military is already gunning for him.

"Don't make that face," Mina said. "We are at peace right now. No one expects him to go into battle. Besides," she gave me a wide grin. "If you and Gideon ever make your engagement official, I'm sure your parents would agree—"

"Stop!" I said and held my hands out. "Not happening." With wide eyes and crimson cheeks I added, "I am not ready for that."

Oliver piped in, saving me from Mina's teasing.

"Mina was right," His eyes moved to the card in my lap. "You did come over to ask about the invite."

"Of course I did!" I said, happy for the reprieve.

"We've decided to marry early, when I turn twelve," he said and puffed out his chest. "Because I'm exceptional."

This direct and very Oliver-like reason, which left out every detail that Mina had explained, made me laugh.

"That response is so you."

Mina was equally amused and had a difficult time suppressing her laugh. "So true."

"What's so funny? I *am* great!"

His lack of humility made me laugh harder. "Buddy, you need to grow up a little more if you hope to marry Mina."

It rarely happened, but for a moment Oliver's perpetual smile slipped. "I will. It's not like I have a choice." His brows furrowed. "There are some people I need to take care—"

"Oliver," Mina said severely. "Don't you dare." She breathed evenly. "That is not your problem to solve, okay?"

His eyes went to Mina, then to the floor. This repeated a few times before he walked off and left the dorm suite.

"What's going on?" I said. "He looked so sad."

A faint sonic boom caught my ear.

Did he just jet off?

Mina's voice was calm and collected. "Nothing you need to worry about." She spread her arms. "Just politics."

I grunted. "Oh. Even though Oliver's the stronger of you two, please protect him as much as you can from that."

She smiled. "I endeavor to do just that."

That was the first time Oliver has behaved like that. Is his outward confidence fake?

CHAPTER TWENTY
A SECOND AWAKENING / WHAT'S IN A CHAMPION?

Octday, Lokandae 21st, 1737

BLACK GOLD IS a composite of several elements, I'd learned. Whatever it was made of gave it an almost dingy gunmetal appearance, which seemed rather inconsistent with its outrageous value. Before me was a sapphire-colored dress held together with black-gold stitching. An burnished gold hammer emblem rested over the chest on my left side.

I pulled my palm across its lustrous surface and was surprised that it was almost like water, but there was just enough grab that it's not quite accurate.

Weird, I thought then asked Sarah, "What is this stuff, it's so smooth."

Sarah worked me into the shift that accompanied it, then picked up a pair of boy shorts that I wear with everything. Except these were equally soft.

"This is vicuña silk," she said and slid the shorts up. "Very expensive, even by your standards."

"I thought vicuña was a wool from alpacas?" Part of me noted that the word translated perfectly. *Odd that two different worlds would have alpacas, but then again they have humans, despite the presence of beast-kin.*

She shook her head. "First, vicuña are not alpacas, but they are similar looking. Second, this is from the vicuña silk worms in the north. They only export enough to make ten garments this size per year," she pointed to my dress, "and no more."

"Oh," I said and pulled on the bodice. "Man that's so soft. Just… how much is this dress?"

Sarah said, "Just the shorts are your allowance for three months."

"Seriously!" I said with my mouth agape. "That's outrageous."

She smiled. "There are over ninety thousand countries on Anfang. With only ten exports a year, the price gets out of hand." Her smile broadened, "I recall Oliver bought *three years* supply worth with his allowance. He wanted to monopolize it for Mina, but Her Imperial High Grace, Lily put an end to that."

Her comment about the number of countries on Anfang made me take a second to reboot. *That's nuts,* I thought. "Wouldn't that be more than his allowance since we started receiving one?" I asked in a whisper.

Sarah pursed her lips. "I may have said too much," she whispered back.

He gets a much *bigger allowance than I do,* I thought to myself. *Saying any more out loud could put Sarah at risk of being punished, since there are other maids around us.*

"Anyway, why is my outfit so grand this time around? During my first ceremony, I wore the simplest outfit."

She said, "It's because of what you have worn, on average, over the past four years. You've been a proper Imperial High Duchess during that time."

"Oh," I said and sighed. "I don't feel like one, if I'm honest."

Sarah nodded. "Agreed," she said and winked when I furrowed my brows at her admission. "You and your brother have unusually kind hearts for nobility. I'd say it's something you share with your cousin, Rina. The three of you have pure hearts. A rarity among the ruling class."

Her words made my nose tingle and I wanted to give her a hug. "Thanks. Despite the teasing, that was nice."

Once I was ready and she gave me the thumbs up. We exited my dorm suite. Across the Imperial Royal dormitories I caught Oliver and Mina exiting just as we had.

Oliver bowed, Mina curtsied, and then they continued on. Despite Mina's height advantage on Oliver, he was catching up fast. She still had about a foot and a half on him, being more than twice his age. As they exited the suites he walked by her leisurely, his usual energetic bouncy self tightly restrained.

I'm happy he's growing up, but at the same time it pains me. It's just confusing for me to want him to stay as he is but also grow up!

"Anessa," Sarah said. "Please remember that you and Gideon are supposed to arrive before Oliver. We should not tarry."

In the commons area at a tea table Rina waved me over. "It's a big day for you, isn't it?" she asked and dipped her head in greeting.

"It is," I said and held a fist against my chest. "Every day, I'm stronger than the last. I'm hopeful I'll finally awaken. It's really strange to be stuck in an in-between state."

Rina smiled weakly. "Good luck. I will have my own final awakening in Ylldriae." She cast her eyes to the table between us. "If I awaken it will be a miracle."

"I'll pray for you to awaken, okay?"

Her face brightened. "Thanks, I'll need all the prayers I can get."

Remembering Sarah's words to hurry I said, "If you'll excuse me, I do need to get going."

Before I could take a step away, Sarah blocked my path and whispered, "Anessa, please sit down for a moment."

Since she had never done this, I followed her guidance and sat.

Then, to my side, a pair of steel gray eyes met mine. Lukas seemed intent on walking through the commons to his own dorm suite, the largest of them all.

As he walked past the scowl never left his face, and he glared at me the entire time.

The hell did I do to him, anyway?

Once we broke eye contact he continued as though I didn't exist.

When I was sure he couldn't hear us I asked Rina, "Does he always have to make sure everyone knows he's the biggest cock on the block?"

Rina had been taking a decorous sip of her tea and spat it out, all over me. Once she was done, she laughed in a brilliant timbre. "You're always so on point with your expressions. Biggest," she mumbled the second word, "on the block," and continued to laugh, holding her hand to her stomach.

Arching a brow at her I said, "It isn't quite that funny."

"It is. First calling Juntaro Imperial Duchy's second heir 'stabby,' and now the perfect line to sum up Lukas's behavior." She breathed out a content sigh and said in a sombre tone, "I needed that, thank you."

Wow, does she have perfect recall? I said that almost two years ago!

We arrived at the church fifteen minutes later. Our services usually occurred at school, so this was the first time I'd been to the church in Ersta.

In Redwood's capital, where our home is located, the church was easily eight stories tall, with leaded stained glass windows at least half that height all around.

Here was a simpler affair. As our carriage came to a halt, the commoners were leaving the church. It seemed positively modest to me, at not even a tenth the overall size of Redwood's.

Still separating us by class, I see.

My eyes locked onto Gideon as I entered and I smiled. Until I saw who was standing next to him. *Why is* she *here before me?*

Taking my seat next to the blue-haired tsundere I thought, *She just had to take the spot next to Gideon.* Mom waved at me to my right. In the much smaller church, parents were separated for our ceremony.

"Good morning," Yukirei said as I sat down. She leaned in and whispered, "And how's this little baby today?"

"Really?" I said flatly, "Stop. I am not in the mood."

She held her hand up to her mouth, "Oh my. You *are* in a mood this morning. Is it that time of the–"

Without saying anything I slammed my foot onto the top of hers, and glared at her.

Pursing her lips she said, "I actually felt that. It tickled, but I felt it."

"You went too far, and I only just got here. I'm only eight years old."

"And? From what I hear that's plenty old."

Eying Gideon made him look away. *Traitor.*

"Based on how strong that kick was, I think you'll awaken today," she said and smiled. Taking Gideon's hand she added, "I hope he has a second awakening. He really could do with a boost to his confidence."

Crossing my arms I said, "You're... not wrong."

Yukirei poked my puffed out cheek. "Is it so hard to agree with me?"

"Yes, you're so... prickly. Why do you have to take every chance you can get to pick on me?"

She turned her eyes to the ceiling and her finger on her chin. "It's probably because you're so cute when you're mad."

"Cute?" I stammered and a light blush bit my cheeks. "If you think that, quit making me mad on purpose. I don't like it, and frankly so far I don't like you."

She pulled her hands into her lap and dipped her head to me. Apparently, my blunt statement had an impact. Her smile vanished and she said, "Understood."

Over the next hour we sat in silence.

I used the time to admire the reliefs carved into the supporting pillars of the church. Though it was smaller than the other church, it was no less decorated. *There's always money in religion,* I thought, then realized that it changes things when the deities really visit with the populace.

The usual depiction of angels and demons was there. Not favoring either species, with angels winning on one side, and demons winning on the other. *That's so strange.* One of the demons sat at the top the front-right pillar like a gargoyle. An angel opposed him on the left.

Maybe it's just the usual good versus evil?

Gideon would eye me every so often. It was clear he knew he'd messed up, but he didn't speak up.

This is hardly the place anyway, it would do to let him stew over his mistake a little while. With a huff my thought continued, *Seriously, why did he tell Yukirei that I've already entered puberty. That's none of her business! He should know better!*

Once our turn came up we stood together. Yukirei went first, and I was oddly pleased when she experienced no Divine Link at all. It took everything I had to keep a smile off my face.

On Gideon's Awakening, I feared it would be a dud. *He's worried about staying a third-rate cultivator.* As my thought concluded, he raised his hand toward Eloria. This caused a quiet murmur that died down when the head priest, or the *Father* of the Scripture's Children, coughed.

I gave Gideon a broad smile as he was pulled aside to meet with her.

Then Oliver stepped forward.

He created a Divine Link with all four deities with a statue.

"Father" gave me the usual line about stepping onto the spot of awakening, marked in tape on the floor. *Still weird they use something as ordinary as tape, instead of inlaying a fancy design in the floor with tiles or something. Do they base the location on something in particular? Does it shift around?*

Like last time, stepping onto the "X" made my body numb until the minute passed. Once again, I had a perfect dual Divine Link with Eloria. The highest form of connection.

Great. Behind me all eyes were on me once again. *Yeah, yeah. Nothing to see here. Pick your jaws up off the floor.*

"This way," Daughter Hy said. Her usual boisterous demeanor was absent. She'd met me at my dorm suite, but hadn't really interacted with me.

"Are you okay?" I asked.

She said, "I am, it's just the gods and goddesses have their way of challenging the Scripture's Children." Shaking her head she added, "That is not something you need to worry about, though. It's my own issue to resolve."

"Okay, if there is anything I can do, please let me know?"

A smile graced her face for a moment as she nodded.

"Please wait here until Gideon's link has concluded," she said and stood to the side.

Four minutes later he exited the meeting room, beaming. Pressing my essence vision with what little essence I could control, a faint brown hue surrounded his body.

Neat. Brown's the Earth element, he's just like…

As Gideon passed me he said my name and nodded.

His height, the Earth element, and the broadness of his shoulders reminded me of someone.

The someone that came to mind made my eyes widen and my heart race. *Gods, I'm not going to marry someone who's just like my Dad am I?*

Sitting down on the pillow they provided me in the pure white room, I closed my eyes. All it had in it was a window and a blank statuette. I called out to my patron goddess, *Eloria Kirzington von Addenal.*

"We meet again, my champion," she said, her presence taking over the miniature statue.

Thoughts sped through my mind, as I worried about what I wanted to ask her.

"Goodness, I can't read your mind like that."

Huh.

"Yes, 'huh.' They're all jumbled and chaotic. Though I suppose it's somewhat my fault. You know the date, you shouldn't even be yourself right now." She buffed her fingernails on her robe.

I was wondering about that. She can stop this infernal behavior all on her own?

She grinned. "It's not something I can do too often. You'll pay for it tomorrow." With a snicker she continued, "Not that you'll remember it."

Great.

Waving her hand she changed topics. "I have good news. Your dantians will sprout tomorrow." Holding up a hand she adds, "Though your first god-given gift will take a bit longer." My patron moved forward and motioned for me to lean down. "Though they're called god-given, it's actually something innate to you, your genetics and soul. Don't repeat that, though."

Nodding I said, "Okay." Taking a moment to breathe I started, "I wanted to ask you something about two thousand years ago."

Her smile dropped and her posture straightened. She crossed her arms and said, "What about it, and what have you heard?"

"In Maaka's library, I found a book called The Accounts of the Day of Death."

Her eyebrows rose at the name.

Returning to a closer position, I whispered, "It covered several hundred personal accounts of a beast-kin purge."

Eloria sat down on the spot in a huff. "I thought I destroyed them all. Guess not." Her eyes became distant and she swiped in the air a few times, before going still. It almost looked like she was swiping through screens on an invisible phone or tablet. "So you did find a copy," she finally said with a sigh.

"Also it…" I started, but realized if she wanted to she could just pick it from my thoughts. "When I found out I'm a beast-kin, the book made me fear for myself. Keeping such a book, as your champion and a beast-kin no less, I reasoned it might offend you."

She nodded slowly, but her face gave no indication of annoyance.

"So I tossed it in the fire."

"Good," she said with a smile. "That means they're all–"

Holding up my hand I added, "After I was sure it was gone, I went to change. But in my drawer, the very book I'd burned was there, with just a single corner singed." Then I explained the English message appearing before my eyes.

All color vanished from the statue and it once again returned to a near-formless rock. Though it was still sitting in a cross-legged position.

"That's unfortunate," a louder version of Eloria's voice said as she stepped into the room directly from some unseen door.

A personal visit again. Mom was more surprised by that than me being Eloria's champion.

Stepping forward she crushed the stone statue beneath her bare feet without so much as wincing, then she sat in front of me. "I'm afraid to tell you, Anessa, that you might have a connection with my... darker side. The biggest folly of my life was that very purge." Her hand went to her belly. "It was driven by feelings of revenge, fear, and petty thoughts. Never should I have killed even one innocent, but I cannot change the past. Let me tell you something: I had a child once, long, long ago. Her life was forfeit, due to a run-in with a beast-kin that was unable to control their primal urges.

"To say that I held a grudge is obvious. Over the eon that followed, it festered and turned into something more, something worse." She shook her head. "Don't let that happen to you. During the purge I…" her words caught in her throat, "killed a child, barely a beast-kin, that looked much like my own. She was no older than you.

"As she laid there, dead on the ground," her voice shook as she continued. "Her human mother picked her up and wailed into the night. That little girl was just another victim to the Art I unleashed onto the world."

Taking a breath she wiped her eyes. "Monikers are something you get because you earn them, or are destined to become them."

Holding her hand out to me she said, "Yours is the latter," returning her hand to her chest she continued, "mine is the former."

Eloria went silent for a few minutes.

"Why are you telling me this?" I asked finally. *What must it be like living with the burden of knowing you killed so many innocents?*

She pursed her lips, reminding me she could read my mind. "Because, it helps to understand how your patron goddess received her title. A title you will eventually inherit. Know that I'm not a monster, and that being destined for such a title is far less… tragic than earning it."

Smiling weakly she said, "That saying about great power, from your original life, is quite true. You can help so many with power, but in one careless action, throw all of that good will away. Be not afraid, for you are not alone. Though… it does change things."

I had a million questions, but I knew this wasn't the best time to ask them.

"Anessa," she said, her voice suddenly seemed to make the world shake, carrying a weight over my whole body. "I am Eloria Kirzington von Addenal. Principal Goddess of Death on Anfang, and High Goddess of Craft of the universe at large."

The hairs on my skin raised and my skin prickled. "I call on you, Anessa Jean, of the Imperial Carlyle Duchy, to become my True Champion."

A faint weight settled on my shoulders and sunk into me. *Her title for crafting is over the entire universe?!* Then my heart ached, and a few beats in my chest spread fire throughout my body and I curled in on myself, overwhelmed. *What the hell?*

"Don't worry," she said. "I would never do anything to hurt you."

Those simple words were spoken with conviction and my body relaxed, shredding my concerns, but it wasn't willful. I sat up, despite the pain.

When the burning died down my sapphire dress and red hair were soaked with sweat, making them stick to me. My usual braid had wicked the sweat from my head and was equally sopping. *Eww.*

"That won't do," Eloria said, and blew toward me over her palm.

Instead of a cool breeze, as I expected, my dress was dried in a blink. More akin to a towel after a shower than a hair dryer.

"Now then," her regal air returned and she smiled. "Be sure to tell your mommy, Lily, about this." Her tone firmed, "However, don't tell anyone else. Not Sarah, not Gideon, no one. Lily has good judgment and will ensure that only those who need to know, do know."

Her hand reached out toward me and stopped before it touched my cheek. She curled her fingers in and withdrew. Through her smile, a profound sadness hit her voice, "There is more I need to tell you, but now is not the time."

She feels so bad about the purge. It doesn't excuse it, but when you're a goddess… recalling her words, I thought further, *of an entire universe, who brings you to task for such a crime?*

After I exited the divine audience room, I met up with Mom.

"How did it go?" She asked.

"G-good, I suppose," I said and motioned for her to come closer. "Can you join me as we return to our dorm suites?"

She smiled, though her eyebrows said she was worried. "Sure. I was planning to, anyway." Looking over at Oliver and Mina she said, "I need to have a talk with your brother." Picking up my hands in hers she added, "But his talk can wait until after ours. Now go sit down, they're about to start the Choosing again."

Groaning, I complied, although I was not looking forward to this. *A bunch of noble idiots trying to push kids together. I'll never find that normal!*

Several nobles clustered around Oliver the moment the Father announced its initiation. Taking Mina's hand, he denied all of them.

"That's one way to send a message," I thought aloud. Then the nobles turned onto Gideon and Yukirei, walking past me as though I were a third wheel.

Great. I suppose after talking to Eloria I finally understand why people fear her, and by extension, me. If they knew about my True Champion title, they'd likely flee in terror.

It suited me fine, if I were honest with myself. Though I was upset about them completely dismissing me, the nature of the Choosing rubbed me the wrong way, and I was happy for my invisibility.

Gideon turned all comers down, as did Yukirei.

Despite how much the girl pissed me off, each time she shook her head, I smiled inside. *Is it because I don't want her adding to our... what was the word Mom used, Polycule?* I'd come to accept that the girl was an inevitability in my future as a metamour, but I didn't have to like it, or her necessarily. *Though liking her would help.* Her smile when she called me cute intruded on my thoughts. *Not like that!*

Ignoring the noble rabble, I focused my sights on Eloria's stained glass depiction at the far edge of the church, behind the sanctuary. Several other gods and goddesses were depicted around the church. Their statues in the fore and in the windows were well defined, but they weren't pristine. Each showed signs of age and dust. Hers, however, was impeccably clean.

Free of even the aged creep that often plagues such windows, making them brighter in the center. Hers were brilliant throughout. *Despite her placement of reverence.* Noting the space around myself I continued, *Fear wins out.*

Stepping into our carriage, I crossed my arms on sitting down. *Gideon didn't have to ride back with Yukirei.*

"What's wrong?" Mom asked.

"Nothing," I pouted.

"Are you upset about Gideon?"

I sighed. "Am I that obvious?"

"You are." She smiled. "He's still young and impressionable. Yukirei is too. Have you thought about hanging out with her?"

I hissed through my teeth and turned to Mom. "Why would I do that?"

"To understand her better. It wouldn't be an accord, unless you wanted it to be."

Thinking of going on an accord with Yukirei made my cheeks heat up a hair. Since young nobility were often in child pacts, or *acpę ħoth*, and they were too young to date, in the traditional sense, they would hang out with the intent of getting to know one another. An accord was hanging out with a similar focus to a date that adults might go on.

"I'm not going to form an *acp ħoth* with Yukirei," I said sternly nearly yelling at Mom.

Mom turned her head down and looked up at me in a disapproving glare. Her voice raised half an octave. "Okay, you don't *like* her, that's obvious." Sharpening her voice she added, "But that doesn't change the fact that you should spend time with her." Placing her hand on her chest she said, "I don't always see eye to eye with Julilah, but I don't let the fact that she frustrates me get in the way with the family's harmony."

I just looked at her evenly.

She coughed and averted her gaze. "There have been times, I'll admit, that I've let my displeasure slip, like when she marred your second birthday with a Genesis test." Her eyes returned to me. "But regardless, I still try. You should too."

Giving me a smile she said, "You never know what the future holds there. Did you know that Julilah and Kristine hated each other at first?"

"That has me curious," I said, leaning toward Mom. "What does Mama-Krissi see in Mama-J? They're polar opposites!"

"While I can't explain everything," she cleared her throat, "the two are similar in one key way. They are both very strong-willed women, just like I am." Her smile broadened, "Your daddy does have a preference there."

Waving my hands down and sticking out my tongue I said, "Bleh, I don't want to know about *any* of that, thank you."

Mom laughed. "Fair enough." She winked at me. "Gideon has one as well. You're even stronger-headed than your step-mommies and me. I suspect Yukirei is similar. You even share mirrored hairstyles."

Holding my braid in my hand I said, "Mine came from the Goddess Eloria. It's not that I necessarily like this hairstyle, you just told me I have to maintain it."

"Yes, if a divine patron makes a suggestion, it's generally best to follow suit."

Crap. Bringing up Eloria reminded me why I'd asked Mom here in the first place. "Speaking of Eloria–"

Mom held a finger over her lips, and took out a yellow-colored block. An S-ROB. Sitting it down and tapping its top, a line along its perimeter lit up.

"Okay, go ahead," she said.

"She told me..." my voice trailed off and I bit my lower lip. Words eluded me and I pensively looked up at Mom.

"What is it, Anessa?"

I said, "Eloria said that I am her–" taking in a shaky breath I continued, "True Champion of Craft..."

Mom smiled.

Until I added, "...and of Death."

Mom's eyes widened and she sat back and fumbled in her purse. She pulled out a red-colored block. Smacking it onto the top of the yellow S-ROB she waited until its side lit up and said, "Son of Griblin's bloody whore." Her face went into her hands and she took a moment to compose herself.

Her choice of words made my stomach churn. Cautiously I asked, "What's wrong?"

When Mom came back up and sat up straight again she took a deep breath. "Nothing!" she lied with a false exuberance, the color slowly fading from her face. "Damn it, I'll need to tell Jorin about this." Exhaling she gave me a smile. "Let's talk about Eloria's past, okay?"

"Um," I said and held up my hand. "I probably already know about it. Maaka's library had a copy of The Accounts."

"Oh dear," Mom said. "You know some gods and goddesses can read your mind, right?"

I nodded. "She can, and has. Because of that, I told her about the book. It was during this discussion that she mentioned me being her True Champion." Explaining the burning sensation I had experienced, mom's pallor worsened.

"That's pretty official," she squeaked out and grabbed for Eloria's hierogram on her necklace.

I'm not saying a word about the book's message or how I couldn't even burn it.

Mom closed her eyes and prayed with the glyph clasped between her hands. "Eloria, protect my daughter and the challenges she must face. Guide her into the future of your calling. Have mercy for anyone who gets in her way." She mumbled the rest, but I caught, "Pity the fools who seek to harm her, for they surely seek Death's embrace."

Her prayer made me seem unaccountably alone in that moment. Fearing our relationship would change, and I wouldn't get an answer in the future, I asked, "What does it mean to be the Champion of the goddess of Death, anyway?"

Shaking her head, Mom said, "You're not the Champion of the Goddess of Death, but rather the True Champion. There is a significant distinction."

"And that is?" I asked.

"It means, that if you live long enough, you'll become a goddess in the future." Her tone saddened, "Specifically, the Goddess of Death."

Her posture had returned to its prim and proper state, but unless I was mistaken, she was sitting just a little further away from me than normal.

"I'm scared, mommy," I said, grabbing the hem of my dress.

Up to this point, Mom had been sitting across from me. She moved to my side and embraced me.

I hugged her back. "It didn't hit me," speaking into her blouse I added, "or feel real until you said what I'd be in the future."

"You'll be a great presence in the future," she said, and pulled me away from herself. "Death is not inherently evil, but it is necessary. That you're also the champion of a high goddess of Craft gives you balance. Some of her greatest creations are *living* golems. Before new life, comes death."

Tears filled my eyes. "So you're not disappointed in me?"

Rubbing her thumbs over my cheeks, she said, "Gods no. I'll love you no matter what, even if you burn the whole world to the ground."

CHAPTER TWENTY-ONE
CHOKE HOLD

Midday, Jothariae 18th, 1737

A FEW WEEKS later I was wrapped up in my thoughts. Mom reiterated that I shouldn't repeat what Eloria said to anyone, which is what Eloria had told me in the first place, and they decided to not tell the emperor, Uncle Jorin Q'Tar.

Sprinting was my latest past-time to burn off energy. I'd run tens of miles a day to merely gain a semblance of normalcy. It was during one of my runs that I happened upon Gideon entering a shop in Ersta. Before he did, he checked around himself a few times and then entered.

He doesn't have either of his sentries with him.

When he'd looked my way, because of how oddly he was acting, I ducked around a corner until the door clicked shut.

Waiting a minute after he entered, I turned to the female guard that was following me. "Would you mind leaving me for about ten or twenty minutes?" I asked.

She nodded and walked the other way.

Before I awakened, they would've resisted this request vehemently, despite my increasing strength. The difference in power since was incomparable.

After I was sure I was alone, I approached the building. "Nora's Essencial Goods." Its sign was a girl's face in an anime style. Sticking her tongue out and winking cheekily with an innocent face. *What was that Japanese animation gesture called, "teehee?"*

Was this the café dad was going to take Gideon to? He never gave a name… I looked back up at the silly sign. *That is giving off café vibes.* Shaking my head I thought, *But it says essential, or excuse me, essencial goods. Wouldn't that be more of a goods and services establishment?*

Reaching my hand out toward the door handle I paused, hearing a familiar and distressed voice, "Please, let me go Your Royal Majesty."

Along the side of Nora's was a small alleyway that I could *just* squeeze through, but had to gather my dress up so that it wouldn't rub along the walls.

On the other side of the alleyway on the back side of the shop was Wyn, Rhis and Mina of all people.

Wyn was firmly grabbing Mina's wrist, glaring at her.

Before I could move forward to stop him, he let her go, pushing her wrist.

Mina stumbled at the force he used and almost fell over.

Rhis was looking between the two, not helping either party.

"You should break off your engagement with Oliver," Wyn said and took a step forward. "Then marry me, instead." He snorted. "I'm twice the man he is."

His words caused my pulse to flare along with my eyes. *What is it with these two's sense of entitlement? Don't they realize that forcing themselves into a situation with a girl is not how it's done!?*

"No," Mina said harshly and brought her hands defensively to her chest. "That's not going to happen. Oliver doesn't like you, and either do I."

Wyn snorted. "Is that so. Remember who you're speaking to, whelp."

Mina flinched.

He continued, "I know all about your story. You're disgraced, and have lost your place in the noble hierarchy." Taking another step toward her he added with disdain, "You're now just a filthy commoner."

Despite being over six inches taller than Wyn, Mina shrank back at his verbal onslaught.

"T-that may be so, but I have no interest in you," she said and momentarily straightened out, towering over the boy. "In fact, I'll soon have a station far above yours, so there's no reason I should listen to anything you say."

Way to go Mina! I cheered internally from the alleyway. *Put that asshole in his place.*

Wyn's voice gained an air of false acceptance. "You know what, you're right!" His tone dropped. "But that's in the future. Right now? Mina Aramon and the rest of her family could disappear tomorrow, and no one would care."

"Oliver would care!" she said. "He'd have your hides if anything happened to me."

With a sigh Wyn shook his head slowly. "Yes, he would, if he were smart enough to find out." He grinned. "But he isn't, and we *both* know that. He may even kill me or Rhis before he can be stopped," he said making Rhis's jaw drop.

Wyn said, "But do you know what they do to unchained dogs who bite without cause?" He ran a finger across his neck and intoned, "They put them down."

The boy's words made me see red, and I wanted to knock his block off, but I bit my tongue. *Words are cheap, and until he does something that is more than hot air, I would be the one in trouble if I stepped in without cause.* It pained me to admit it, but Wyn would've made a great politician. *Bal must be a genius at manipulating people to raise someone like him.*

Mina had her hands clenched at her sides.

Keep it together Mina, Wyn isn't worth it.

Her posture relaxed as she breathed.

"I could find out what happened for you, and even get you the 'justice' that you seek." He crossed his arms. "But you know what? Everything has a price, and mine just went up." He spun his finger in the air. "You need to show me how strong your conviction is."

"What do you want? I'm not marrying you."

He laughed. "We'll see. What I want you to do is strip."

She covered her chest with her arms. "Excuse you?"

Yeah what she said, what the hell Wyn.

"I'm pretty sure you heard me," he said and looked to his younger brother. "You heard me, didn't you Rhis?"

Rhis nodded.

"I mean," Wyn said, "it would be a shame if the field you get those flowers from were to be…" he tapped his chin, "torn out to make a nice pig-sty."

"Flowers?" Mina asked unease crept into her voice.

Smiling he said, "Yes, the field with the Yalif flowers. They're excellent for the creeping weakness that I've heard has plagued your region."

Mina's eyes went to the ground and she clenched her skirt.

CRISTOPH A. T. 289

"Come on now," Wyn said. "Show me your 'conviction.'"

Enough, I thought and rounded the corner, out of the boys' view.

She hugged herself and stepped closer to the building. Glancing in both directions Mina's hand went to her shoulder and she briefly showed her shoulder before I cut in.

"Just what the Nether do you think you're doing, Wyn?"

Gods this boy has gotten worse *over the last year. The goal of having the boys leave me alone for an orbital year was to hope they'd mature. Seems* I *was the fool there.*

"What a pleasure to see you," he said in a mocking tone while giving me a bow. "Your Imperial High Grace, Anessa Carlyle."

"Save your pleasantries," I said.

He grinned and said firmly, "As for what I am doing? Well…" his voice trailed off as though this exchange was beneath him.

"You know full well what you were doing."

Wyn crossed his arms. "It is none of your business."

Stomping my foot I added, "Are you kidding me?" I moved forward toward him. "It most certainly is my business. I don't know about her current circumstances, but she is Oliver's fiancée now, officially. Making her look bad, in public, affects him." Hiking my finger toward my chest I added, "By extension it affects me. We're in public, and you just asked Mina to strip. What kind of message do you think that sends?"

"I have no intention of apologizing," he said and narrowed his eyes. "It's beneath me."

"It's an abuse of power, Wyn."

"The worst I'll get is a slap on the wrist," he said and shrugged.

"Like the Nether. If you don't apologize, I'll report that you threatened her life and that of her family."

He narrowed his lips. "You were eavesdropping, huh?"

With a sigh he said, "Nal, Via, take a hike."

"What?" I said, then heard two bells ring out on either side.

"Just what are you trying to tell me, Anessa?" Wyn asked, "Are you threatening me?"

"I'm warning you," I said sternly. "Such behavior and abuse of power could lead to your execution if I were to report it to the proper authorities."

"You wouldn't dare," he said with a smile.

Crossing my arms I said, "Try me."

In an instant he rushed me, having apparently learned nothing since our duel.

I waited until the last moment and stepped aside.

His face met the ground.

It might have been aided by me tripping him.

Before he could move, I placed my foot between his shoulders.

"Attacking the daughter of an Imperial Duke, and an Imperial Princess, no less, is a far graver crime than what you did to Mina." Leaning in I whispered to him, "I'm talking about me, dummy."

Each time he tried to push off my weight with his strength, I'd apply pressure to his spine and he'd cry out and go still for a second.

Wyn grabbed a handful of dirt from on top of the stone bricks as he tried to get up.

Yeah, dig your hole buddy.

Pressing on his back, I said, "Apologize to Mina."

He squirmed beneath my boot and looked at her. While saying "Sorry," sarcastically he tossed the dirt in my face.

I had seen it coming from a mile away, so I closed my eyes and wafted my hand in front of my face. *Enough of this. Why did I hope he'd change?*

Picking him up by his jacket I hoisted him onto his feet. Then grabbed him by his collar, then by his neck.

He failed to pull away.

Was his strength overrated? Making my intent clear I squeezed and said, "You are trying my patience, Wyn Blackwood."

Rhis was to the side, still being an idiot, standing there doing nothing of use. Or rather, perhaps I wasn't giving him due credit. Staying out of this was probably a very smart move for him.

"Anessa," came a voice.

These two make me sick. Pride, pomp, and prejudice all rolled into one.

The voice urged again, "Anessa."

He put his hands on my wrists. While he was touted as being able to crush rock in his fists, but after my awakening, his efforts were like a baby was trying to pull away from my grip. The power was intoxicating.

"Anessa!" Mina shouted with her hand on my shoulder.

I released Wyn.

He bowled over onto his rear. Taking a deep straggled breath he began to cough.

What the hell was I doing? My skin tingled and the reality of nearly killing the boy hit me. *Gods, is this what being the champion of* Death *is about? Justifying myself before nearly killing someone?* Lightly taking a hold of Mina's wrist on my shoulder, I let her guide me back by a step. *If Mina hadn't been here, he'd be dead.*

"Leave," I demanded. For a moment, they remained where they were, frozen. Removing Mina's hand from my shoulder, I pushed forward toward them. I added, "Now."

Wyn scrambled to his feet and grabbed Rhis by his shoulder and they fled.

Before they could get out of earshot, Wyn yelled, "Oliver and Anessa won't protect you forever, Aramon."

Turning to Mina, she was gripping her shoulder. The very one Wyn had made her expose a few minutes ago. The intense frown on her face said she wasn't sad or scared.

She was disgusted, and so was I.

CHAPTER TWENTY-TWO
MINA'S DILEMMA

"THANK YOU FOR your help, Your Imperial High Grace," Mina said formally as she curtsied.

Waving my hand I said, "Enough of that. We'll be sisters in a few years."

She said, "I take it your dantians came in?"

Holding out my hand and spreading my fingers I said, "Yeah."

The female guard I'd dismissed earlier exited the alleyway.

Eloria mentioned my dantians would bloom, *but I never imagined it would make me so murderous. Is it my awakening as a cultivator that made me lose my cool with Wyn?*

The roped section of the library came to mind. *No, it would be foolish to seek yet more power–* turning my hand over I made a fist, *–if I don't even understand what I already have.* Remembering the feeling of Wyn's throat against my hand, and how my fingernails dug into his skin made me relax my fist and shake my hand.

"They did finally come in, but it's been an adjustment." I sighed. "I've worked on keeping my cool in times of stress, but something about what he asked you to do set me off." Smiling I said, "Sarah said violence is the final option."

"He attacked you first," Mina said in my defense.

Shaking my head I said, "Yeah, but I could have done other things to deescalate things. I saw him pick up the dirt, and I..." my voice trailed off. Waving my arms I said, "Didn't care."

Mina hugged me from my side. "Ollie struggles with the same thing, you know?"

"He does?" I asked, noting the nickname she called him.

"Yes, ever since he could walk," she pinched her fingers. "he's been trained to use as little force as possible."

"I remember. Daddy didn't give me any of that. I thought you meant he had issues with anger."

She laughed. "He does at times. There are a few things I've been dealing with that really push his buttons." Her gaze became distant and her smile broadened. "Your big brother cares the world for me, though I don't know why."

"When did you two become so close, anyway?"

Taking some of her hair in her hand she flicked the ends mindlessly. "Did you know he has visited me every single day since you two started school?"

Blinking at her a few times I gasped. "Seriously?"

She nodded. "He always gushes about his days at school, the friends he's made." With a laugh she continued, "He has a lot of friends. A year ago he was really mad when he couldn't visit you for a while. Then once a week he pouts for three days for the same reason."

Clearing my throat I blushed and turned away.

"He'll understand one day," she said and put her hand on my shoulder.

I sent up a prayer. "Let us hope that I never need to tell him myself!"

Giggling she said, "Agreed. That would be quite awful."

With a growl I frowned. *I really don't want to talk about this with Oliver's fiancée!*

It seemed Mina took the hint. "I'm the lowest-grade cultivator, and will likely never advance. From what I do know, aggression isn't usually tied to dantian blooming."

Dantians, I thought, but didn't feel correcting her was helpful.

"Perhaps," Mina said, "it's tied to *that* since it's so... early?"

"Maybe," I said and exhaled. "It's scary. I almost choked him out. A child no less." Catching myself I said, "I know he's older than me, but it doesn't change the fact that he's of an age where he can become a better person, a better man."

Opening and closing my hand I said, "He's older than me, taller, and weighs more than I do." Returning my hand to my side I added, "But he was as light as a toy, and weaker than a baby. When we had our duel, he could easily have trounced me if he weren't toying with me." My eyes stung. "But now, now…"

She dipped down and hugged me. "Now we're okay."

"Yeah. That we are. I should have started with asking how you're doing." Giving her a hug back I said, "Thanks."

"I'm okay, but I'm also pissed at that boy," she said. "I nearly bared myself to him, in public no less!"

"Yes, don't do that."

She laughed. "I'll try."

I vocalized in a short burst, and said, "Gods, I just need to get out of my head!"

"You and Ollie are a *lot* alike in that regard. I always have to tease out what's bothering him because he bottles it all up." She regarded me for a few seconds and said, "Do you have anyone you can say literally anything to? Someone you can trust, who isn't a servant?"

"Why the condition?" I wondered.

"It's nothing big, it just helps to ensure that when you tell them, you're telling only them. Unless you hired them yourself with your own money, they likely have another master or two they speak to."

"Oh," I said.

With a smile Mina said, "It hadn't ever occurred to you, had it?"

"No." Weakly laughing I said, "Not at all."

"Before all this," She gestured around us. "I was actually meaning to talk to you."

"Oh?"

"Yes, but not here. If I'm being honest, I'd like to get away from here."

▼ ▼ ▼

"I was hoping you could help me with some family issues," Mina started as Sarah poured us both some tea in my dorm suite.

"Sure, but is this something Oliver could help you with?" I asked.

Mina's hands went to her chest. "He might be able to, but…"

Holding up my hand I said, "It's not that I don't want to help! Oliver cares for you, and I know he'd do anything for you."

She smiled. "You're right. But he is a little too eager. Would you hear me out before deciding?"

"Of course."

"I'm no longer Her Royal Majesty, Mina Aramon," she said.

For a brief moment, Sarah paused, but then moved to clear the room.

Thanks Sarah. Remembering Mina's words from earlier, I wondered, *Or is it for someone else's sake you are helping?* Shaking my head I realized, *Doesn't matter, right now. She's always there for me, but I guess I should be more cautious with what I tell her. Since it will most certainly get back to my parents.*

"Wyn did say something along those lines, didn't he? How did he find out, anyway?"

"Certainly a good question. Dad was set up by the chancellor." She placed her tea down shakily on her saucer, rattling it. "They found 'evidence' that he was trying to betray the Westwood Empire to a member state of the Tanis Region in the south." Her hand met the table and it rattled once again and bitterness entered her voice, "He would never do that. His entire life has been in service to our empire!"

She huffed. "Sorry. It hasn't been an easy thing to deal with."

"Why *not* ask Oliver to help?" I asked with an arched brow.

"He's overeager." Shaking her head she said, "I don't imagine he would think it through before he started smashing things." She pointed to me. "You, on the other hand, would." Smiling she added, "At least, if what Ollie says about you is true. 'She's always been the smart one.'"

Her comment made me almost spit my tea out, but I covered my mouth to be sure.

"I can see him saying that," I said. "He always has been the kind that hits first, and asks questions later." Recalling my encounter with Wyn, I continued at a whisper, "I'm starting to wonder if we share that in common."

"Don't be so hard on yourself Your Imperial Grace, Anessa," Mina said, making me wince at the formality of it.

"Please, call me Anessa."

"Maybe once Ollie and I are married, I can do so, but as a commoner, I would be breaking decor—"

"Sarah," I said, cutting Mina off. "If I ask a commoner to use my name in my chambers, is that permitted?"

"No," Sarah said simply.

When I gave her a glare she continued, "But, if there's no one around to report the decorum break, I suppose there is no issue."

She looked pointedly at the guard at the door who exited. Then she curtsied and went upstairs.

"I'll see what I can do to help," I continued, "Though I'll be honest, I have no idea if it'll amount to anything."

"Thank you. I would love to have asked Ollie, but there's also propriety and how people would take it."

"What do you mean?"

"Even if we could get him to not 'punch first', they might question his involvement as being only because I'm his fiancée."

"Ah. Yeah. People do love gossip, and noble life is all about the appearance over the facts." Her comment and my rebuttal reminded me of Earth, and I had a light epiphany. *Holy crap, do they care about decorum so much because it's a way to keep "cancel culture" at bay?* I internally reminded myself that cancel culture for nobles from commoners tended to be a bit more fatal.

"I've never actually used my political power to any degree," I said. Remembering the message I sent Bal Blackwood I added, "Well, there may have been this one time I sent an annoying King a warning, but I don't even know if it made it to him."

Mina smiled. "It most certainly did reach Black the Terrible."

"Oh, how would you know?"

"Blackwood is south of the Honeybur Nation, my homeland. When His Royal Majesty, Bal Blackwood received your letter," tears entered her eyes. "Father sent me a message personally."

Why is she crying? I wondered and asked, "What did it say?"

She laughed. "It read that Black the Terrible is throwing a fit. He held a parade for the shield saying it was nearly lost in a foolish bet, but he had it restored to its former glory."

"How is that throwing a fit?" I asked

"Word is, his parade was intended as a public defiance of your message." She held up a finger. "When you didn't react to his provocation, you sent the message that he wasn't even worth the time. He fired all of his court staff, including one my father had been pining over for nearly a decade."

How he'd reacted made me chuckle. "I didn't even *know* about his parade. What, am I supposed to send someone to watch him and tattles when he does something stupid?" The reality of it hit me and my laugh deepened. "I guess he wasn't worth the time. He was right to be mad."

Mina joined in on my laugh. "Oh gods, that's hilarious." She covered her mouth. "You made Black the Terrible look irrelevant by mistake! He'd be livid if he found out." Her smile and joviality fell. "I pity Wyn and Rhis, you know?"

"Yeah. Their dad really *is* Terrible."

She shook her head. "No, not that." Tilting her head she corrected, "Well somewhat that. It's sad that they have that man as a role model." Her eyes went to her lap. "It makes me miss mine that much more."

"What happened, exactly? I know you're no longer a Royal, but is there more to the story?"

Nodding she wiped her eyes. "Daddy didn't make it when we fled Honeybur. His sudden execution was what tipped us off, and led to our escape."

I gasped. "Oh Mina, I'm sorry."

"It's not your fault. There was no trial, and when we appealed to Imperial Bur Barony, we were almost captured ourselves. They held us there long enough for the chancellor's men to arrive, to 'Get to the bottom of this mess.'" She held herself. "We lost some good men that day when they helped us escape."

"Again, I'll do what I can. I'm not sure it will amount to much, but I'll be in touch. Stay in Oliver's dorm suite until we arrange for some guards to watch after you, as I'm guessing they didn't let any of them into the suites?"

She nodded.

If the Imperial Bur Barony is corrupt too, how far up the chain does the problem go?

CHAPTER TWENTY-THREE
AGGRESSION AND INVESTIGATIONS

LATER THAT EVENING, I pointedly asked Sarah, "If I asked you to keep something between us, would you tell my parents anyway?"

She'd been brushing my hair, and her hand stopped when I asked the question. "It depends."

"On?"

"Why don't you answer that question yourself?" she said.

I sighed. "How is that helpful?"

Insisting, she said, "Please?"

"Were I to guess," I said and exhaled. "You would tell them if you thought I would hurt myself, or your silence would hurt me."

Sarah nodded. "You're partly right. There are also legal or ethical considerations. You or your family's reputation."

The brush snagged, pulling my hair. "Ouch."

"Sorry. If I believe you've misjudged the situation, or there are religious implications to my silence. You are the champion of the High Goddess of craft, after all."

And Death, though True Champion on both, I thought but didn't correct her. *I'd hate to know what Her Goddess Eloria would do if I went against what she asked me to do.*

"I've been wondering about that," I said.

"What's that?" Sarah said.

Tapping the hierogram on my mantle I said, "If I'm Eloria's champion, will I need to learn how to craft?"

Sarah shook her head. "Not unless she explicitly directs you to do so. Monikers are complicated. It could mean crafting alliances, nations, or—" her voice trailed off.

"Or what?"

She leaned in and said quietly, "Children."

I turned toward Sarah in a flash, and regretted it. The brush was on a particularly large snag and I think I lost a few strands of hair. "Ow," I held the spot on my head.

"You asked."

With rosy cheeks I crossed my arms and said, "I *really* hope my connection to the High Goddess of Craft is not focused on bearing children."

"They would be children in her name, if that were the case," Sarah said.

"Not helping," I growled.

"Apologies my lady."

"There is something I wanted your advice on, though," I said and hoped it wouldn't get back to my parents. "Wyn was harassing Mina today behind a shop..." I explained our encounter and how I'd nearly killed him.

"Is it normal to be so aggressive after awakening?" I finally asked.

Sarah resumed detangling my hair. "Not necessarily, but you've also gone through several drastic changes lately." She sat the hairbrush down and sat next to me.

"In particular, your beast-kin heritage showing the way it did. Your first duel with Wyn two years ago may have lacked closure for you after you realized he was playing with you."

Her comment made me purse my lips. *She's not wrong.*

Sarah took my hair in her hands and started to re-braid it. "Finding out you're Eloria's True Champion of Craft." She winked at me and said, "Her Imperial High Grace, Lily filled me in on that."

Putting my hand on my chest I said, "Yeah I'm still not sure how to process that." I thought, *Or my connection to death.*

"Yukirei."

Her name made me clench my jaw. "Yeah. Yukirei really chaps my ass," I said and covered my mouth.

In the mirror Sarah sported a smile, but she was silent. She pulled out a letter from my chest of drawers. Waving it by an end, she said, "You still haven't sent her a reply."

"Of course I haven't!" I said and almost stood, but Sarah's gentle hand on my shoulder stopped me. "She asked for an accord." I turned to Sarah and she held my braid near my head so I wouldn't undo her work. "You know that means. She wants to *date* me. I don't feel that way about her, and I'm not sure if I ever can."

"Is it because she makes you upset?" Sarah asked.

"Not entirely that." I put my hand on the side of my head. "I'm not sure how I feel about… girls, you know?"

Sarah nodded.

"Gideon is infatuated with her, and he's said if I want him to stop going on accords with Yukirei he would oblige, and even break off their *acp hoth*." I lowered my voice. "But I couldn't do that to him."

Sarah must've sensed my frustration, she continued, "You've also stopped training since you found out about being the True Champion of Craft." She tied the end of my braid off. "Is it because you're afraid your untamed skill to erase things runs counter to how you personify Her Goddess Eloria?"

"Mostly, but there are other things mommy knows that I can't talk about. It is my decision though, and no one else's."

"See," she patted my leg. "You're stressed. Going back to your training could do you wonders. Pretend the dummies are Wyn and Rhis if you like." Playfully she made a fist and tapped my shoulder. "Beat the stuffing out of them."

"Maybe so," I said and made a tight fist. "Getting the hang of this might help me defend myself, and not accidentally kill anyone."

Her voice raised a half-octave, "That's important to do, too."

"Do you think Anult and Binault are still available to continue my training?"

She shook her head. "Not really. You said to give them a month's allowance as their pay when you started. When you stopped training after your awakening, I paid them, and they both… retired."

I laughed nervously. "Yeah. A month of my allowance could let most people do that." Nodding to her I said, "Would you find a suitable replacement, and pay them what's actually appropriate for their efforts?"

Sarah pulled out some parchment and a quill and wrote it down. "Any other purchases at this time?"

"Not really," I said and a flash of picking up Wyn flickered through my mind. "It was strange, you know?"

"What?" She asked.

"He was so light. I thought I was 'strong' before my ceremony, but now… it's scary."

"If I may be permitted to know, how many dantians do you have?"

Tilting my head to the side I said, "Seven. You were there when I told Kile."

"Yes, but…" She placed her quill to the paper and lifted it again. "It's not normal to have seven. Even if you have seven buds. Can you check?"

Giving Sarah a pointed look I sighed and closed my eyes. Looking inside your Personal Space is second nature to cultivators. Think of it like a really detailed map of how you look on the inside of your own body.

One behind each of my eyes, another in the center of my head, inside my heart, then in my diaphragm, behind my navel and finally my groin. All seven were there. As buds, they were nebulous voids. After they "bloomed" they became like a thick polychromatic mist.

"Still seven," I said.

"Hmm," she said. "I'll need to consult your parents about that."

Giving her a tone of disbelief I said with an arched brow, "Why?"

"Oliver has three dantians, you know that, right?"

I nodded.

"The chances that someone is born a future cultivator are one in ten thousand. The rate is higher in the nobility because they tend to gravitate to cultivators." She looked to the side and pursed her lips. "How rare do you think it is to have two dantians, and then three?"

"Um, I have no idea, because I have no context to draw from."

Sarah widened her eyes at me and gestured with her hand encouragingly.

Got it, I'm supposed to try anyway, I thought then said, "One in a hundred thousand, and one in a million?"

"Not quite. The odds of having two dantians is one in ten million. Oliver is one in twenty billion, but that's not factoring in his innate talent for drawing in essence, which is even rarer."

I just blinked at her. *That's insane. What? If the odds are so stacked against even Oliver having three, what are the odds of me having all seven?*

"There's only a single record of someone with four dantians, and that's Lady Undine. She, like Oliver, was a paragon. Though she was far rarer, being born at the peak of the Sky Realm."

"But…" the odds had my head spinning. "Wouldn't that make me as rare as Oliver is to mortals on Anfang, when compared to a world full of Undines?"

"Rarer, perhaps."

Sighing I said, "That math makes my head hurt." I thought, *She's got to be pulling my leg. Oliver's so much more powerful than me.*

Waving my hand I said, "Moving on. I wanted to get your input on Mina. Are you aware of her circumstances right now?"

Sarah nodded. "Yes. It's a sad state of affairs." She looked away. "The coup was done by the book. They followed all the correct procedures."

At her words, I almost screamed. "They *what?*"

"Um…" she said and leaned back. "The previous chancellor of the Honeybur Nation secured the backing of the Imperial Baron above him."

I exhaled, realizing I was pressuring Sarah. *It's not her fault.*

She relaxed. "As a result, the Palace Coup was legitimized." Holding up her hands she added, "That doesn't make it 'okay,' exactly, just that the Imperial involvement after that is minimal unless there's reason to believe otherwise."

"Then Mina needs to handle her next moves carefully, right?"

Sarah nodded. "Very carefully."

"Alright, you said Imperial involvement is minimal due to following procedure. That means it's not zero." Thinking about how corporate hierarchy worked, I asked, "Does that mean Mina should go up the chain, and seek aid at each juncture? If she manages to reach the Carlyle house along the way, we could step in and do a proper investigation at that point?"

Sarah smiled. "Yes, that's it exactly."

I closed my eyes and exhaled. "Why didn't one of my parents tell Mina this herself? She's important to Oliver."

"Because he's not marrying her for her station, she hasn't asked them, and as you rightly pointed out, there's procedure to follow." Sarah shook her head. "If they were to tell Oliver or Mina directly what to do, it would be bad form." She pointed to me. "You on the other hand, are not under as many restrictions as your parents. They also did not tell you to do anything about Mina's situation."

Sarah went to prep my bed. "Now then, this also doubles to find additional dereliction of duty. The Imperial Bur Baron legitimizing the chancellor's plan, and going as far as to hold onto Mina and her family, stinks of foul play."

Oh, I'd assumed she'd need to visit the other nobles. But finding corruption is a bonus, I thought, then said, "Mina will have to visit each of the Imperial noble houses in person, won't she?"

Sarah nodded. "Unfortunately." She sat back down next to me. "Let's hope the Carlyle house handles the situation well."

"What do you mean?" I furrowed my eyebrows. "We wouldn't do anything to Mina!"

"Not what I meant," Sarah held up her hands. "Your house is not just your family. Who knows what might happen if she's turned away before even being seen in an official capacity, is what I mean."

"Oh, that makes more sense," I said. *Yeah who knows what the guards might say. They should all know M...*

Realizing the issue, I said, "She's really recognizable, that might be a bad thing." I pointed to my hair. "Her silver hair is very rare, isn't it?"

"Yes, it might even be best if she hides it." Sarah motioned toward my bed, giving me the hint that it's time for me to lie down. "Southern Westwood doesn't have a rail system yet. She'll have to travel by carriage."

"Crap, so her trip will take her…" doing the math in my head my eyes widened, "years?"

Nodding Sarah said, "Yes, probably around three years. She'll be away from His Imperial High Grace, Oliver for quite some time." Pursing her lips she added, "That might make him a bit upset with you."

"Couldn't we just hire someone in the Sky Realm to…"

Sarah shook her head. "That's an expensive ask. It would show she had a very substantial backer. Any chance we have, at her trip uncovering something of worth, would vanish. Especially if she showed up with someone of that stature."

There's also only seven *Sky Realm cultivators in Westwood. And I know three of them. Five if you count my "lovable" cousin Lukas, and his father, Jorin but I've never met him.*

"While it's much slower," Sarah said, "a land trip would be more believable."

Nodding to Sarah's comments I thought, *Were she not deposed, she would be able to afford it. Dad did something similar for the guests at Oliver and my's second birthday.* I laughed. *My gut tells me they didn't pay him a single Ŵua for his efforts.*

The run-in I had with Wyn sprang to mind and I sighed. "We need to prepare some form of insurance for her, don't we?"

"Insurance?" Sarah asked.

"You know, some form of 'get out of jail free' card she can use to contact me in an urgent moment?"

Her face brightened. "Yes. Something like that would be useful. She could put it in a secure place, but we'd need to hope she doesn't need it. A life tablet would also be a vital necessity."

"Life tablet? Is that something she can eat?"

A light smirk bit at the corners of Sarah's lips. "No, it is not something you can eat. It will tell us about her health. If it cracks, she's critically injured." Her tone went sombre, "If it breaks…"

"Oh. Gods, yes. She'll need something like that. And I'll pray daily that it never breaks *or* cracks."

CHAPTER TWENTY-FOUR
IN THE HEAT OF THE MOMENT

Hexoday, Jothariae 19th, 1738

I HAVE A bone to pick with the gods above. All eyes were on me this morning after I'd just "vanished" a portion of my school desk with the touch of my hand.

Less than a minute ago I'd groaned and rolled my eyes at Max. He'd made a tasteless joke comparing me to Oliver.

Max laughed and said, "You're a bit testy this morning Imperial Lady Anessa."

Breathing out through my nose usually worked to calm myself, but this morning it didn't work. "Do you ever shut up!?" I yelled, then I lightly "slapped" my desk. The stillness in the room, in finding a hand-shaped hole in my desk that perfectly fit my palm, made my scalp tingle.

Turning my head towards my classmates, all eyes were on me, but that ended the moment our eyes met. The weather must've been particularly noteworthy today since they all looked outside. Desks gently screeched as a few students decided they were too close.

With everyone's eyes on me, I wanted to yell at whatever god or goddess that made my hormonal situation possible. Worse, the *cycle* I experience is every ten days on the dot, and lasted three. On the day that I return to my senses, my clarity and temperament are still affected. Clearly to my detriment.

In the mornings I'd even picked up running, martial practice, then a bath before classes. Usually, the routine did well to level me out, but not this morning. Slumping over my desk I turned my attention to Portia who looked between me and the teacher several times. It seemed she wasn't sure how to handle my outburst either.

Two *years* had already passed since Mina had started her journey up the Imperial chain of command, and the further she got, the more apprehension I had for her.

She missed her regular check-in last week.

A bell chimed ending our class. I released the breath I'd been holding.

"Portia," I whispered as everyone moved to exit the class.

"Yeah?"

Tracing the smooth edges of the hole I'd carved from my desk I said, "Would you have first lunch with me today?"

Her smile and furrowed brows said she wasn't afraid of me, more concerned. "Sure. But you'll need to accompany me, they won't even let me in if you aren't there, or it's arranged in advance." She sighed and gave a light laugh. "I know, I've tried."

"Okay," I said and picked up the donut pillow I always used the day after my cycle ended.

Max continued to try my patience and asked, "Why do you have that pillow once a day every week, anyway?"

His comment made me stop on a dime. Measuring my breathing, and hoping I didn't repeat my incident with the desk, I said, "That question is not one I am willing to answer."

Before he even opened his mouth, I noticed Portia begin the motion of face-palming.

"Why not," he nudged my shoulder. "Is it embarrassing?"

It's not his fault he's insensitive, I can't tell Max what it's like to taper off from eighty times *what full human women go through.* Heat graced my cheeks and I shook my head.

He took a step back when I turned to him and gave him a look of disdain.

"Never mind!" His pitch went up, and he realized his folly. With his hand behind his head, he chuckled nervously.

Portia gently moved him to the side and took my hand. "Come on Imperial Lady Anessa, let's go have first lunch."

▼ ▼ ▼

As we entered my dorm suite, Portia asked, "What's wrong?"

"Can I trust you?" I asked.

She nodded.

I steeled myself as I said, "I'm a beast-kin."

Portia sat down and didn't say a word.

Say something.

Sarah brought some tea by and gave me a knowing look with one arched eyebrow.

"That's why I'm gone every week for three days," I explained after the silence went on just a little bit too long.

Portia asked, "Oh, do you change into something else?"

Tilting my head to the side, I turned to Sarah.

"Some beast-kin transform, involuntarily with certain stimuli," she explained. Her eyes focused off to the side. "Lesser werewolves, for instance, are strongly affected by Anfang's Lokar, the red moon of war."

"Wait, so some werewolves *aren't* affected by the moon?"

"Correct," she said then coughed. "Though I doubt you are telling Portia that you're a werewolf, since you're not."

"Right," my eyes returned to Portia. "I'm a cat-kin."

My commoner friend looked at me from my head to my toes and frowned. "You don't look it, if I'm honest."

With a sigh I said, "I know. Apparently something about my daddy's lineage hides it until I hit a certain… age, then I should be able to learn to control how much 'cat' shows."

"Mhmm," she said.

"After every seven days, I have my," I started, then lowered my voice and leaned forward, "cycle, and during that time I can't attend classes."

She covered her mouth. "Oh, is it messy?"

A heat settled in my chest. "No, it's perfectly clean, but I behave differently. Weird, and in ways that would break decorum." I thought, *I'm not telling her any more than that, all that stuff was so embarrassing I could die.*

"What's the pillow for, then?" She asked. Her tone of voice was generally curious, so I knew she wasn't being judgmental.

"The day after, I'm super sensitive. It just helps." A blush covered my cheeks. "I'd rather not say more than that."

"Oh, I see," she leaned in equally. "Your bottom hurts, doesn't it?"

"What?" I said a bit loudly, "Heavens no."

She dipped her head to the table. "Sorry. I meant no harm." When she came up her face lit up. She continued, "Oh... that's so much worse."

Her realization made an apple red blush bloom on my cheeks and ears. "Yes," my voice squeaked. "Let's move on from that already."

A single chuckle came from Sarah, earning her a glare from me.

She set her jaw low to hide her grin and her eyes ran from mine.

Clearing the air, we talked more about Portia's troubles with Max, a topic that was a relief to us both.

As she stood to leave, I breathed out, and the tension in my neck, back and forehead faded. *Who knew talking to anyone about this would do wonders.* Turning to Sarah I continued my thought, *Sarah sadly doesn't count, because it's as though she shares everything with me already. I'd be lost without her.*

Sarah caught Portia at the door. My lady's maid curtsied and said, "Please consider everything you discussed a private matter."

Portia smiled. "I will, don't worry. Not even Max will hear about it." She laughed. "He's terrible at keeping secrets anyway."

Turning to me she said, "Thanks for the meal, Imperial Lady Anessa. That's the best food I've ever had."

When the door clicked shut, Sarah said, "Please be more cautious."

"What about?"

"Discussing beast-kin. The ruling ranks do not take kindly to *them*," she said, though I might have colored her emphasis in my head.

"Them?" Putting my arms on my waist, I said, "I'm not a 'them'. I am a beast-kin, and it's not my fault."

She pursed her lips and bowed. "My apologies Lady Anessa, that's not what I meant. I am merely worried for you. With His Imperial Majesty Lukas the way he is, it would do to remain vigilant."

With a sigh I said, "I know," deflating I continued, "But I needed someone to talk to. That's why I told Portia. I know I can tell you anything, but it's not the same."

Sarah raised up and said, "I should be more mindful of my words. I did not mean to diminish who you are as a person." She raised a finger. "Please remember though that you being a beast-kin is *not* common or public knowledge.

"Yeah. That's the other reason I invited Portia here." I cast my eyes to the floor. "Because I guess I knew that others hearing it would be bad." Looking back at Sarah I asked, "Is the treatment of Beast-kin really so poor? They're the majority, so how is it they're so marginalized, just the same?"

"Another ugly part of nobility is their preference for pure blood. Namely human blood," she said and snorted. "It's stupid."

"You make it sound like you're speaking from experience," I said and laughed ruefully.

Sarah stammered, "No, th-that's not the case. I've just seen the prejudice all too often."

Remembering my connection, I asked, "Does it stem from Eloria's purge?"

Sarah nodded. "It does. After her purge, many noble families were…" She shook her head. "Never mind. You may really be an agent of change."

"How so?"

"Being her champion as a beast-kin, that alone sets you apart."

Her words made my stomach roil. *I could do* without *the Death part.* Pushing that aside I said, "It's nice though to be able to talk to someone closer to my age."

Sarah tilted her head. "Whatever do you mean? She's eighteen this year."

I merely waved my hand at her, hoping to dismiss that I'd called someone eight years my senior *"closer to my age"*. "Don't worry about it." The concern I'd had since morning weaseled its way back into my head. "Have there been any updates on Mina's investigation?"

Sarah nodded. "During your lunch, in fact, new information came in." She cleared away the tea and lunch on the dining table and waved her hand. An array of paperwork appeared before us. "The 'evidence' the chancellor used to depose the former Honeybur King is fake." With a sigh she tapped a short stack of paper, "Not even convincingly fake. It's rather sloppy."

Looking through the paperwork I spread the pages out on the table even further. They were numbered at the top, and there was one thing clear. "There's nothing here. It's just... normal reports on politics," I sat one down, "weather," tapping a third I said, "and rumor. The top of the pages say, 'The King's Trust is Broken', but what the Nether is this?" I said and shouted. "You're telling me someone lost their life over this drivel?"

She remained silent for a minute as I calmed down. "These files were pulled from the record of why the king was deposed. Looking for ten seconds would show that it's nonsense."

Sitting across from me, something she rarely does as my lady's maid, she said, "Sometimes the powerful seek yet more power." Sitting another page in front of me, she said, "This is their most likely goal."

On the page was a geological survey, along with a hand-drawn map of a *vein* that covered a hundred miles. There was something notably absent, though. What the vein was.

"Why would you believe this is why he was deposed?"

"Some materials are very rare, to the point that you don't even write down what they are until you're certain," Sarah said. "We have someone looking into the details now. Based on the history of the region, I have some ideas, but…"

Her silence spoke volumes as her eyes scanned the room.

Got it. Whatever it is, they'd kill for it. Though I didn't understand the numbers on the page, I memorized what I could. My gut told me I'd never see this again. *Even talking about it here where I should be safe, is dangerous.*

Sarah tapped the edge of the page and it went up like a magician's flash paper without singing any of the others around it.

Good thing numbers are easy for me. It was then that I realized Sarah had also placed an S-ROB between us, so no one could eavesdrop on our conversation. *Wow, she's really worried about this.*

Moving through the paperwork further, I noticed there were compelling reasons to have deposed a leader, but something stuck out that bothered me.

Comparing the dates on the clearly junk files and the others, I asked what seemed to be obvious, "When was Mina's father deposed? What is his name, anyway?"

Sarah said in a solemn voice, "His name *was* Hammid, and he died on Hexoday, Jothariae 18, 1737."

Right, was. Her reminder that he was dead made my flub sting. But the date brought me up short. "Wait. So he was deposed before the date on this file?" I said and tapped the document on the so-called legitimate acts he was responsible for.

She nodded. "That's right, and it's also why I said this is sloppy. They're drumming up the 'evidence' after the fact. For someone who's guilty without measure, as noted in their official documents, the two don't match up."

Acid bit at the back of my throat, and heat covered my chest. *Those bastards killed an innocent man.* It redoubled my concern, and I asked, "How is Mina doing, anyway? She hasn't checked in lately, is her life tablet okay?"

Sarah had stored the white jade tablet in her storage ring. When she brought it out, we saw that it wasn't cracked, which was a relief, but the body of the stone had gained a faint yellow hue.

"That's weird. Is it normal for it to change color?"

She furrowed her eyebrows. "I'm not sure." Stowing the tablet she added, "But I'll find out."

My lady's maid's secrecy, Mina's silence, and the suspicious resource made me wonder, *What have I stepped into?*

CHAPTER TWENTY-FIVE

NORA'S ESSENCIAL GOODS / SOME EXPLAINING TO DO

A FEW WEEKS later I found myself back in front of Nora's Essencial Goods. Yet again, I happened to see Gideon exit the place.

He stretched and deflated after closing the door behind him, and then bumped into some stranger, laughing.

They shook their head at him and the two went separate ways.

What is that store, some drug house? He's acting like he's high.

Once I was sure he was far enough away, I turned to my guard and asked her to give me a few dozen minutes.

Her look was as if she were saying, *Remember last time?* She regarded me for a moment, but complied.

It took me a few minutes to gather the courage needed to touch the door handle. *Get a hold of yourself. It's just a door.* Grabbing it firmly I pulled it open and roast boar and mint hit my nose. *That's not half bad.*

The hostess, a dog-eared woman was writing on the podium in front of herself. Without looking up at me she said, "I'll be with you in a moment."

It's just a restaurant, I thought. Shaking my head I was humored at my mistake, until the hostess looked up at me.

Her tone soured and she pointed down the hall at my right, then back to me. After doing this twice, she said, "Io, what were you doing outside? Especially in *that.*" She exhaled. "You know you're not allowed outside of your room." She pulled the glasses she had on down her nose and looked at me over the frames. "Especially not in character."

In character? Do they do plays here? Since I had literally no clue what the woman was on about, nor who Io was, I just arched an eyebrow at her.

Her tone harshened, reminding me of a dog barking, which I found amusing. "Io, what exactly were you doing outside? Answer me this instant."

Despite my confusion her tone made me cross my arms.

She smiled. "I'll admit, you play the part well, but right now I'm asking you to stop goofing around and return to your room."

Seeing me do nothing the woman pulled a pendant from behind her dress. She held it up for me to see. It was a silver pendant with a large ruby-colored cabochon set in its center. "Do I need to force the issue?"

She's pissed, but I still have no idea why. I couldn't remove the smile from my face and gestured toward her. "By all means." I thought, *Let's see what this* "force" *is all about.*

Narrowing her eyes at me she said, "Alright. You've left me no choice." Her hand closed over the pendant's frame and the stone flared red. Down the hall we both turned toward a scream that called out.

Her eyes snapped back to me and she said, "Shit, you're not Io. Who *are* you?" Then quickly releasing the amulet, she bolted down the hall.

Having nothing better to do, I followed. *I really must be a cat-kin. Even though I don't know what's going on, there's an urge inside me, nudging me toward that scream. Curiosity killed the cat-kin, right...?*

As I walked, I noted the decor. Deep hardwoods lined the hall and every room had the telltale sign that there was a built-in S-ROB. *There's money in this place.* Noting the regular accents of gold I continued, *A lot of money.* The devices required essence to function, so I wondered, *If the barrier had been active, would the hostess have even heard the woman's scream?*

The hostess was standing in the doorway with a complex expression I couldn't quite sort out.

Is she pissed, anxious or remorseful? Rounding the corner I froze. On the floor was a woman several years my senior, who otherwise looked exactly like me. Freckles, red hair, student uniform. All identical. With one major change: she was older, which made no sense.

The skin on her hand turned pink at the tips, then a vibrant cherry red. The color shifted down her hand, arm, and suffused throughout her body. Horns then sprouted from her head, and her legs and arms grew by several inches.

Is she a demon? I thought and stood in shock.

Once the change was complete the frozen hostess seemed to thaw and rushed to the stranger's side. She hoisted the woman onto a bench she popped down from the stone in the wall.

Neat trick.

Shifting my weight onto my right leg I couldn't do more than glare at the two. I'd been partly responsible, but at the same time I was just an unwitting participant in whatever this was.

A pointed tail dropped from the bench and I realized what the girl was.

She's a succubus!

"So…" I started drawing my word out. "Would you like to explain to me why the Nether she looked like a taller version of me?"

"Older," the hostess corrected, her glare could bore a hole through steel if that were a thing.

"Sorry?"

"She was an older version of… you, I suspect."

"How and why exactly?"

She pinched between her eyes and sighed. "With the right blood, Io is able to take on the likeness of individuals at clients' requests."

Mom asked for a blood sample, and Dad took one of the samples. That they mentioned a café made sense now.

"Was the client Gideon Varn?" I said in a flat tone.

She thinned her lips into a line but nodded.

Placing my hands on my hips I said, "That answers how, now the why… what does Gideon do here?"

"I'm not at liberty to say. Our clients' confidentiality is paramount."

Io moved and her hand went to her head. "Damn, what the Nether happened?" She stood and yelled, "What was the big idea, woman! That zap came out of nowhere! What did I do wrong?"

Dog-ear motioned toward me and the red-skinned woman's raised fist lowered.

"Oh. Oh *shit*." Io sat back down and crossed her legs with a wide stance, more closely to how a man might. "Well, what do we do now?" She asked and rested her chin on her fist.

The hostess said, "That's a good question."

With her tail pointed up behind her head she scratched behind her ear with it. Her outfit was a copy of the one I wore when I went to classes. That on its own wasn't hard to explain, since students visited Ersta on a daily basis.

Though the hostess had told me, I wanted to hear it from her.

"How was it that you had my face when I entered this room?"

She raised her arm at me and said dismissively, "It's my talent, or blood-born gift, if you will. Give me someone's blood, and," she raised up and widened her hands, "Poof! I can become them when I want to."

What annoyed me was the fact that the outfit was clearly made for "me," but on the real form of Io it was bursting in a specific area.

I asked, "You are taller now than you were before, why is that?"

"Mirror, the name of my blood-born gift, allows me to accurately reflect anyone's appearance at any age." She smirked. "That's why I was taller than you are now."

"Uh huh. Can you…" I started but my stomach churned when I thought about the reality of it. "Turn back into me for a little bit." Before she could do anything I added, "Same age as before?"

Io looked at the hostess who simply nodded.

"Okay, sure," she said and her "sure" came out closer to my voice, which was downright eerie. Her skin shifted back, in reverse this time, going from red, to pink to peach, like mine. Freckles popped into place all over her face, neck and along her collar bone. Her height shrunk by several inches.

Her bust, nearly escaping the outfit before, didn't even have cleavage.

Gods please don't let this be me as an adult. I'm a short washboard! Beyond assessing her general appearance, seeing someone else with my face, outside of a mirror made my skin crawl.

"H-how old am I," I gestured vaguely at her, "at this height?"

"Eighteen."

Damn it! I slumped at her admission.

Walking around her once, I tried to make myself feel better. *At least I'll have* some *"back."* It was little consolation. Io stood no more than five foot tall and being given the opportunity to see your future was bizarre.

"Is this really how I'll look?" I asked, in a downtrodden voice.

"With a few exceptions," she said with a nod.

"Exceptions?" I said and perked up.

She tapped her cheek. "If you get a scar, for instance. I can't copy that kind of thing."

"Oh," I said with disappointment. It brought me to my next question. "What was Gideon doing with an older version of me?"

Both women avoided my gaze, and said nothing.

Crossing my arms I said, "Did he lose his virginity?"

"No," the hostess said resolutely. "This is not that kind of establishment."

Io smirked and pointed to her mouth.

This earned her a smack on the back of the head by the hostess who raised her pendant and gave Io a death glare.

The succubus just turned her head away, a pleased smirk still on her face.

▼ ▼ ▼

On my way back to my dorm suite a storm brewed in my mind. The clouds parted briefly as I chanced upon Portia.

"Hey!" I called out.

When I caught up I asked, "Do you mind if I borrow you for a minute? I need to vent."

"Sure, what about?"

"Gideon."

She tittered, "Did you two get in a fight?"

"Not yet," I said. Then I shook my head. "But we might."

"Oh my," she said and followed. "Do tell."

When we entered my dorm suite, I complained the instant the door shut. "I can't believe him!"

Hearing my tone, Sarah rushed over and pulled out an S-ROB, holding it in her palm between Portia and me.

"What did he do?" Portia asked with her head to the side.

"I mean, I'm not *exactly* certain, but I think he's visiting a pleasure house!"

While Portia's eyes widened and she gasped, to my side Sarah's gaze evaded mine.

She knew!

"That's terrible," Portia said. "What are you going to do?"

"I... don't know," I said and turned to Sarah. "You knew, didn't you?"

"Yes, Lady Anessa, I did," she said.

Shouting at her I said, "And you were okay with it?!"

"It is not my place to express an opinion here, Lady Anessa." She sighed. "This was not a decision made by me, and I was told to not speak of it unless asked."

"Why would they even set up such a thing?"

Sarah motioned toward the couch and chairs, and we all sat.

"Tell me, Lady Anessa, what would you do if Gideon was unable to control himself?"

"What do you mean?"

"If he were to either attack you, or was unable to resist your peculiar situation every week, what would you do then?"

All I could say was, "I..." before I came up short. "Why would he?"

Sarah tapped her nose. "He's part beast-kin himself. Just as you have your difficulties, he has his. He said to His Imperial Grace, Roland that he needs to stay far away from you."

"Isn't that a solution?" I asked.

"That means breaking off your engagement, Lady Anessa. Or sending him to another school."

Turning my head to the floor I said, "Oh."

"You're no longer a little girl," Portia said gently. "At least, if I'm understanding Sarah right."

My lady's maid nodded.

Portia laughed. "I mean you *are* little. But you're not a girl, you're a woman despite your young age. Some beast-kin have difficulties controlling themselves," she said. "For males, it's especially troublesome."

"It's creepy, though," I said.

"What is?"

"That he's meeting someone with *my* face."

"Oh?" she said with a smile. "She has *your* face?"

"Yeah, but older. As an eighteen-year-old adult. I mean I'd be equally annoyed if it were someone else, but with what Sarah said I'm just confused."

"Isn't it also somewhat awesome though?"

"How?" I said pulling my head away from her.

"In a way, he seeks comfort in you, on some level."

"I mean… I guess." Io's prone form came to mind and I asked Sarah, "When I entered the 'café' the hostess thought I was some lady named Io. The hostess threatened me with a pendant of some kind because 'I' was outside the room I was designated. When I called her bluff, it made the actual Io collapse. What kind of pendant was that?"

"That pendant was most likely a slave collar control pendant," Sarah said. "To be clear though, the key there is the word control. If it were a key, it would be a control key. A bracelet, would be a control bracelet." She twirled her wrist. "And so on."

"Io was a slave? I've never met one before her, I guess." The benefits of noble life had shielded me from the uglier parts of Anfang society. Though with the fear commoners have towards us, I wasn't too surprised that slavery was legal, we just didn't have any in our estates. *That I know of, at least.*

"Given the… nature of the work," Sarah said, "It's likely active only when she's at work, and not a permanent thing." She coughed. "If things were to get a little too… heated, it could have a constant command that would *encourage* proper behavior." Shaking her head she added, "It's like an electric shock. Some cultivators can push back against it, but not for long. They get a headache, then a nosebleed. After that, they'd bleed from their ears, and eyes."

With a sigh she said, "And if they continue resisting, there is just one other outcome."

"What?" Portia asked, leaning forward.

Oddly, I found myself doing the same. Despite the gruesome effects, I wondered what could be worse.

"Death."

CHAPTER TWENTY-SIX
OLIVER'S CONCERN

Triday, Ylldriae 16th, 1738

"HEY SISSY," OLIVER said at my door.

In a rare effort, I had answered the knock myself and smiled.

Though Oliver and I saw one another daily, personal issues aside, we didn't visit one another's dorm suites regularly.

Today, though, his jovial smile was absent and his eyebrows were furrowed.

"What's wrong?" I asked in an instant.

"Have you heard from Mina?"

Stepping to the side I motioned for him to enter.

"I know she's been visiting the Imperial Nobility throughout our domain, but she was supposed to return last month."

He pulled a communication jade out of his storage ring. "No matter how many times I've tried to contact her," he said, fear entering his voice, "she doesn't respond." He seemed like a ghost of his usual vibrant self.

"Sarah," I said and turned to her. "Could you bring me her life tablet?"

Pulling it from her own ring, she joined us and set up another S-ROB. Lately, I'd had more chats with one than without.

Mina's life tablet remained unblemished aside from the odd discoloration.

"Last I knew," Oliver said, "she was headed toward our home. I've checked around our home and inside it, even." He pressed his hands on the table between us. "At least three times, and she's nowhere to be found."

Sarah piped up to try and sooth him. She said calmly, "We're still looking into the chancellor, from—"

Oliver made fists at his side and the teacup she'd sat in front of him cracked on its own. "I could kill him," he said in a throaty tone.

Pinpricks of numbness shot across my skin as the very air around him became charged. A thick burnt metallic taste clumped in the back of my throat.

His pupils had narrowed to a point, as Oliver's frightening amount of power began gathering like a thundercloud. It was clear my brother was having a difficult time with Mina's absence.

"Whoa there, Oliver," I said and moved around to his side of the table. Despite the tiny hairs on my arm rising as I inched closer to him, I grabbed his hand, and said, "Calm down, don't think like that."

"It's his fault, Anessa!" he shouted, his voice thumping in my chest. "All of it! She wouldn't need to be on a mission to get justice if it weren't for him!"

"Yes, but you can't go around killing people." I said, keeping my voice level. Oliver's temperament was infectious because heat spread over my chest as I added, "Even if you're right, without proof, it would just make you a murderer in the eyes of the law."

Stomping his foot, he broke the tiles beneath his feet. "I don't care!"

I snatched my hand away as a jolt went up my arm.

He held up his hands and added, "It would be so easy," his laugh made me take a step back. "All I'd have to do is snap–"

Tears burned my eyes as I slapped him across the face. "No," I said in a growl. "That's not the way. Your power should never be used like that."

Hitting his face was like smacking a stone pillar, so I grabbed my throbbing hand.

His hand went to his cheek and the look on his face pained me more than anything else he'd said or done, with his slack jaw and astonished gaze.

My heart broke as he shifted from disbelief to understanding over the next minute.

I'm so sorry Oliver. Turning my eyes to the table I blinked tears from my eyes as the tea spilled out of his teacup. *I didn't know how else to get through to you, no way I'm going to let you go down the same path that Wyn or Rhis tread.* Though I wanted desperately to say it to him, the weight in the air sealed my lips.

Finally, he said, "You're right, sissy," he bowed deeply to me. "I'm sorry." His tears wet the floor.

Pulling his head into my arms I gave him a hug to let him cry it out.

Though I wanted to tell him I knew what he was going through, because of what the Blackwood brothers "allegedly" did to Gideon, now wasn't the time for that.

After a few minutes he'd calmed down and retook his seat across from me, though in a different chair as two maids hurried in to clean the floor.

They really do work quick around here.

Once the maids left us, he asked, "How have you been doing yourself? You've been missing a lot of school. Have you been feeling unwell?"

"I'm fine," I said. Then I remembered a visitor we'd had a few days before Mina set off on her trip. "Do you remember that beast seeker daddy called for? You know, after we turned eight?"

"That weird hairy man with the funny eye?"

His description made me smirk. "Yes, that guy."

"What about him?"

"I'm like daddy, a beast-kin. A full cat-kin at that." I shrugged. "Though I honestly don't know how it happened."

Breaking out into a wide grin he said, "That's awesome! So you'll eventually have like... ears and a tail like Mama Krissi and big sis Nicole?"

"We're not really sure, but it's possible I won't have any traits if I don't want them to show." Seeing him almost back to himself made my smile broaden.

"What features would you like as a cat-kin?" he asked.

Leaning back I turned my attention to the ceiling. "You know, I've never given it much thought." Remembering the cat-ears I wore before and how I'd embarrassed myself, I said, "Probably just claws, I guess?" Though I wanted to tell him about my weekly troubles, I bit my tongue. *He's had enough things stain his innocence, he doesn't need another.*

In the moment the door closed, I asked Sarah without preamble, "What did you find out?"

She shook her head. "Nothing, so far. At least, not from the people we have looking for her. Your brother provided a clue without knowing it, though."

I stood. "Why didn't you say anything?"

She looked down. "I'm sorry Lady Anessa. It didn't feel appropriate. When His Imperial High Grace Oliver lost his temper, it made my teeth ache."

"It's fine. I shouldn't have asked that of you." Seeing her relax I said, "He was a bit scary, wasn't he?"

With a nod she said, "The high-class communication jade he has is actually non-functional. They usually emit a dim glow from their center at all times. Unless they need to be recharged."

She pulled out another jade like his. "His manservants wouldn't allow that to happen. This is our jade for Mina. It's also lost its luster."

"I thought breaking them was how you activated them. Have I been using them wrong?"

With a smile she shook her head. "No. Those are lower class jades. You didn't use them enough to warrant more than that." She rubbed her thumb over the ridges in the engraving along the stone. "These require essence to use. Before your last awakening ceremony, you couldn't use a high-class jade."

Huh.

"Gideon should be arriving shortly," Sarah said, changing the subject.

Pursing my lips I sat heavily in my chair. "Yeah, I know."

"Are you sure you want to… confront him about this?" she asked.

"I have to at least see how he reacts. It'll help me clear my mind. Lately I've found myself getting angry just thinking about it, so while I'm not looking forward to this chat," I said, as a knock came at my door, "it's necessary."

Our eyes met as Gideon entered the room. I sat a little straighter and narrowed my eyes.

He'd been smiling, but his face fell the moment he saw me. His pace slowed and he eased himself into the chair across from me. "Did I do something wrong?"

With false levity in my voice, I said, "That depends."

"On?" he asked, unsure of himself while taking a careful drink.

"Have you heard of Nora's Essencial Goods?"

He coughed as he spat his coffee out to the side. His eyes widened. "Um… yes," he said and sat his cup down.

The moment was disrupted by an unexpected arrival. In a rare first, one of Oliver's manservants entered the room and stood off to the side between us, handing something to Sarah.

Sarah said from behind me, "I've been summoned back to the Carlyle estates, urgently. I should return by late evening." She entered my field of view from the side, and curtsied. "Mr. John here will stand in my place until your fiancé, Sir Varn, departs."

Another one of my maids stood beside her. "Fina will stand in for my usual duties until I return this evening."

Damn it, I thought. *That takes the bite out of what I wanted to say. It's more difficult with someone other than Sarah by my side.* Shaking my head at myself internally I thought, *I guess I've become too dependent on her.*

When Sarah was out of sight, Gideon continued.

"It was His Imperial Grace, Roland's idea," he said, and I held up a hand for him to stop.

Since I wasn't familiar with our chaperones, I placed my own S-ROB between us for privacy and motioned for him to continue.

His body closed off to me, and he shifted in his chair. Fidgeting with his thumbs he said, "Around when you became a woman, and I visited on Triday," moving his right hand behind his head he continued, "I'd always seen you as a delicate flower that needed protecting, even though you were stronger than I was." He shook his head. "When I entered the room I had a hard time even thinking straight. Like someone else was in control. The smell was…"

My right eye twitched when he mentioned *the* smell, but I didn't say anything.

"Intoxicating. After Sarah took you into the other room and she asked me to leave, it took me a few minutes to–"

"Stop," I said and shook my head. "Relax. I didn't bring you here to embarrass you." His reaction to the smell was different than I was expecting, but I didn't want to think on it. We'd get far too off topic. "I met the hostess and Io."

The color drained from his face in an instant.

"Don't freak out," I chastised. "As I was trying to say, I wanted to hear the truth of it from you. I mean, I'm not jumping for joy or anything about the café. But at the same time, we can't have *that* kind of decorum break between us, either." A thought entered my mind, *Certainly not until we're married and I'm an adult at least,* then I blushed furiously.

"I am…" I started, while playing with my braid, then paused to phrase it right. "Pleased that you are content with how I will look in the future, for what it's worth."

Without warning, he rushed forward and gave me a hug. "Absolutely, little kitten."

To my side Mr. John was giving me the stink eye. He couldn't hear us through the S-ROB, but he could certainly see us.

Great, I'm certain to hear about this from Sarah.

CHAPTER TWENTY-SEVEN

SARAH'S INVESTIGATION DEEPENS

Midday, Hanvarae 9th, 1738

"IT'S AMAZING," GIDEON said. "Ever since I created a divine link with Eloria," the excitement in his voice was palpable, "my strength has increased by the day."

"Yeah?" I said. Taking the final bite of my meal I listened curiously.

He nodded. "There's even talk that I might become a Martial Core student." A smile bloomed across his face. "I have only dreamed of that."

"Isn't that great," Yukirei said, somewhat spoiling my mood.

"It is," I said looking at her. "If he keeps it up he might become another Martial Core Scholar, like you."

She smiled. "He just might. Though I suspect you'll make it there before he does," turning to the side she said, "no offense, Gideon."

"None taken, even if I improve over the next four years at my current rate, Anessa's still out-pacing me."

"How fast can you run, anyway?" Yukirei asked.

"What was it, Gideon?" I asked turning to him. "With the cultivator carriage, was it two hundred miles an hour?"

"Yeah I think so," Gideon said and nodded. "I'm only able to hit fifty, but it beats the *six* I was doing before."

"What's this cultivator carriage?" Yukirei asked me.

"It's just a carriage set up to be pulled by a cultivator instead of an animal. Generally used for training, or for transit in bigger towns."

Patting Gideon's hand she says, "That's a nice speed." Her eyes turned to me. "When I fly I can hit about a thousand."

This little… her words hit a nerve. She complimented Gideon then trounced my efforts directly. Closing my eyes I thought, *I hope I can hit Martial Core Scholar before Yukirei did at eleven.* Shaking my head I realized, *She's been in the Sky Realm for two years before that. Even if I get titled as a Martial Core Scholar, she'd come up with some reason to lord over how much better than me she is.*

Strength wasn't my issue, it was the Scholar part. I needed to master five-digit multiplication, whose answers often hit ten digits. The mind of a cultivator is amazing, as it's almost easy for them to perform mental feats such as this, but with some combinations, I knew it was unlikely that I'd master it by my next birthday.

But to my surprise, Yukirei pursed her lips and mouthed, "*Sorry*" to me.

It made my eyes widen for a moment. *Maybe she is learning. I doubt we'll ever go on an accord, though.*

She pushed her finger against the wood of the table absentmindedly. As she chatted with Gideon she avoided eye contact. I saw that around her neck was Eloria's hierogram, something she started wearing when I told her I didn't even like her due to the way she was acting.

Her fingernails were painted with yellow, Gideon's hair color. Her pinkie nails were painted the same emerald green as his eyes, but her earrings were the color of my hair.

Amending my thought, I added, *It depends.*

"Lady Anessa," Sarah said and curtsied. "I have some *business* to attend to over the next few weeks."

Pulling her to the side I asked her, inside an S-ROB, "Is it about Mina?"

She nodded.

"Are you sure I can't go?"

She shook her head. "It's too dangerous." She put away the barrier, telling me we were done talking about Mina.

"Since I will be gone so long, you'll need to pick a temporary replacement for me," looking around the room, Sarah added, "the Carlyle estates have added some exceptional new talent of late. One in particular stood out, although I didn't get her name. Last time I went there, I was a bit busy."

Tilting my head to the side, I asked, "Doesn't a trip home take as long as you'll be gone?" Arching a brow I added, "Longer if you include the return route?"

"Not if you *run*," she said with a smile.

"I mean, I guess, yeah. That's possible," I said and sighed. "I'll need to leave shortly if I want to get there tonight."

"You're going home today?" Gideon asked as he approached me from the side. "Would you mind if I tagged along? Mama-Lily has a long-distance communication orb. I'd like to say hi to my Mom." He paused and said, "If that's okay?"

"Of course it's okay," I said and smiled.

"This sounds fun," Yukirei said from her chair. "I'd like to see your home, assuming you don't mind my tagging along?"

"What do you think?" I whispered to Gideon.

He looked between the girl and I. "I'm good if you are, but," he whispered back, "I know you two can get a bit catty."

Locking eyes with him I thought, *Gods, why is he so cute. He's a tall, well built man...*

He realized his inadvertent joke and snort-laughed.

...but at the same time he's a huge dork.

"Oh," he said and scratched the back of his head. "I'm not as fast as you. We'll be four times slower if I run alongside you." He held his hand vertical and added apologetically, "Every hour I'd also need a break."

"Yukirei," I called and waited for her attention. "Can you fly us there?"

She crossed her arms and turned her head away. "No. I'm 'grounded.'"

"Why?"

Looking back at us she said, "I don't want to talk about it."

Returning to my seat I said, "Tell me," I smiled and prodded, "and you can go with us."

Though she tried to hide it, the corner of her lips edged up. "I almost dropped someone," she confessed.

Widening my eyes I pulled back a hair. *Yeah maybe it's best she doesn't fly us.*

Yukirei added, "On purpose."

My jaw could've fallen off. *That's psychopathic tendencies right there, girl!*

"I was only playing around! Unlike His Imperial Grace, Roland Carlyle, I haven't advanced enough to carry someone without placing my hands on them. When I take multiple people, I pick up a carrier they can rest inside." She put one hand under her armpit. "But when it's just one, I tend to carry them." Her body closed off further and her eyes darted to the side as she remembered.

"The scaly old coot asked to ride on my back. I obliged, not thinking anything of it." She spread her arms out. "It's not like I let him step on my back in public, we walked a ways out of town before we headed out."

"Why'd you almost drop him?" Gideon asked.

"He got a bit handsy halfway through. I might've turned upside down," She failed to stop her grin. "Then carried him by his robe."

Okay, not a psychopath. I would've done the same.

"If you are going," Sarah said from our side. "You kids should head out soon. Despite your speed, Lady Anessa, after third six, your guard detail won't permit you to leave Ersta." She winced. "There are also three-person cultivator carriages on the back side of the dorm suites. They'll allow you to get there in comfort."

"Couldn't her guards pull us?" Yukirei asked.

Sarah nodded. "They could, but Anessa has been slacking on her training. A good six-hour run pulling a three-ton carriage would do her good."

For the second time in a short span, I had to pick up my jaw. *Gee thanks Sarah!* I would've complained, but I saw something that worried me. "Are you okay Sarah?"

"Yes, why?" She asked.

"There's a drop of blood on your outfit," I said.

"Oh," she pulled out a handkerchief and dabbed her nose. "I'm okay. The weather's just been a bit dry lately." Giving us a curtsy she said, "I'm going to take a brief nap before I head out." Her eyes focused on me. "Would that be okay with you, Lady Anessa?"

"Sure, you're going to be busy w—" I stopped myself before I said what she would be doing.

Pulling a carriage like a common horse sucked. Though I had a sense of pride, despite that, in knowing that I was faster than any horse could hope to be. The weather had turned as we went. The carriage had a gyroscopic wheel that whirred as it spun down. It took up most of the carriage's size and weight.

"That's tiring," I said as Gideon exited.

"Comfortable though," he said and smiled. "I didn't even feel a bump." His attention turned to Yukirei whose hand he took, and he guided her out.

She walked over to me and said, "Indeed," she put her hand on my head and said, "Who's a good hor—"

The glare I shot her made her remove her hand and laugh.

"Who's a good what-now?" I asked in a deadpan.

"Horsey?" she said, and her voice squeaked.

"Think about where you left off in that word," I said and shook my head.

"Oh my!" She covered her mouth and promptly curtsied. "I am sorry, I didn't think that through."

Lightning cracked, lighting the courtyard, and thunder rumbled for several seconds afterwards.

"Let's just move past it," I said in a sigh. Looking at the sky I said, "We'd better get inside before it starts pouring."

Yllia met us at the door and promptly ushered us inside. "What a pleasant surprise, Your Imperial High Grace, Anessa, young master Varn, and…?" Her eyes stopped on our third member.

"Her Imperial Right Honorable, Yukirei Truval," Gideon said for her. "She's the daughter of Westwood Empire's Grand Master General, Eugene Truval."

Yllia chastised, "Young master Gideon, while the titles are long, if his daughter is Her Imperial Right Honorable, through Rang en Absentia, her father must be His Imperial Most Honorable, or His Imperial Grace." Her eyes returned to Yukirei for confirmation.

"Most Honorable," she said simply.

Gideon's supposed to say, "She's the daughter of Westwood Empire's Grand Master General, His Most Honorable, Eugene Truval?" Yuck, it's a mouthful as it was!

Gideon bowed and said, "I meant no harm."

"It's fine," Yukirei said. "I'm not bothered by it," she eyed Yllia and added, "I doubt any of us are interested in filing paperwork about a simple mistake."

There's paperwork for that?!

Yllia merely said, "Very good. What brings Your Imperials to the Carlyle family home?"

As she shut the door the gust of wind that slowed her efforts brought with it the tell-tale moisture of rain.

Barely made it.

She curtsied and said, "Your Imperial High Grace, Anessa, I must insist that you return to your quarters to change," she said before I could get to why we were here.

Down at my feet I noticed my shoes were trashed from my run. I'd even inadvertently torn part of my dress somehow from my ankles all the way to my hip. The shift I wore beneath was visible on the side and also showed signs of damage. *Crap.* My face heated up as I covered my left side. I recognized my folly, *It was impractical of me to wear a dress to run hundreds of miles.*

Yllia took a piece of cloth from a cabinet in the foyer and wrapped it around my waist. She then fastened it securely.

Gideon and Yukirei sat at a side-table near the foyer. A maid had already approached them to serve them tea.

"I can change myself Yllia," I said at my bedroom door.

She nodded. "Do you still need me, ma'am, or should I call for someone else?"

"Please stand by for a bit. I have a few questions, and I think you'd be best able to answer them."

Giving me a curtsy she closed the door.

Inside, I realized that in fact my entire outfit was shredded. The gold leaf layer on my skirt had broken down and had flaked all over. *Don't run in your school outfit.* It wasn't something I had done before, but since I'd noticed the clouds in the distance, I skipped changing.

Huh, Sarah said it had been dry lately? Shaking my head I thought, *She's probably just tired. Every time I'm awake, she's there. That she asked to take a nap was almost shocking.* Looking over my tattered school outfit, I realized, *Huh, I must've forgot my travel belt.* Shaking my head I mumbled to myself, "Should be okay, I'm at home."

After making myself more presentable, I reconnected with my entourage.

"Yllia, could you please have the latest new hire maids join us in the great room?" I asked.

She curtsied and took off.

"I really am sorry about earlier," said Yukirei with a bow. "When you glared at me, I stopped talking."

I exhaled. "It's fine. If you're really still worried about it, it's clear you didn't mean it."

"Thank you." She smiled. "You have a really nice home," she said, then added in a whisper, "Though it's a bit light on security."

Wondering what she meant by that, I sat down on a bench near the two and relaxed in a sigh. *Running twelve hundred miles is tiring.*

Closing my eyes, I let the back of my head rest against the wall until someone sat next to my left.

It was Yukirei. She took my hand in hers, and said with a smile, "The color lavender suits you." Holding our hands up she asked, "I hope you don't mind."

CRISTOPH A. T. 365

I just gave a soft grunt in acknowledgment and closed my eyes again. I was too tired to fuss about her presumptuous token of friendship. *Tolerate her for Gideon's sake.*

He was about to sit next to her when I shot a look at him. Freezing on the spot, he decided he'd sit to my right.

Good job paying attention, I thought and smiled.

A light warmness settled over my chest when he took my other hand.

In a few minutes Yllia's polite but firm cough made Gideon remove his hand, though Yukirei kept her grip.

Attempting to extract my left hand myself proved a fruitless endeavor as she simply hung on.

After three attempts she gave a light giggle drawing my gaze. She stuck out her tongue and winked.

I couldn't help but grin, then caught myself. *Don't let her pull you in, Anessa.* Choosing to ignore her I stood and pretended she wasn't there. Which was difficult when she went from holding my hand to interlacing our fingers.

Good grief, Yukirei.

CHAPTER TWENTY-EIGHT
THE MAID NAMED CARAH

"PLEASE, FOLLOW ME," Yllia said.

We did so, and entered the great room. More accurately, the grand great room, as there were three in total.

Lined up in the center were three rows of maids, five wide each row. There was ample walking space between each row. *These were just the new hires?* I tended to forget how many people our estates employed. They were so vast that you never got a sense of their entirety, being several times the size of the school I was attending. *Unless you're miles away, you don't think about it. They're hidden behind gigantic walls, and you barely see more than a few people at a time.*

Seeing them here, like this, almost made me a bit squeamish at what I'd requested. They were all perfectly at attention, furthering the awkwardness of my request.

They were relatively uniform in appearance, polished, impeccably groomed and feminine. On the far right in the back, however, one of them stuck out like a sore thumb being six foot tall with dull black hair.

Walking in front of the first row there wasn't anything particularly noteworthy about any of them. Two of them seemed to be bolder or more curious than the rest, and openly looked at me. When they flashed me a smile, Yllia cleared her throat and they returned to staring forward.

On the second row, Yukirei finally let go of my hand as continuing would've been awkward to pull her along behind me.

I asked Yllia, "Is there anyone of particular note?"

"Not that I am aware of Lady Anessa." She followed at a measured pace, looking the women over with a careful eye. "They're all new, within the past month or so. They haven't been fully trained up yet."

In the third row I moved at a quicker pace, somewhat disappointed. *Sarah wouldn't pull my leg, and send me on a fool's errand. What exactly did she mean there's someone with excep—*

The final maid in line made me stop in place and blink. *Wow she looks* just *like Mina.* A light sense of vertigo hit me and my heart started beating faster, as I got an awful feeling inside and realized who I was looking at. *Is this what Sarah was trying to tell me?*

Before she'd left on her journey to try and restore her family's name, Mina had cut her beautiful silver-colored hair and *lacquered* it to a matte black. She explained that her hair is actually made of metal and hence cannot be colored with ordinary hair dye. It wasn't that her hair was rare, per se, though it was. But it was very valuable, and expensive to maintain. When she'd popped a medium platinum coin into her mouth and *chewed* I about fell off my chair. While I didn't know Mina as well as I would have liked, her metallic hair was unmistakable, if you knew what to look for.

And though her gaze was blank and showed no signs of recognition, I was looking right at her.

"Yllia," I said and my voice squeaked, pointing to the tall maid. "What is her name?"

Thinning her lips she closed her eyes for a second. "Carah, I believe."

"Do you know where she is from, by chance?" I asked evenly.

Carah had vacant eyes and didn't budge an inch, even when her name was called. Her attire was identical to the other maids, save for a black choker, an accent that only three others seemed to share.

"No ma'am, I do not," Yllia said. Looking the maid over she sighed, and added, "She was hired directly by Mr. Morris, the head butler."

Sarah's never liked Mr. Morris, and avoids talking about him like the plague. A dot of crimson weaseled its way out of my memory into my head. Sarah's bloody nose, and hint that there was someone at home I should check out, to the point of *running* home. *Gods. Was her bloody nose backlash for defying some kind of control?*

A peal of thunder reminded me it was most certainly not *dry* outside, though we were over twelve hundred miles from Ersta, the clouds covered the sky mere miles from town.

If this is *Mina, her roots should be a different color.* Looking up at the tall woman I lamented my small frame.

"Carah, please kneel," I said.

She didn't even budge.

Yllia repeated the order and the girl complied.

"Why didn't she listen to me?" I asked.

"Unfortunately…" She said and avoided my gaze. "Carah is a slave." Her eyes briefly landed on the other girls with a collar. "As are a few others. Mr. Morris hasn't instructed them to respond to you, which is why she did not."

Approaching Carah, I said, "I see." That was something to address later. I did not like the idea of people in my own home who would not respond to my orders. It implied a general deliberate break in command. Though I didn't like coercing others, it set a bad precedent.

Her hair was thick and most importantly heavy. Despite being a pixie cut, the strands weighed a lot. It was more akin to a soft brush than a person's hair. Spreading the hair to look at the roots I was not happy to see a silver color glinting in the low light back at me.

It made my teeth ache to know my brother's fiancée had been turned into a slave and was sitting in front of me, in my own home.

Slavery itself wasn't illegal in Westwood, and the entrapment variety was reserved for criminals.

Mina is no criminal, so what is going on?

"Yllia," I said sternly.

"Yes, Lady Anessa?"

"Am I correct to assume her slave status is tied to her collar?" I asked. Though I wanted to just tear it off myself, such an act would simply kill the slave. It was a common "protection" against someone trying to free them unjustly.

Yllia confirmed, "Yes, that is correct."

"Remove it, immediately," I demanded. *Mina dyed her hair to avoid standing out. She managed a sixty-thousand-mile trip, only to be taken advantage of at the end.* My blood boiled. *By our own house.*

"Lady Anessa," Yllia said, drawing my attention. She shook her head. "I cannot do that." Before I could so much as speak she bowed. "But Mr. Morris can. Would you like me to retrieve him?"

"Yes," I said flatly.

As she left the room, Carah stood on her own, staring blankly forward.

Weaving my fingers together, I sent up a prayer to Eloria. *Please let this be a horrible misunderstanding.* Though I fervently wished that were true, I feared it was not the case.

Gideon approached from the side. "What's going on?"

Lowering my hands I shook my head. "I'll tell you as soon as they remove her collar, okay?"

He looked between "Carah" and myself and nodded, returning to Yukirei's side, whispering to her and glancing back at the slave with a slight frown. The girl took to pulling her hand over her braid.

Yllia returned a handful of minutes later with Mr. Morris in tow.

He walked slowly with his hands behind his back, and made it clear he was in no particular hurry.

The head maid curtsied and said, "Lady Anessa, if you'll excuse me, I have other matters to attend to." Hearing no complaint from me, she closed the doors behind her as she left.

"How may I be of service," he intoned, "Lady Anessa?" There was the slightest bit of annoyance in his voice as he said *Lady*.

"You are to remove this maid's collar at once, Mr. Morris."

His eyes fixed on the maid. "I cannot do that."

"Could you repeat that, Mr. Morris?" I said with wide disbelieving eyes.

"This one, and three of the others before us, are criminal slaves. I picked them up from the market to help bolster our numbers during Oliver's reception, after his wedding, in just over a year." He approached and stood over Carah.

It reminded me of how tall he was, and how small I was by comparison.

Looking down on me, he said, "Slaves take longer to train." His eyes returned to the girl. "They're in there, fighting the whole time."

There was no smile on his face, that I could tell. His face in general had always been difficult to read. In fact, his features usually shifted and blurred to my eyes. I'd always chalked it up to an oddity of being on a new world. No one else shouted in horror at how he looked, so I'd always done my best to do the same.

The levity in his voice as he said, "As it wears them down, compliance follows," gave me a chill.

CRISTOPH A. T. 373

He enjoys breaking people, I realized. *Just who is this man?* Knowing that showing weakness here would work to my disadvantage, I said, "Remove her collar. I am overruling any concerns you have."

His face returned to me and he said nothing for several dozen seconds. He said finally, "I cannot do that. Whether you say you'll take responsibility or not. If this girl attacks you, it would be my head that rolls."

Putting my hands on my waist, I said in a growl, "Is it that this maid is dangerous, or that you're afraid of people finding out who she is?"

Mr. Morris sighed and placed a hand on his face. "Whatever are you talking about," he said and his tone soured, "child?" His eyes turned to the others, and he barked, "Everyone but Carah is dismissed. Leave, now."

His hand stayed over his face as they departed.

My stomach by this point was doing somersaults.

"Now then, Anessa," arrogance, malice, and disdain dripped from his mouth, "why don't you tell me just who you think this maid is, hm?"

"Mina Aramon-Carlyle, Oliver's fiancée."

He snorted. "Please. Your father has at least a dozen soldiers looking for her." The man grabbed her by her cheeks and pulled her close. Turning her face as he did so. Then, taking a single hair, he plucked it with little effort and stared, transfixed at the silver roots.

"What a shame," he said simply, then a deep, resonant bellow came forth that belied his frame. Like a mix between a motorcycle revving and a pig grunting, I soon realized he was *laughing*. "You know," he said in a smooth voice that suddenly dropped all pretense. "I thought she looked vaguely familiar." He shook his head. "I wanted to break her first before I took her for the first time."

Mr. Morris threw away all chances he had at explaining himself when he caressed her cheek and traced down her form. "It's a shame I'll have to leave this identity behind." Looking to me he added, "A high noble's estates give me wonderful access, you know?"

Before his hand could go below her navel, I shouted, "What exactly are you talking about?"

My brain was not quite processing what I was seeing. But his behavior was so odd that even though I was frozen with confusion, part of me prepared to attack him.

Instead of replying, in an instant, he went from standing next to Mina to grabbing for my throat as my world exploded into a whirl of blinding light and a blast of noise.

What? My head swam as I tried to piece together what was going on. Darkness tugged at the edge of my vision, a ringing in my ear was all I heard after a brief blast of sound. *Daddy,* I thought and pulled the emergency jade from my storage ring. I'd never used one before, so all I thought to put in it were the essentials. Something that could call my Dad in an instant seemed to fit the bill.

But before I could gather the essence needed to activate it, the object was batted from my hand and shattered against the tiled floor.

Gideon, in what seemed like slow-motion, was rushing to my side.

With the barest effort, Mr. Morris smacked him away, sending him careening into the far wall.

No, don't hurt him. I thought and tried the best I could to extricate myself from his grip. Either my usual strength had failed me, or he was far, far stronger than I'd imagined.

With no more than a finger, he tore through my bodice and shift.

Alarm bells went off in my head and I feared what he was trying to do.

To my side, Yukirei was frozen like a deer in headlights, gripping her braid. She was petrified, as I would be in her place.

Holding my free hand out, I managed to get out, "Yuki... rei..." Breathing in was impossible. When her attention turned to me, I added, "help."

Her eyes widened and she gave the faintest of nods.

Before I knew what happened, she'd vanished from my sight and I was tumbling to the floor. When I hit the ground I breathed in the sweetest breath of air I'd ever taken, violently and in a coughing fit.

Then I noticed a hand was still around my neck, and I pulled it away. That was literally all it was, a hand. Throwing the disgusting thing away from me, I sat up against the wall. I wavered as frequent impacts caught my ear.

It was evident now why everything was happening so quickly. The seventh and final Sky Realm cultivator in Westwood was going up against Yukirei, and losing.

Her decision to remove his hand in an instant instead of giving him a chance worked in her favor.

Covering my chest, I thought bleakly on his words. *He didn't care what happened after this, because he was planning on killing us all.*

CHAPTER TWENTY-NINE
FALLOUT - HER REAL NAME

YUKIREI'S FIGHT ENDED as quickly as it began. From start to finish, Morris was outclassed in every way. The intensity of their battle made it difficult to look away, until his head went tumbling through the air after a final decisive strike.

Then I closed my eyes and heard it thump and tumble as the rest of him dropped like a sack of potatoes.

Once I was certain the danger was over, I opened my eyes.

Yukirei was standing near the man's body looking at the ceiling. Blood dripped from the hand at her side. Some very gnarly nails extended from her fingertips.

She didn't even use a weapon, I realized. *I'm definitely going for claws once I can control my cat-kin traits.*

In a flash she disappeared from her spot and appeared at my side. A light wind teased the side of my face, but otherwise there wasn't the sonic boom that you'd expect from such a speed.

"Are you okay?" she asked and took my hand.

With a nod I pulled her into a hug. "Thank you."

Moments later, Yllia entered. "There'd better be a good reason for this—" she had begun but stopped in her tracks.

The junior maid behind her bumped into her.

I'd pulled away from my hug, but I didn't feel like letting go of Yukirei's hand, despite the tiny flecks of blood on it.

Yllia's eyes only briefly touched on the late butler. As quickly as her older frame could carry her, she ran to me. "Take this," she said and put a jade stick into my hands. Though she took to my side, she was very aware of the blood on Yukirei's hand and seemed to avoid it. Not one word was uttered about me holding the girl's hand.

Her gaze went above my head and she said, "Are you alright, Lady Anessa?"

With a nod, I said, "Yes." Curiosity won out over my inclination to remain still, and I turned to look behind myself. My body had left an impression in the stone wall at least a foot deep.

Thank the gods for my cultivator body, I sent in a prayer. Had this incident happened before I awoke, the impact would've killed me in an instant.

The older woman pulled away, yanked a runner from a table and wrapped it around me.

As she did so I pushed my essence into the emergency jade she'd given me, finally thinking clearly enough to realize what was in my hand.

Pulling a bell from a pocket at her waist, she rang it. The maid that responded screamed on seeing the butler. The junior maid that entered with Yllia had been frozen on the spot, enough that I'd forgotten she was there. It seemed the sudden shift made her start to scream as well.

Yllia firmed her voice. "Snap out of it." They both stopped. "You," she pointed to the one who'd just entered, "Go to Anessa's room and fetch her some proper clothes."

The girl shot off without another word.

"And you," Yllia said to the junior maid, "Find Her Imperial High Grace, Lily Carlyle and bring her here. Then take the rest of the day off."

She all but tripped over herself to comply.

A sonic boom outside made me perk up and look around. Seconds later a broad smile covered my face as Dad entered.

Though I tried to stand when I saw him, I was not yet able, and my world spun in my efforts.

He picked me up like a doll, despite being almost eleven years old.

Instead of resisting I just hugged him and said, devolving into a bawl, "Daddy, I was so scared."

While carrying me, he briefly hovered over the former butler and nodded to Yukirei.

"Daddy, is Gideon okay?" I asked while clinging to his jacket.

He looked across the room. "Yllia," he said. "Go fetch a doctor to check on Gideon and then Anessa."

She curtsied and said, "Very good, sir."

"Anessa!" Mom said at the room's entrance. She all but pulled me from Dad's arms and hugged me tight. "Gods baby, what happened here?"

"Mina!" I shouted, finally realizing what set it all off. I pointed at the still motionless maid "Carah," who didn't react in the slightest at anything. The slave collar truly did seal her away from the world. "That's Mina. Mr. Morris put a slave collar on her. When I asked him to take it off, he attacked me."

Dad's jaw fell. "I didn't even recognize her without her silver hair, with such a short haircut." Setting it he shook his head and walked over to "Mr." Morris, then rummaged through his pockets. Finding nothing, he moved to his storage ring, and pursed his lips before putting it on. In an instant a key appeared in his hand. He then took the ring off and sat it on the man's chest.

Though I wanted to look away as Dad searched, I found myself unable to.

He walked over to "Carah" and tapped the collar with the end of the key, saying, "Release."

It fell away in an instant.

Yllia had taken up a place behind her and was talking to the family doctor she brought in.

A second after the collar dropped Mina backed into the older woman, bowling them both over. Her hands went to her face. She was quietly screaming as she processed what was going on. Our eyes met and she looked to the others present.

Her breathing smoothed out and she let her hands fall to the floor.

In a few minutes she stood and approached us. Her eyes landed on Mr. Morris and she choked back a scream, but decided to instead stand as far away from him as she could, even though he was lying in pieces.

"I'm sorry, let me take care of that," Dad said and waved his hand over the late butler, storing the gruesome corpse away in his storage ring.

Dad's passive commentary about the man made me realize he'd seen much worse.

"I'm not sure what the date is," Mina started, "But I arrived here on Ylldriae 5th. The month before, I'd lost my communication jades in a mistake of my own, but instead of spending *another* month replacing them, I pushed on to the Carlyle estates."

She shook her head. "As I had been directed, I did not identify myself with anyone but the master of the house. When…" her eyes turned to the spot Mr. Morris was a few moments ago, "he greeted me at the entrance."

Closing her eyes she said, "He brought me to one of the smaller meeting rooms. And despite my insistence that I be allowed to speak with the master of the house, at great urgency, all he did was offer me some tea." She opened her eyes and grabbed the cloth of her dress. "It paralyzed me," with her other hand at her throat she added, "and I could only *watch* as he placed that blasted thing around my neck."

Midway through her explanation Mom gasped.

Mina began to cry, "After that, no matter how hard I tried, I had no choice but to do everything he said." Covering her face, as though ashamed, she continued, "He said he couldn't wait until it broke my mind. Every day he'd make me und–"

"Mina," I interrupted. "It's okay. He can't make you do anything anymore. We can talk about what he made you do when you feel safe, okay?" Shaking my head I said, "No one's forcing you to talk about it now. Unless you want or need to."

I'm still not sure what made me interrupt her. Perhaps it was how Mom raised me to not feel the need to talk about my trauma, and how I died on Earth.

Mom squeezed my midsection, as I was still on her lap.

"I am ashamed," Dad said, and I'd worried he was talking to Mina, until he continued, "How could I let such a fox dwell in our midst."

"He's always had a weird face," I said.

Dad chuckled despite the tension, "Yeah, a weaselly face."

"Weaselly?" I said. "I could never make out his face. No one said anything so I thought it was normal."

Mom said, "I always thought he looked somewhat piggish, myself."

"He looked more wolfish, to me," Mina said.

"How come we all have such different impressions?" I asked.

"Illusion," Dad said in a cross tone. "Though I think it didn't work on Anessa as well. We most certainly should *not* have a different memory of his face."

The incongruity reminded me of Sarah, then of the backlash she had possibly faced. "Daddy, is Sarah a slave?"

He shook his head. "No. The only slaves we've had are the ones we took on lately, at *his* behest." Making a fist at his side he said, "It's not something I like, but I don't have his experience managing estates."

Before I could ask about Sarah, Dad asked, "Why were you seeking me anyway, Mina?"

Mom sat me beside herself, but held my hand.

Mina replied in a quiet tone, "As you know, my father was deposed. At Anessa's behest, I've been traveling, going up the Imperial noble hierarchy in search for aid. Each time I was turned away without so much as them listening to me. It led me finally here, to the Carlyle estates."

"Anessa," Dad said in a doubly cross tone, "Did you seriously sanction her actions without even informing us?"

Mom squeezed my hand but didn't say anything.

"That…" I said and considered my words. *What the hell Sarah!* She was *supposed* to have informed them, and been giving them regular updates. The fact that they were completely ignorant about it was concerning. Sarah had given me several dozen reports, all of which I'd assumed she relayed to my parents.

Breathing out I said, "Let me start over. I asked if Sarah was a slave, because I feared she was suffering from backlash." Gesturing toward Mina I said, "The only reason I'm here today is Sarah mentioned we had a particularly exceptional maid that could take her place while she investigated Mina's whereabouts. She even suggested that I *run*. It didn't hit me until now that was due to the urgency of the matter."

Leaving a pause for everyone to think about my words, I said, "Since Mina's right here, and Sarah clearly knew where she was, I strongly suspect the bloody nose she had was related to telling me about Mina." Exhaling I finished, "She has been helping me keep track of Mina's efforts for a long time. Clearly the updates she'd been giving me never made it to you. Sarah told me she'd consulted you both before everything was set in motion. It seems that was not true. We haven't seen each other for over two years because," I motioned to Dad, "You're busy, and it's weeks of travel for Mom to visit on her own.

"Oliver's been home a few times to look for Mina, and I knew you had soldiers out looking for her, so I'd thought everyone was on the same page."

Dad nodded. It seemed my answer satisfied him. He held up the key he'd retrieved from Mr. Morris and to my surprise a small screen popped up above it.

The hell? How is it we're stuck riding carriages, and he's using what looks like a smart device!?

CRISTOPH A. T. 387

"How are there so many names," Dad said with wide eyes as he scanned the list. "There are hundreds of slaves under his control." Swiping with his finger, he stopped, but I was too far away to read what he saw.

My frustration mounted. *Seriously, we were barely getting free-floating screens on Earth, how does Anfang have them?* Remembering that he interacted with the screen, I amended the thought, *Touch enabled, at that.*

Waving the screen away he sighed slowly and gripped the key in his hand. He approached me and lifted me into his arms. "Come on, Anessa."

"What?" I said, a bit flummoxed.

"We're returning to Maaka," he said with no humor in his voice.

"Your Imperial Grace," Yukirei said. She'd at some point cleaned off her bloodied hand and was in a curtsy. That she hadn't changed, meant the sight was still a bloody spectacle. "Would it be acceptable if I joined you?"

With a nod Dad said, "As long as you can keep up." Nodding toward Mina he said, "Bring Oliver's fiancée with you, if you would?"

Yukirei smiled.

What followed was the most magical moment in my life so far.

Being on an airplane for the first time is a nervous and uncomfortable affair. Being literally lifted into the sky by your Dad and flown without a metal contraption surrounding you on all sides, was incredible.

The journey took me sixteen days by carriage, and six hours by my own power on foot. With Dad's help? We were back in a little over a *single* hour. I strongly suspected it was only because he was worried about Mina's wellbeing, or we would've gone faster.

Yukirei commented about being grounded before we left, but Dad merely said he knows she wouldn't drop Mina.

The instant we touched down, Mina dashed off to Oliver's dorm suite without a word. We could all hear him shout, "Mina!" before entering mine.

One of my maids was standing near the door to Sarah's room. Seeing us she curtsied, and said, "Sorry Your Imperial Graces, Sarah hasn't left her room since Her Imperial High Grace left for home. I was about to enter to check on her."

Dad said, "You are dismissed, we'll take it from here."

She relaxed and went upstairs.

"Sarah!" I cried as we entered and she was sprawled out on the floor. She'd no more than closed her door and made it one step before falling down.

To my relief her chest's rise and fall told me she was okay, at least as okay as she can be, considering. A trail of blood from her nose was long dried and had pooled some around her face along her cheek.

Dad looked at it without comment, nodding to himself as if a theory had been confirmed.

After I put her in bed, Dad said, "You might be surprised at what happens next." He placed the key against her collar bone and said, "Release."

A simple white choker appeared from nowhere around her neck and fell away. Sarah's pitch-black hair transformed from her roots out, to a platinum blond. Her once-obscured features cleared up. Before, her breathing was a bit labored. It smoothed out and her face relaxed.

My jaw went lax. Though I'd spent nearly every waking hour with Sarah for a good chunk of my life, I was now seeing her real face clearly for the first time.

I looked at Dad in amazement, but his expression showed that he was not pleased. He ran his fingers through his hair and paced around the room.

"What's wrong?" I asked.

"Sarah," he began and pointed to my Lady's maid. "More accurately, Sarah Greensbaro, is supposed to be dead."

CHAPTER THIRTY
SHAKING THE EMPIRE

Triday, Hanvarae 25th, 1738

ALTHOUGH IT HAD been a little under a week and a half, I was still at home, nursing my play fiancé. There were other things that were delaying my return to school.

"What do you mean Sarah's under house arrest?" I asked Dad. "That makes no sense." I crossed my arms and stomped my foot. "Who knows what that man would've done to Mina if it weren't for her!"

Dad sighed. "Anessa, it's not that simple."

I was in the middle of feeding Gideon an apple slice in one of our guest rooms. The only reason I was allowed in here with him was due to his injury. He'd broken his dominant arm when Mr. Morris had slammed him into the stone wall.

Shaking his head Dad laughed. "You're eating this up, aren't you, boy?"

Gideon froze with a thin cut of fruit between his lips as though he was caught red-handed.

Patting Dad's arm I said, "Leave him alone." Lowering my voice I said, "What's so complicated about Sarah's situation?"

Grunting, Dad held out his hand with an S-S-ROB, a super-short-range obscuring barrier, meaning it was between him and I only. "Her family was purged. Believed to have been pulled out from the roots for the treasonous crimes Red Greensbaro committed against His Imperial Majesty, Jorin Q'Tar."

With a nod I asked, "Isn't there a chance for clemency? You know, for doing what's right despite her own risk of personal harm?"

"Yes, but here's the complicated bit," he said and scratched his cheek. "It's hard to determine her motives. Do you know what her station was before?"

I shook my head. *All I know is the Greensbaro family was the former head of the Imperial Duchy we maintain. Any and all information about the family was purged, as though they had never existed. Even Sarah's chair at school was destroyed after she ran off from it. They thought she was afraid of being associated with the family.*

He pointed to me. "Your position," he started, then pointed to the ceiling right after. "Well, more precisely Oliver's position. If they deem her actions to have been solely self-serving, there is nothing we can do about what happens next." He put away the barrier

Turning away from Gideon I said in a level tone, "And just what is *next* exactly?"

Dad looked between Gideon and me. "Boy, you have a firecracker in this one." He chuckled. "She's already got her mom beat on intensity."

In the corner of my eye I saw Gideon nod, which earned him a side-eye from me.

"Mmm," he said, "This is good." Then decided to stare out the window.

"I'm not going to tell you what happens next, because it's not clear yet." Dad shrugged. "If I'm wrong, I'll worry you over nothing, and conversely giving you the alternatives on what's next could provide false hope."

Looking to the ground I said, "I just hope I don't lose her as a lady's maid."

He cleared his throat. "That's… one possibility, yes."

I sighed. "It makes me feel guilty for thinking that way. What if Sarah wants something else?"

"You *could* ask her, but I'd wait to see how things shake out. There is some good news, though."

"Oh?"

"Despite the fact that Sarah was reporting everything to that," he made a fist, "man. I was never informed, because he was destroying the information."

Tilting my head to the side I asked, "How's that good news?" Absently offering a piece of fruit to Gideon I managed to squish it against his cheek, since neither he nor I was looking.

Dad coughed and nodded toward the young man.

"Oh, sorry," I said and wiped off Gideon's cheek.

He leaned toward me and winked, showing he really was enjoying our time together, despite the required chaperon.

Smiling Dad said, "Sarah apparently made copies of all those reports. If anything, that should do well to work in her favor. It confirms everything Mina's said."

"Is there any bad news?" I asked.

"Depends on who you are," he said with a half-smile. "The 'leaders' of the Honeybur Nation, the chancellor that betrayed Hammid, has been arrested along with his entire family. The Bur Imperial Barony, the Anston Imperial County, *and* the Hardwood Imperial Marquessate were taken into custody as well."

Dad shook his head. "I wouldn't want to be the former chancellor or a member of his family."

"Attainder, was it?" I asked.

His eyes widened. "I'm surprised you're familiar with it. Yes. It's... likely being carried out as we speak."

I only discovered the term after I learned Sarah's family name. It took looking in our private library along with a minder as I read through things. His entire family is being executed. Sarah's face came to mind, *Just like hers was.*

Breaking me out of my stormy reflections, Dad said, "It was fortuitous that you were so closely involved in trying to help and protect Mina."

"Why?"

"There were no documents of us being involved in whatever that group was. However," he paused, "Mina went through a terrible ordeal right under our noses. Worst case for us would have been loss of status, if she had died. Especially if you weren't involved. We likely would have been demoted several ranks to one of the newly opened Imperial seats."

"Newly opened?" I asked. "They aren't," I lowered my voice, "killing all of them are they?"

Dad sighed. "The Imperial nobles *directly* responsible? Yes. Their families will lose their status, with no chance of regaining any formal noble title. Not even in the lower caste at the kingdom level. The entire lot of them are commoners now, or more accurately, disgraced nobles."

Pursing my lips, I said, "We really kicked a hornet's nest, didn't we?"

He nodded and stood. Walking over to the open window, he continued, "They're investigating all of the families' business dealings. Depending on what they find, His Imperial Majesty may focus on our sister dukedom, the Juntaro Imperial Duchy." He exhaled. "That false king has it the worst."

Joining him I asked, "In what way? He will just..." I hesitated since I was about to say, *"die like the rest of them, right?"* That I nearly reduced someone to a footnote like that bothered me.

Around the edge of the window was a dim yellow glow, a tell-tale sign that the entire room had an S-ROB applied. *He doesn't need to worry about people hearing us, at least.*

A hand landed on my back. Dad said with a weak grin. "I'm glad you think through your words. He has a front row seat. His crime does not absolve him of his fate, but having to sit through it? Watching your whole family..." his voice trailed off and he shook his head.

Turning back to Gideon, for the briefest moments an image of him in the gallows, or under a guillotine sent a chill through me. *Yikes, that'll never happen. Not by my hand, at least.*

"Back to Sarah. His Imperial Majesty, Jorin Q'Tar has received your request. You'll have an answer within a week. Until you have your answer, you're expected to attend classes as normal."

Right. As though I'll be able to focus.

396 CONNECTIONS

▼ ▼ ▼

Triday, Fandariae 7th, 1738

Returning to school was an odd affair. Students avoided me, though no one said why. Portia wasn't even much help here, as she wasn't sure herself. What—figuratively—struck me, was my cousin.

It had almost been a week since Dad had told me to wait, and my cousin happened upon me exiting the dorm suites. Far enough away from the common area to take a seat.

To my surprise, he nodded and continued on.

I pinched myself. *Ouch, no, I'm not dreaming.*

Doubling back to talk to Rina, who always seemed to have extra time in the mornings, I asked her, "Did you see that?"

She nodded. "I'd say he must be sick, but daddy's likely to blame."

"Blame? I could kiss him!" I said and face palmed right after. "Not literally, of course, but not being the target of unjust malice is nice for a change."

"Just don't expect it'll last forever. Daddy will expect you to eventually take care of your own problems."

An mental image of slapping Lukas came to mind and I laughed. "Yeah, I probably need to mature more before that happens. My current plans mostly involve physical violence."

Rina was mid-sip and stopped looking at me over her cup.

"I'm not going to actually hit him or anything!"

She closed her eyes and lifted her tea a hair and giggled. "The look on your face was priceless." Peering over the top of her cup she sat it down and said, "I'll admit I've reveled in such thoughts before." Winking she added, "I was about your age."

Her efforts earned her a glare. "Ha-ha. Very funny." I sighed.

"I'm only teasing," she said and smiled. "Please don't take it personally."

"I didn't. I do need to get to class, though." Giving her a curtsy I said, "Thanks for your time and the chat." As I walked away I wondered, *I wonder why she always has mornings free.*

After second lunch Portia and I were headed to my dorm suite.

"Any progress with Max?" I asked tentatively.

She batted my shoulder with the tips of her fingers. "Stop. You know I can't be with him," she interlaced her fingers and held them out in front of herself while smiling at me, "despite my interests otherwise."

"A girl can dream, can't she?"

She sighed and said, "Of course I can dream, but dreams don't change much."

Though I wanted to discuss what was going on with Mina and the other Imperial ranks, I knew Dad would disapprove. Their grim fates were hardly gossip-worthy, given the strict need to maintain decorum.

Thinking on how I should approach my next question, I asked, "Has he… found interest in anyone else yet?"

She looked up into the sky. "Hmm. Not seriously, no." Leaning in she continued, "Although, I think Paul may interest him some."

My voice raised a quarter octave, "That mousy boy we eat with every Triday?"

Portia nodded. "I caught them holding hands the other day, though I pretended not to notice."

While it was less and less frequent as time marched on, there were days where the culture shock would still hit me hard. *Max and Paul? I would've never guessed. They're so different!*

"Who's stronger, anyway?" I asked.

"Between Max and Paul?" she asked incredulously. "Max, without question. Though Paul is a master tactician."

"Ah, Max will out punch you, but Paul would out-think you?" I said with a laugh.

"Exactly."

"Oh," I said and blinked in her direction. We shared a moment of silence then laughed together.

A few hundred feet from the Imperial Royal dormitories Portia asked, "You haven't been glaring at Yukirei as much." She whispered. "In fact, you were almost flirting with each other at first lunch. What's with that?"

Portia's comment made me stumble and almost fall over.

"W-we aren't flirting!" I defended. "Why would you say that?"

"Okay, maybe I'm exaggerating," She looked at me with her face forward. "A little. You're laughing and smiling more, though. When she touched Gideon's hand during lunch you didn't so much as bat an eye."

Narrowing my eyes I exhaled. "Yukirei, she…" I said, then caught myself. Shaking my head I added, "It's complicated. She may have done something that really helped me out, is all."

"Is that why you actually let her hug you?"

Turning my eyes away I said, "Maybe. I don't want to talk about that, though." Her question made me think, *She actually apologized for calling me a baby. I didn't know how much it was bothering me until she did.* Yukirei explained that it had been part of her upbringing, viewing mortals beneath cultivators. *At least she admitted her dismissive nature toward me was wrong.*

"Hmm…" With a smile Portia said, "You're smiling, seems like things are complicated."

My smile dropped and I gave her a glare, then suck out my tongue.

"Your new lady's maid is a stickler. She would've chastised you for that."

Portia's comment made me stomp my foot. "I know! She won't even let me sit closer than twenty inches to Gideon." Growling I said, "Yesterday, she got an actual ruler out to check. Can you believe it?"

"Pfft," Portia laughed. "That's a bit much. How is Sarah, anyway?"

"Don't know. That is also complicated," I said and moved closer to her, whispering, "Please don't ask me more, I can't talk about her right now."

Portia nodded and replied, "I hope everything's okay. She's really nice."

I smiled back. "That she is."

As I entered the Imperial Royal dormitories Mina met up with me as Portia departed.

"Everything okay?" I asked.

She tucked a lock of her long platinum hair behind her ear, which glistened in the light.

I can't believe the hair she chopped off was able to be… melted and fused back where it was. At the same time, it made me happy she didn't have to part with her hair, long term.

"I'm good. Though I did want to talk to you for a moment." She looked around us, then into the air. "Your birthday is coming up, and I'd like to get Oliver a gift."

Leaning up and toward her, I put my left hand on my hip, and my right on my chest. "Oh, no gift for me?"

She laughed and placed her hand on my shoulder. "Don't be silly, I can't ask you for advice about yourself."

We entered my dorm suite and sat across from one another. Over the past few weeks we'd found we shared a lot of the same worries, kidnapping and enslavement aside.

My temporary lady's maid rushed forward as I'd just gotten comfortable. With a deep curtsy, and a bow to boot, she said, "I'm terribly sorry to interrupt you, Your Imperial Lady, Anessa, but…" She paused and looked at me pleadingly.

"Yes?"

"Your father requests your presence at home immediately. He says he has received a missive from His Imperial Majesty addressed to you."

My stomach churned and my palms began to sweat. *That the message didn't come here means it can only be about Sarah.*

CHAPTER THIRTY-ONE
VERDICT

OUR TRIP HOME was quick and uneventful, but the worries that found me were unnerving. Since I was so wound up, my guards decided it appropriate to power my trip home.

To my surprise, they were slower than I was, and we were only entering the Carlyle Estates as the sun set.

In the short time I had to prepare, only Gideon and my temporary lady's maid had been able to join me.

"Sorry we couldn't invite Yukirei," I said to Gideon.

"It's okay, I think she's a bit spooked from last time."

I nodded. "Yeah, I would be too in her situation." Playing with my fingers, I asked, "Do you think it's good news?"

He shrugged. "Not really something I can even guess about. The Varn Baronetcy is so far beneath His Imperial Majesty's notice, the most we'd interacted with higher nobility before you and your family was the local Count."

Turning the page on his book titled *"To be Among the Select. A Guide to Imperial Nobility,"* he said. "It's anybody's guess. He's the father of both Rina *and* Lukas, which might put his temperament somewhere between the two?"

Lukas. Great. The Imperial Prince's steel-gray eyes flashed in my mind, and I got a chill.

"Yikes, yeah that's either way." Turning to my temporary lady's maid, Tania I asked, "What do you think?"

Her eyes widened and darted around the carriage, hoping I was talking to someone else. Realizing that I wasn't, she bowed her head, and finally said, "It is not really my place to comment, Imperial Lady Anessa."

I sighed. "Okay." Her denial made me think to myself, *Was Sarah unusually open, is Tania new to being a lady's maid, or both?*

Inside our main estate, I was greeted by Yllia, who led me to Sarah's room. To my surprise, Yllia was taking us to a guest quarters, instead of a servant's quarters.

Must be because they knew she was an Imperial Duke's daughter at one point?

Inside the room, Sarah smiled and waved.

But thoughts of joviality in me fled at the harsh clanking of the steel cuffs around her wrists and chains that connected them. Intricate engravings on them made me wonder, *Is that to suppress her strength?*

Sarah was a late-stage Ascended Realm cultivator. It's why I'd struggled to keep up with her when she would join me on my morning jogs. Despite awakening as a cultivator when I turned eight, I still couldn't catch up to her nearly three years later.

Taking a seat next to her bed, which she seemed to be chained to, I pursed my lips.

Tania coughed as Gideon sat down. It seemed she took offense to him being less than twenty inches away from me.

How can she tell anyway? She uses a ruler!

"Don't be so hard on those two. They know the proper decorum," Sarah said.

Tania ignored her and proceeded to use her hands to get the right distance, nudging Gideon over as she did so.

I wasn't in any mood to argue with her. "How have you been? Are they treating you well?" I asked Sarah.

Sarah's laugh told me everything I needed to know. "I've been well," she held up a lock of her platinum blond hair. "Though it's been almost ten years since my hair was its natural color."

She's been a slave to that man for so long? How wretched.

A knock came at the door. As we turned to it, my parents entered.

Dad was carrying a scroll in his hand, and Mom was being reserved with her hands behind her back.

"This is for you," he said and held it out for me to take.

Without wasting any time I removed the ribbon around the wound up paper. It read,

"To her Imperial High Grace and Imperial Princess of the Westwood Empire, Anessa, High Duchess of the Carlyle Imperial Duchy, Daughter of His Imperial Grace, Roland Carlyle and Her Imperial High Grace and Imperial Princess of the Westwood Empire, Lily Carlyle and Niece of His Imperial Majesty, Jorin Q'Tar."

Seriously? The first paragraph is nothing more than my byline! It continued:

"Your deeds in helping Her Royal Majesty, Mina Aramon-Carlyle, uncover deception, and high treason in several Imperial Ranks speaks volumes to your dedication to the Westwood Empire, despite being in the throes of youth, and have not gone unnoticed.

"However, it pains me to inform you that your request for Sarah Greensbaro, of the <u>disgraced</u> *Imperial Greensbaro family line, to receive full clemency for her assistance in resolving Her Royal Majesty, Mina Aramon-Carlyle's issue is denied.*

"Such a request comes from a place of personal ambition, is highly emotional, and is largely self-serving. You must be aware that some things are above yourself, your wants, and needs. The Westwood Empire is one of them.

"Instead of full clemency for the misdeeds and treason her family committed, Sarah Greensbaro, of the <u>disgraced</u> Imperial Greensbaro family line, will remain your lady's maid, in perpetuity. Enforced through a slave contract.

"The contract is a necessary evil. Once others see Sarah Greensbaro, of the <u>disgraced</u> Imperial Greensbaro family line, for who she is, her status as a Greensbaro will be evident. Now, more than ever, the empire needs to send a message that corruption, theft, treason, and deceit will not go unpunished. Her enslavement is a necessary corollary of this fact. Full clemency would invite those who seek a similar line of thought to follow through with their misdeeds.

"Despite being my niece and your efforts outlined above, there must be a cost to placing yourself over the empire. There will be no announcement of your good deeds to the Empire. Your part in this investigation will be buried, and there will be no award.

"Please understand that this is for your own good.

"-H.I.M. Jorin Q.Tar"

Crap. He really likes to let me know that her family is disgraced, doesn't he?

Dad held his hand out for the scroll as Mom brandished another from behind her back.

"You have a choice, it seems," Mom said and gestured toward Dad's scroll with hers. "Accept Sarah back into your fold, or…" she offered it forward.

Raising an eyebrow I accepted it. The start of it was much the same, except that I would be awarded five-thousand large black gold coins from the Imperial Royal vault.

That's so much money it's stupid. Part of it explained,

"You will be recognized for your efforts to stabilize the empire. An Imperial Court meeting with you to cover your part for personal recognition of your meritorious deeds.

"Your status as Her Goddess Eloria Kirzington von Addenal's champion of Craft will be announced to the Westwood Empire at large. This will not make you any friends, admittedly, but it will send a message to those who wish to harm the Westwood Empire.

"Your request for Sarah Greensbaro, of the <u>disgraced</u> Imperial Greensbaro family line, is denied in full force. She will be remanded into Imperial custody. The empire will make good on her being struck from the Imperial Register. It will be confirmed once she is…"

I almost ripped it in two. *I thought it was too good to be true.*

"…summarily executed in private.

"Please understand that this is for your own good.

"-H.I.M. Jorin Q. Tar"

Both say that this is for my own "good." It was all I could do to not shred it on the spot. Taking a breath, I looked back up at Mom, and said, "I hope this isn't some test and I'm being evaluated to see whether I choose the 'correct' option."

410 CONNECTIONS

She shook her head. "No test, honey. Though, I think I already know which one you'll choose."

"They both suck!" I shouted.

"Calm down," Dad said in a stern voice.

I growled back, "When in the world has 'calm down' ever worked for you?"

He put his finger on his chin and went quiet.

"What does it say, Lady Anessa?" Sarah asked meekly.

"Right," I said and retook my seat near her. "This most certainly involves you." Handing her the one I was not interested in, in the slightest, I held out my hand for my Dad to return the other one to me.

"You're right, it hasn't ever worked," he chuckled. Though I suspect it was to diffuse the tension, he earned himself two glares.

One from Mom, the other from me.

Accepting the scroll, I waited for Sarah to finish reading the first one.

Tears entered her eyes as she accepted the second scroll, returning the other to me.

When she finished the second scroll she said, "I'd admit that I'd like to ask that you *not* take the money, but that isn't fair. You'll likely never see that much in one place again." She waved her hand. "Mostly because it's too dangerous to store it all in one place."

CRISTOPH A. T. 411

Her comment made my decision easy. I took the scroll with the offer of money in exchange for her life, and tore it into two.

Looking back at Mom I said, "I don't really need to think about it any longer, but what I am worried about is the part where Sarah has to be a slave."

Mom pursed her lips and looked to Dad who shook his head.

"I'm afraid that is not negotiable, honey," Mom said.

Moving toward her I said, "She's been a slave for almost *ten* years already! Isn't that enough?"

"Anessa," Mom said but she wasn't able to meet my gaze.

"It's fine," Sarah said. "Dad was never really a good man, and I wasn't entirely innocent, either."

Her comment made me return to my seat once again.

"You know, he was taking girls he found pretty and selling them. I'd heard the rumors, and didn't think anything of it. One day there was a girl in our great room that was just 'there'. She didn't respond to anything I said, and I'd assumed she was mute." Sarah gripped the cover over her bed. "She was actually a nobleman's daughter dad had 'picked up' because he knew the nobleman's chances of getting justice were low."

Large tears flooded down her face, despite the calm demeanor she presented.

"Dad was also taking more in taxes, and skimming a lot off before he sent the rest to His Imperial Majesty," her voice grew quiet, "There's truth in the rumors. I thought the noble girl looked familiar to me, but I didn't ask any questions when Dad carted her away later that night. Who she was only crystallized when the Imperial Enforcers knocked on our door."

Her hands went to her face. "The head enforcer thought I was pretty, but he told Mr. Morris that he couldn't take me himself. But for a price, he was willing to let Mr. Morris have me."

Moving to her side, I pulled her head into my chest. Turning to Mom showed she was equally distressed.

Gideon, as wonderful as he was, seemed beside himself. He seemed like he wanted to reach out to me, but stopped himself.

"Sarah, are you sure this is what you want?" I asked quietly. "You were under his control for so long."

"You are NOT that man," she said in sobs, heavily emphasizing "not." Sniffling she wiped her eyes. "You won't treat me the way he did." Her eyes found my Mom. "If my only other option is death," she let a pregnant pause hang in the air and Mom nodded.

"I would gladly serve you," Sarah said.

I asked, "Promise you'll tell me more about it later?"

She nodded.

Dad held a black collar out for me to take, which I did.

Though it was a simple silk with an engraved disk in the front, it seemed far heavier than it ought to. Holding it out to Sarah, she shook her head and curled my fingers around it.

"You have to put it around my neck yourself." She smiled. "That's just how it works."

Don't smile. This is not the time to smile. It made my own fight against the salty torrent I'd been battling that much more difficult.

"Do I need to say anything?"

Dad cleared his throat and told me over the next few minutes. "If you forget anything, I can repeat it as you say it. Just try not to veer too far off course."

With I nod I started, "Sarah Greensbaro," I held the collar up to her neck, "for the crimes the Greensbaro Imperial Duchy committed against the Westwood Empire," I looked to Dad who provided what I said next, "you should be dead. It is by the grace of His Imperial Majesty, Jorin Q'Tar, that you have been given this clemency. You shall no longer be a Greensbaro."

That line made me lose my fight, and tears flowed. "Henceforth, you shall be known as Sarah-Knecht von Anessa." The name meant Sarah, Servant of Anessa.

She sensed my trepidation and leaned forward into the choker.

I fastened it, and said, "You shall serve me for—" a part of me wanted to say *the "rest of the day"*, but when I paused, Dad said what I echoed, "the rest of your life." Touching the black disk, I finished, "Activate."

CHAPTER THIRTY-TWO
POWER / CONSORT

FOR THE BRIEFEST moment, Sarah's eyes flared violet as the slave collar activated. Dad quietly relayed my decision to let her live in service over some communication device to the Emperor.

Although I was still torn up inside over everything, it felt good to have Sarah back. Over the next few hours, I told her about the humdrum things she missed in the last week. It was nice to see her laugh. Our joviality was dashed when a crisp crack brought silence throughout the room.

It originated from Dad, and the telltale signs of a distant look and shuffling eyes told me he was looking into his storage ring for something. In a moment he went white as a ghost and brought out something into his hand.

"Gods," was his only word before he showed something to Mom.

"No!" She screamed and collapsed into her chair, her face wrought with horror.

"What's wrong?" I asked, my tone laden with concern, and stood.

Instead of responding, he turned his hand around to me, showing a cracked, and nearly broken life tablet engraved with a name I never thought I'd see in a critical state.

Oliver.

I imagined his cheery face, and insane speed. He was a force of nature, indestructible. I couldn't imagine anyone being able to get the better of him. *What happened to Oliver?!* Though I wanted to scream, I was interrupted by Dad dashing to the closest window and jumping out of it.

He didn't think too much about his departure as all of the windows in the room, and likely the entire side of the house, shattered in an instant.

Thankfully Mom was far enough away that she was unharmed. Sarah's bed had a headboard that blocked all the glass.

Gideon, to his credit, dodged a fairly large shard of glass that was sitting right between his legs. Were I not freaking out, I might've found his dumbfounded expression humorous.

Mom had yelled down the hall for assistance, then went to pacing about the room. "I need to have them prepare our fastest thunder oxen and head to Maaka…"

"Mommy, how long would they take to get there, top

speed?"

"Ten days if we pushed them to death," she said, my question caused her to cry. "I wouldn't want to do that, they're such good boys, but we need to hurry."

Shaking my head I put my hand on hers. "I can get us there in a few hours if I pull us." Turning to Tania I said, "Would you be okay if I left you here for now?"

She merely nodded, as she was in the corner of the room hugging her arms. The spray of glass had rightly startled her.

"Do you know where the key is for Sarah's cuffs?" I asked Mom.

She shook her head, "Sorry, Roland has them. Would it be okay if we came back for Sarah?"

"Go to your brother," Sarah said. "I'm fine here." She pulled up her sleeves and smiled. "I can help put this place back in order while you're gone."

"Thanks, Sarah." I picked up the shard of glass Gideon seemed terrified of, which I noticed was precariously close to cutting into him in a fairly sensitive area. Tossing the eight-inch dagger of glass to the floor, then wincing when it shattered into a thousand smaller pieces, I said, "Let's go."

It was past fourth-twelve, by the time we arrived. When

pushed, due to the emergency, I was able to burst to a substantially higher speed, but my pace had ebbed and flowed as we went. Our guards collapsed at the entrance to the Imperial Royal dormitories and asked a change-over to occur.

To their credit, I did much the same and collapsed to the ground as the cart came to a halt. Each breath was like a raging fire in my lungs.

Gideon's immediate reaction was to pick me up into a princess carry.

He was warm, and the closeness let me feel his calm heart beating. I knew it wasn't something I'd soon forget, short-lived as it were.

Mina met us at the entrance. "He's inside, His Imperial Grace, Roland told me you should be here soon." she said and ushered us into their shared dorm suite.

Gideon deposited me into a chair near the end of Oliver's bed.

Dad had his hand on Oliver's chest with a strange triangle sitting on top of him. Our Dad was keeping the device in place.

My brother was sweating, to the point that his hair was matted onto his forehead. Whatever was going on was making him thrash about. Despite his strength, he was grabbing onto the bed's comforter and though it stretched, he was causing it no harm.

Dad's knuckles were white, and every few minutes he was looking through a loupe.

Mina sat beside me and said, "Someone has poisoned Ollie. We have no idea how they did it. He was in the back training under a barrier, when he knocked on the door and fell inside."

He grew still and I had recovered enough to go to his side. Next to Dad was a hole in the wall, I'd assumed one he put there.

To say he was furious would've been an understatement. The energy in the air was akin to Oliver's when he almost lost control over himself. It made my teeth tingle, which I didn't know was something they could do.

Dad breathed out slowly. "There was a second decree," he said. "Should you save Sarah, Oliver would get all the credit for helping Mina." His voice took on a gravel quality, "Few people were informed before the public announcement." He motioned toward my brother. "The poison is tearing his meridians apart. Two of his three dantians have actually ruptured."

"What, so the poison only attacks the thing that makes us a cultivator?" I asked and took a hold of Oliver's hand.

"If his third dantian goes," he held the loupe up to his eye again, "He'll be a mortal for life." Then he snapped the handle of the looking glass and shattered it against the floor, making us jump.

"D…" I started, and feared I knew the answer, "Did the last one rupture, too?"

He looked up at the ceiling and closed his eyes. "Yeah."

He bolted out of the room, and a loud boom shook the dorm suite. That I didn't hear any windows break mean he likely used some restraint.

"Where's he going?" I asked, hoping for anyone to answer.

"To see my brother, most likely," Mom said. "Whoever did this," she said flatly, "will pay. I've never seen Roland that angry."

"Mina," a weak voice called. It wasn't until I looked at him that I realized it was Oliver.

He continued, "Could you get me some water?"

I moved to the side so Mina could see to him.

Despite hearing he'd be a mortal, and the impact that would have on his future, she moved to fulfill his request herself.

Listening to the two, it broke my heart to hear him say that he feels weak.

"I couldn't do anything for Mina, and needed help," I said quietly. "Sarah's still a slave." Blinking a tear from my eye I finished, "And there's nothing I can do for Oliver." It made me wonder, *If I'd chosen to forsake Sarah, would it be me lying there?*

Mina said, "We should probably let him rest. He just fell asleep. Would you all join me in the living area?"

Mom paced back and forth once we moved. Sitting down, she ushered Mina to sit across from her.

"Mina, if Oliver is… a mortal moving forward, will you still–"

"Yes, I will not forsake him." She smiled. "You and your family didn't forsake me. The soular kinship we felt when we first met?" She looked towards his bedroom. "It hasn't changed." Shaking her head she said, "No, that's not exactly true." Her grin broadened, "It's stronger than ever."

At her reflection, I looked over at Gideon, who'd been quiet lately. He looked perturbed, almost shell-shocked.

It's been crazy lately, and he hasn't had a chance to process what we've all gone through. None of us have.

He turned to me and our eyes met.

Staring directly into his eyes wasn't something I did often. Not because I was embarrassed, but because there was strong pull in my chest every time I did. Thinking on Mina's words, I realized, *Our connection is stronger, too. I'd thought he was just a tiny little bookworm, but when I can't turn to Sarah, he listens. How do I tell Gideon that if he were to become a mortal overnight, or hurt in some way, that I'd support him regardless?*

▼ ▼ ▼

Deuday, Polarae 24th, 1738

Three days after we turned eleven, Oliver was packing up his effects. I had been indisposed on the day of our birthday, but due to poor timing on the carrier's part, he received a letter on that same day.

Oliver's loss of power had led to a corresponding loss of status. He had been stripped of his title as the Imperial Carlyle Duchy's heir presumptive. The school took away his Martial Core student status. What had happened to his cultivation base was irreversible.

"I'm really upset, Oliver," I said.

"I know."

I stomped my foot, "Aren't you?"

He paused and looked at me. "Of course I'm mad," he said and closed his suitcase as hard as he could. Ire creeped into his tone, "But being mad doesn't fix it."

"I know, I'm just upset that the moment you aren't a cultivator, everything you are to them changed," turning to Mina I amended, "Present company notwithstanding."

She flashed me a smile and directed a few maids to bring things to Oliver.

"Why are you packing yourself, anyway?" I asked.

Holding up his hands, he said, "I wanted to feel like I was doing something. It's such a change," he wiped the sweat from his forehead, "to not be a cultivator." He gave me a grin. "This is like when daddy made me pull fifty-ton weights on each ankle behind myself."

His nonchalance at saying he used to be able to pull a hundred thousand pounds as easily as packing a suitcase made my eyebrow twitch.

"Sissy," he said, in a surprisingly serious voice, "Thank you for caring, but I'm not very smart. Without my strength, I don't have a lot going for me." He shook his head. "I'm no scholar, my grades are barely passing, and I think that's only because of the teachers being," he sighed, "very lenient on me."

With a click-click of the latest suitcase being loaded he handed it off to a maid.

Watching it as they went, I saw they were just taking it into another room nearby and immediately repacking it. When Oliver's eyes caught mine I pursed my lips, hoping I didn't give them away.

In spite of his false levity, his slip made me keenly aware of how poorly he was handling his situation.

Hang in there.

He blew through his teeth. "Anyway! When Mina and I return to the Honeybur Nation, His Imperial Majesty, Jorin Q'Tar will appoint her personally." Leaning forward he whispered, "He's even stronger than daddy, can you believe it?"

Seriously? That little admission blew my mind.

"Uncle Jorin gave me a demonstration of the half-step of the Otherworldly Realm when we turned ten. Daddy didn't last one strike. It was almost as bad as me losing to Master Kile." Saying Kile's name made him look down in front of himself and laughed. "I mean Mr. Kile, he's not really my master anymore, I guess."

I couldn't take it any more and pulled Oliver into a hug. "You're going to be okay, you know?"

"Ouch, too much!" He said and I let him go. "Sheesh, is what I've been doing to people? I think my back popped!"

His return to optimism made me smile.

"When we turn twelve, I'll take to Mina's side as her King Consort. That's still the plan, at least."

Mine widened her eyes and held an article of clothing out in front of her, "Yes… the 'plan.'" She shook her head. She winked at me. "You can imagine what that involves, given that my family isn't exactly large."

Her admission made me gasp and point at him. "He'll only be twelve!"

"I will delay it as long as I can," she said. "Hopefully until he's sixteen at a minimum."

Clasping my hands I sent up a prayer, "Please Eloria, help Mina maintain Oliver's innocence as long as she can!"

"What are you two talking about?" he asked bluntly.

His cluelessness made me scowl and look to Mina who was equally aghast.

"Ollie," Mina said. "You do know where babies come from, don't you?"

Shaking his head he said, "No, not really. I mean, a man and a woman get married and then… babies?"

I couldn't help but hug him again with a little laugh. "This is what I mean. Let him keep this as long as possible."

Mina nodded and smiled broadly. "I will."

"You know," Oliver said as I let him go. "We had some fun times, didn't we?"

"Oh?" I said and arched my brow. "Like what?" With my hands on my hips I said, "Remember that I don't count the time you sent me through a wall when training last year as 'fun'."

"I meant when we were at home, before school. Running from a treant, when you awoke half-way when you turned four." He turned to Mina, "When I met my future fiancées, though I only ended up needing one." Dipping in he added, "And you met yours."

His comment made me laugh and I batted him on the arm. "Stop. Gideon and I are…" I wasn't able to finish the comment. *What are we?*

"When I first met Rufus," he said and turned to the mantle. "I'd already outgrown him by the time we turned nine." Pausing he sat down the item he was packing and walked over to Rufus. "I suppose it *is* about time you two officially met, huh?"

Oliver tried to pick him up with one hand, and realized he could no longer do so. Even two hands was a struggle, so he moved closer. "This sucks," he puffed while shakily holding the sword.

"What? I know Rufus is heavier than he was," I said, "but you'll get used to it."

Oliver turned to me and was crying. "I can't hear his voice anymore!" He fell to his knees holding the sword in his arms. "I'm so sorry that I didn't get to say goodbye."

Gods this is breaking my heart. Why did someone do this to Oliver? Wiping my eyes, I thought, *It's not fair.*

"Rufus used to sing to me," he said, "he has a good singing voice." He laughed. "Though daddy says that I'm tone deaf."

His admission made me laugh. "Yeah, even Yllia would leave the room when you'd join Rufus in his songs."

"Hey! I wasn't that bad," Oliver objected.

With a smile I said, "You're right," I nodded, then winked. "You were worse."

He puffed out his cheeks and turned his head away in mock defiance. Giving his sword a hug, he turned to me and held it out for me to accept. "He's... yours now."

"I can't take him!" I said and took a step back. "Rufus is too important to you."

"Rufus, before he and I became friends, was alone, in the dark. He used my essence to see and experience the world around him. Without it, everything goes dark for him." He gripped the sword tighter. "I can't do that to him."

That changed things a bit. I could tell that taking the sword really would be doing Oliver a favor. "Okay," I consented, and held out my hand.

In the instant I touched the scabbard, a quiet voice nudged its way into my head, *"Hi."*

The suddenness of the voice made me withdraw my hand.

"I wasn't expecting that!" I blurted out.

"You heard him?" Oliver said with a broad smile.

"Yeah," I said and thought, *The voice sounds so young. Like a five year old.*

Accepting "Rufus" from Oliver, the voice continued. *"Did I scare you? I didn't mean to scare you. It's nice to meet you."*

"Can you hear me?" I thought back.

"I can! Though if it isn't too much to ask, can we make a contract?" The voice saddened, *"My contract with Oliver broke. I'm worried about him."*

"Rufus says he's worried about you, because your contract broke?" I said disbelievingly.

"Please tell him I'm okay," He skipped over to one of the maids and took a knife from them. His nonchalance at moving around with it made me nervous.

You're not durable anymore, be careful!

"Oliver," I said sternly. "Do not run with knives. You will hurt yourself."

"Sorry sissy," he said and lowered his head.

"It's okay, it just scared me, is all."

He held out the knife to me.

"What am I supposed to do with this?" I asked.

"Right. Um. Poke your finger, and put a line across Rufus's blade." He mimicked the gesture himself as though he were doing so. "That's what I did."

"And this is safe?" I asked.

Both Oliver and Rufus replied, *"Yes."*

"This will take some getting used to," I said to Rufus, *"A voice in my head, that is."*

"You are funny. People have a voice in their head all the time," Rufus said, a bit of smugness and humor carried over.

"I mean," I sent back, *"I suppose you're right, but I do remember reading that not everyone does."*

"If it bothers you, don't worry. We can only talk when you're actually touching my hilt or scabbard." After a few seconds, Rufus continued, *"I suppose you* could *touch my blade, but that would be strange."*

His bubbly nature reminded me of someone and my eyes landed on Oliver. *"You're a lot like my brother. Remember not to tell a girl to touch your blade."*

"Yes, I'd hate to hurt you."

My mind swirled with inappropriate thoughts. Sadly some of it got through to the sword.

"What? No, that's weird! Have you always been this weird?"

I caught myself laughing out loud, until I noticed a few eyes on me. Clearing my throat I said, "Rufus is funny."

Following Oliver's instructions, I bound Rufus to myself, though it gave me a pang of guilt. It was painfully similar to Sarah's situation in a way.

"Sarah will be fine," said the sword. *"You seem like a caring master."* After a pause I heard, *"Weird, but caring."*

"Enough about the weird," I sent, *"You'll find I'm not weird at all, just... a little older than Oliver."*

"Let me show you how to secure him around your waist," Oliver said.

Before he could do so I gave him another hug. "Thank you. I'll treasure him, okay?"

"I know you will." Oliver beamed. "He's wanted to meet you since I met him, but you couldn't hear his voice."

After securing him to my side, Oliver gave me a warning with furrowed brows. "Just a warning: do not draw Rufus unless you're prepared to take someone's life." He scratched his cheek. "Training is different, though you might want to practice alone some before training with another person."

His lecture made me smile. *This is the first time he's lectured* me.

Oliver went to securing Rufus better, since it sat on my waist differently than his. He whispered to me, "Have you made up your mind about Gideon?"

Raising an eyebrow I said, "How would you know what I've been thinking?"

Satisfied with how secure Rufus was, he stood. "I always have, since day one."

"Day one?" I said blankly. I was astonished at this revelation of unknown depths in my brother.

"Since we first saw each other when we were born. I didn't understand your words so much as warm hugs of intent. I knew how much you loved having a brother." Shaking his head he said, "It's not words, really, but I always get the idea of what you want or mean."

Approaching me, he said, "Don't worry, your secret about your past life is safe with me." His voice was but a whisper, eying Mina in the background, who smiled.

Oliver pulled me into a bear hug. "I can't lift you anymore, but always know that I love you sissy."

Looking up at him I grinned and hugged back. Picking him up I spun him around a few times. I may have held onto him for a few minutes. *I've always taken him for granted, but he's always been there for me.* A gnarled tree with a face entered my mind's eye. *And protected me.*

As I held him I said, "Promise you'll write."

"I will."

It took me a while to let him go, since I knew we'd see each other far less in the future. *This royally sucks.*

CHAPTER THIRTY-THREE
DECISIONS AND THE FUTURE

Finday, Zenthriae 4th, 1738

"I'LL NEED TO stand on a chair, won't I?" I asked.

"Probably," Sarah said, with a light laugh as she brushed my hair. "You do need to make sure to preserve decorum, after all."

Flipping the page on the gigantic tome on Westwood Empire's traditions I sighed at the nauseating rigmarole in some of them.

Clenching my fist over my chest, I said, "I'm nervous, is that normal?"

Sarah sat down the hairbrush and turned me toward herself. "Are you sure this is what you want?"

Her brilliant blue eyes and platinum blond hair made me a bit envious. I was astonished that I'd never questioned my inability to see my own personal attendant clearly before. Now, her lovely face, sparkling eyes, and shining hair were crystal clear.

How is this person Sarah!

Nothing about her prior appearance, save for her height, was the same. Porcelain skin, azure irises, wavy hair she puts in a thick braid behind herself. It was obvious that she came from nobility. Dad had relaxed the strict dress code for servants at the lady's maid or higher rank, so they could wear almost whatever they wanted, so long as they made sure they didn't outshine their lady.

Sarah had chosen a white blouse with filigree along the neckline, flared with a bertha-like gollar. It was pinned with a diamond-shaped sapphire cabochon. A black and gray corset framed her long faded black to gray skirt.

If someone were to ask me, I'd say she toed the line on outshining me.

I didn't care.

Thinking about the invisible black slave choker resting on her neck made me frown internally. Though she might not be free, if dressing this way gave her some solace, I'd gladly permit it.

"Anessa?" she asked.

"Sorry, I'm not used to the new you, yet." Her comfort in her new clothes made me smile. Tapping a page in the book, I said, "I'm sure that this is what I want. It's long overdue."

Sarah looked at what I'd pointed to and raised a brow. There was confusion in her voice, "You want to safely bleed game?"

Quickly looking down at the page, I saw she was teasing me. "Very funny."

"I thought so," she said with levity.

"You're being a little more ornery now. Is there a reason for it?"

"Yes and no." Aggression slipped into her tone, "Morris had a background rule of obedience set for me." It softened, "When you chose to save my life over leaving me to my fate, it made me realize, that I truly, honestly, do not mind serving you. Part of that service, is being open and honest."

A grin spread across my face. "Then your honest self likes to tease?"

"Of course. If I didn't tease you, you'd think something was wrong, right?" She resumed brushing my hair.

"I suppose so. Even before you were occasionally a little snarky, though I couldn't read your facial features through the illusion enough to get a read on your intent."

"To me," she said and paused the brush mid-stroke, "you're somewhat like a granddaughter."

Turning back towards her with my mouth agape, I said, "That might require some explanation." Pointing to myself I said, "I mean, granddaughter?!"

With the brush in her hand she put her hands on her hips. "How old do you think I am? If I had kids, which I never had the opportunity to, they would have kids of their own…" Tapping her chin with the brush she said. "Oh. Even *they* might have kids your age."

Her comment made me bark a laugh. "You'd have to be seventy!"

She nodded. "Precisely."

Louder than I ought to, I shouted, "What!?" I could only blink at her as she shook her head ruefully.

"Come on then, let's get you dressed." Sarah said, stepping over my outburst as though it didn't happen.

"Yeah," I said in a whisper. "Seventy? That's crazy," I said to myself.

"You do know how long cultivators live, don't you?" she asked.

"I know Dad's older than Mom, but not by how much."

"His Imperial Grace, Roland Carlyle will be three hundred and two years old next month."

"W…" I wanted to say something, but didn't know what *to* say. *No wonder he doesn't celebrate his birthday. I didn't even know what month it was in!*

"Do you know how old you'll live to be, assuming you never train again?"

Tilting my head to the side, I said, "No."

"Tania," Sarah said.

My newest lady's maid said, "Yes Sarah-Knecht?"

Her use of the hyphenated form of her name made me thin my lips out, but I didn't say anything. This was something not even my parents would budge on. Every time someone talked about her, they'd call her a servant. It was a big ask for them to permit me to drop it in private company.

"Be a dear and bring me these two books," Sarah said and wrote something on a piece of paper.

Tania merely curtsied and dashed off.

"What is she getting?"

"Some books about cultivation. I don't remember everything off hand, so it's easier to look it up."

When Tania returned she had two thick tomes in her hands. Their titles were simple, "The Elements," and "Dantians."

Sarah flipped through them and wrote some things down.

She'd written several numbers down, and multiplied them together, then took it times three hundred and circled her answer. "It's a bit difficult with your situation of seven dantians, since," she tapped the book on

Dantians, "it's so rare that the tables in this book don't cover it. But by a low-ball estimate, you'll live to be at least eight-hundred-twenty-five."

I squeaked, "Huh?"

"Let's see, and Gideon…" she said, and returned to the book. She whispered to herself, "Earth, Darkness and three dantians."

I found myself keenly interested in her efforts. It reminded me that Gideon's final awakening granted him *two* additional dantians. Darkness and Earth canceled one another out on their effects. Her answer was a little troubling to me.

"Gideon would reach six hundred total, though if he keeps up his current progress he'll hit the Ascended Realm in four years. If he pushes himself, he'll be middling Ascended Realm. That puts him at about two thousand-eight-hundred."

"That's… no, is that real?" I said and took a seat on my bed.

Sarah clapped her hands. "Now then, while you might be a bit surprised, that doesn't change the fact that you need to get dressed." With a wink she added, "You might even like your outfit."

"Yeah," I said, still a bit dazed.

It was as though they'd taken my school outfit and cranked it up to eleven. Instead of a white base, it was teal, my school outfit's secondary color. Gold was spread throughout the outfit. The skirt itself looked to be a web of gold at the hem.

Even Rufus received a treatment of his own, being granted a gilded sword belt. They also platinum plated his pommel and quillons. Though I thought the process might hurt him, he said it felt like taking a bath.

They'd upgraded my preference for modesty by giving my shorts a garter belt, designed to my specifications. *No more near accidents.* I thought as I went to pick them up.

"Would you like some help?" Sarah asked.

With a sigh, I said, "Sure."

On her own, Sarah was able to assist me from one outfit to the next, in five minutes flat. With Tania's help, it took twenty.

As Tania slid a stocking up my leg I said, "Why is it that you insist I wear these?"

"For modesty, ma'am."

Looking pleadingly to Sarah she shrugged.

"Did Mom approve this?" I asked.

"Yes ma'am," said Tania.

Now, before I was able to go from one outfit to another, I was forced to wear leggings before I stepped out of one shift and into another. It was an aggravating and, to me, pointless extra step.

In the thirty *seconds* between one shift to the next, my top and midriff were wrapped, complicating the whole affair.

Sarah and Tania were also required to wear gloves at all time when contacting my skin.

Something had changed, though I wasn't yet clued in on what.

Between the ages of zero to four, my family had kept Awakening Ceremonies from me, and cultivation knowledge. In the end it was a massive disappointment. So I shrugged the difference off as something I'd find out, and would likely laugh at.

The two went on to braid my hair in its usual Dutch plait.

Sarah ended it with a tan-colored bow, then handed me a mirror.

"How's that?"

Exhaling I said, "It looks like me. I hope someday I can have a different hairstyle."

"I wouldn't count on it," Sarah said.

"Yeah, I know. Because Her Goddess Eloria herself gave this hairstyle to me." Playing with the braid I continued, "Doesn't mean I can't dream, does it? Since I don't talk with her that frequently, what needs to change to permit me a new hairstyle?"

"You could wait until your next Awakening Ceremony and ask her," her eyes darted to the side, "Or, Eloria would need to fall."

Tania gasped. "Sarah-Knecht, please take that back."

Sarah dipped her head and shoulders. "Sorry, Tania's right, such talk is blasphemous." Her voice shook, "Please pretend I did not say it."

"It's fine, I've already forgotten," I said. Despite her comment being genuinely free of malice, the way Sarah's eyes widened when Tania chastised Sarah and the immediate prayer she gave told me she believed she'd messed up.

The two whispered between one another and I heard Tania say urgently, "You need to pray tonight and tell Her Goddess Eloria you did not mean anything by it."

Sarah said back, "I know, I will, I was merely answering our lady in earnest."

"Okay," Tania sighed. "I understand that, but be careful."

Sarah coughed and picked up Rufus. She began fastening him on my belt.

I said, "I guess I need to be prepared, huh?"

"Yes," she said. "His Imperial Grace, Roland said that you are to not go anywhere without your sword. You'll attend classes with it, even."

"Rufus is a 'he,'" I said, then laughed. Placing my hand on his scabbard, I asked, *"Rufus, do you care whether people call you he or it?"*

"Why would I?" he asked nonchalantly. *"I'm technically neither, but most people seem to call me he, because I guess I sound like a boy? I can't really talk to anyone but those I say are worthy, and I can only hear your voice when you want me to. Did someone call me a bad name?"*

His admission gave me a sense of unaccountable loneliness for him. *"No, no one said anything bad, I was just wondering."*

Thinking to Rufus for a moment. *"You'll protect me, right?"* I asked.

"Always! Oliver told me about that meanie Mr. Borris or whatever his name was. If I were there, he would've lost an arm."

"He did lose his arm. A friend of mine, Yukirei, made sure of that."

Contentment came through our connection. *"I like this Yukirei. For her to step in and protect you like that, is she one of your mates?"*

"No!" I shouted aloud, drawing my lady's maids' attention. "Sorry, Rufus asked me something weird."

Returning my hand to his scabbard I said, *"Why would you ask that?"* Shaking my head I thought to him, *"Now they think I'm weird."*

As I caught a glimpse of him turning his nose up at me, he said, *"I've seen thoughts like you sent before from prior masters, when I told you not to touch my blade, and you said it was normal. Now you're saying it's weird. What's the difference?"*

Face palming I said, *"Point taken. It's a matter of context, I don't have those thoughts toward Yukirei."*

"I sense something about a name, Gideon, running through your head. Is she different?"

"Please don't read those thoughts. That's personal."

Rufus sent an image of him bowing to me, which was strange, since it was just a sword lifting up onto its pommel and smacking down onto the ground. The intent came through clearly, though. *"I'm sorry."*

"It's fine, this time. Gideon is a boy, not a girl. It's possible you sensed his name because I'm about to go talk to him. To be clear, all I'll be doing is talking. Nothing weird. We have something very important to discuss."

▼ ▼ ▼

I smacked my face before approaching Gideon's dormitory. The usual wide-faced boy was on guard, but this time he just sighed when he saw me. Without saying a word, he opened the door for me.

CRISTOPH A. T. 445

As I approached Gideon's dorm room, his voice filtered into the hall. It made my heart skip a beat until another joined it.

Yukirei. Although we were on better terms, given my aims, my mood soured.

Ignoring the fact that she was there, I knocked.

A woman answered the door I'd never seen before. Dressed in a Gothic Lolita outfit and makeup to match. In broad daylight, I would avoid her on a public street on Earth. Her left hand was missing three fingers, leaving a pinkie and a thumb.

"Lord Gideon," she said, in a clearly fake high pitched voice. "You have an armed visitor."

When her face returned to me, she merely glowered, waiting for a response from Gideon.

"Aul, did you say armed?" He replied and approached us, concern in his voice. When he managed to get a good sight of me, he said, "Anessa!"

"Hey."

"We were just about to have second dinner, would you like to join us?"

I pursed my lips. *There are times when I'm allowed to be a little selfish.* With a smile I said, "Actually, I was hoping you could join me instead."

Aul stepped to the side and Yukirei waved at me from a small circle table. Based on her outfit, Aul must be her maid and probably her protection, not that she needed it.

"Yukirei, I'm sorry," I gave a curtsy. "I'm going to borrow him for today. I'll make sure he makes it up to you, okay?"

She put her hand on her cheek and waved. "Okay." Then mouthed, *"Good luck."*

Shaking my head I smiled and tugged on Gideon's arm. He hollered to Yukirei, "Can you lock my door, Yuki?"

"Sure."

Yuki, huh? I pushed the thought away. *She didn't know when I was going to do this, just that I'd been thinking about it.*

At that, we both left his dormitory and made our way toward my dorm suite.

"They've already got everything prepared," I said and slowed down after we were a fair distance. "Sorry to pull you away."

His smile made my worries fade. "It's okay. I know you wouldn't pull me away like that if it weren't important." He said, "It *is* important, isn't it?"

Turning away I said, "Hmmph, of course it is!"

During our meal, Gideon asked, "Are you upset with me?"

"For?" I said.

"Yukirei."

"No." Taking my braid in my hand I traced a "Y" in my palm with the end, then a "G". I said, "I'm not mad about *Yuki*."

He winced. "You seem mad though."

Letting my braid go, I said, "Just nervous."

"About?"

After I started into his eyes for several seconds he continued.

"Is it being the Carlyle heir apparent?"

My eyes widened. "Shit," I said aloud and covered my mouth.

Both Tania and Sarah shook their heads.

Lowering my face to the table, I said, "Um," I laughed and looked up at him, "Until you said that, I had not thought about it, at all." Waving my hand to clear the thought, I said, "Now, about Yukirei," I said. "I know you and her get along well."

He nodded.

I stumbled over my words, "You will be my only husband, you know? If you and Yukirei marry in the future, so be it." Pressing my splayed fingers together I added and my cheeks burned, "B-but I'll be your first wife."

"I'm okay with that." He smiled and my heart skipped a beat. "I expected as much, whenever that will be."

"A-about that," I said, and our plates were cleared away. "Please stand up."

He did so, but his off-kilter brow said he was confused.

"Please stand near the window."

Taking my chair with me, I sat it near him and stood on top of it.

His eyes widened in recognition, but he dropped to the floor and held his hand up while prostrating before me.

What is he doing? I'm not making him keep his initial titled standing here. I crossed my arms. "Gideon, what are you doing. I said to *stand* near the window, didn't I?"

He lifted up onto his knees and said, "Are you sure?"

Nor am I making him my lesser. Furrowing my brows I hardened my voice, "You *are* going to make me mad if I have to repeat myself," I paused for effect, "Again."

He stood, and despite standing on a chair, he was *still* taller than I was.

Damn being two-foot shorter than he is!

Taking a breath I closed my eyes and told myself, *You can do this, it's just procedure.* Once I'd calmed myself enough, I opened my eyes and fixed them on his forehead, then our gazes locked. "Your Imperial Low

Presumptive Duke Consort Gideon, oldest son of the Varn baronetcy, we began our *acp hoth* over seven years ago, originally under our parent's well-intentioned guidance. Through that time we've grown closer, would you agree?"

He said, "I do agree."

"Then it is my great pleasure that I ask of you, Gideon, to make our acp hoth more formal, and engage to be married as my equal when I am eighteen on Octday, Lokandae 21st, 1742."

Giving me a grin he said, "I would be delighted."

His hands were at his sides the whole time, where they stayed. Since I was still over six inches too short, I placed my hands on his shoulders, and he dipped his head down.

With the quickest peck on the forehead, I let go and hopped off the chair.

"That was so embarrassing!" I said.

"Congratulations!" Tania and Sarah chimed in together.

Their efforts only made me blush further.

"I'm overjoyed, Anessa," he said. "What brought this on, though?"

"It's not polite to prod too much into your maiden's heart," I said and turned away. Turning my eyes to him I said, "It's clear some people wish my family harm. I just figured you'd be easier to… protect if you were closer."

Realizing I'd just thought of him as a damsel in distress, I envisioned him in a dress, making me laugh. *A very tall damsel.* But my mood sobered quickly as I thought about the dangers. *If anyone tries to hurt him, they'll have to go through me.*

Thanks for making it this far!

Ratings and reviews are the lifeblood of a series. If you have time, please take the time to leave one.

This series will be releasing often, so look forward to the next book, and follow me on Amazon for updates!

Thank you to Alice Waites (Damson) for the illustrations in this story. It wouldn't be the same without her help. Her X account can be found @damson_fox

Another thank you to Danny DeCillis, my editor. For making my words not trip over one another.

Thanks to the talented Ashley Gatti for her voices in the audiobooks.

For posters, stickers and other merch, visit my website at cristoph.net. You can find my X account @cristoph_a_t

ESTAR TRANSLATION GUIDE

Days of the week:
Unday - First day of the week.
Deuday - Second day of the week.
Triday - Third day of the week.
Quattoroday - Fourth day of the week.
Midday - Fifth day of the week (midweek).
Hexoday - Sixth day of the week.
Septaday - Seventh day of the week.
Octday - Eighth day of the week.
Finday - Ninth day of the week.

Month names (and their English equivalent):
Runariae - January
Crotariae - February
Totharae - March
Evantaiae - April
Lokandae - May
Jothariae - June
Mankae - July
Ylldriae - August
Hanvarae - September
Fandariae - October
Polarae - November
Zenthriae - December

While Runariae is positionally equivalent to January, that's where the similarities end. Months are 27 days long (three weeks).

Äneaca is Anessa's name in Estar.

UNITS / CONVERSIONS

Standard minute - Sixty-four seconds.
   Standard hour - Sixty-four Standard minutes.
   Standard day - Twenty-four Standard hours.

   Anfang day - Forty-eight Standard hours or two Standard days.
   Anfang Week - Nine Anfang days.
   Anfang Month - Twenty-seven Anfang Days or Fifty-four & 2718/5411 Earth days long.
   Anfang Year - Three-hundred-twenty-four Anfang days, twelve Anfang months, or six-hundred-forty-eight Standard days. With one leap Anfang day every nine Anfang years.

CHARACTER GUIDE

Anessa Jean Carlyle - Our protagonist. Her death on Earth is somewhat of a mystery. She thought at first it was her best friend that took her life, but things might not be as simple as that. Early Nascent Realm.

Bal Blackwood (Black the Terrible) - King of the Blackwood Kingdom. Father of Rhis and Wyn Blackwood. Julilah's second husband. Mortal.

Eloria Kirzington von Addenal - Anfang's goddess of Death. She was once viewed as the goddess of craft.

Eugene Truval - Grand Master General of the Westwood Empire, Yukirei's father.

Evan Q'Tar - Heir to the Redwater Empire. Late stages of the Ascended Realm.

Fan Mul - Lily's former Lady's maid. Her role changes throughout the book. Mortal.

Hammid Aramont† - Former king of the Honeybur Nation, Mina's father.

Jorin Q'Tar - His Imperial Majesty, the Emperor of the Westwood Empire. Sky-Realm, half-step in the Otherworldly Realm.

Julilah Carlyle - Roland's first wife. Veronica's on-pa. Anessa's step-mother. Mortal.

Kile - Oliver and Anessa's combat trainer. Unknown Realm.

Kristine Carlyle - Roland's second wife. Veronica's on-ma. Anessa's step-mother. Middling Ascended Realm.

Lily Carlyle - Anessa's mother and Roland's third wife.

Lom Carlyle - Kristine and Roland's son. Anessa's younger half-brother. Early Nascent Realm.

Lukas Q'Tar - Anessa's cousin. Heir presumptive and Imperial Prince of the Westwood Empire. Middling Sky Realm.

Max Winnie - Portia's love interest, son of Baron Min Winnie. Late Nascent Realm.

M. Gideon Varn - Son of the Varn Baronet from Rhinebur. Anessa's Fiancé. Late Nascent Realm.

Mina Aramon-Carlyle - Oliver's fiancée. Early Nascent Realm.

Mr. Morris† - Former head butler of the Carlyle estates. Was in the Sky Realm.

Nicole Carlyle - Roland and Kristine's oldest daughter. Anessa's oldest half-sister. Mortal.

Oliver Sil Carlyle - Anessa's older twin brother. Former heir of the Carlyle Imperial Duchy. Was in the late Sky Realm, but due to poisoning he is now a mortal.

Pia and **Roa** - Two of Oliver's former fiancées. Mortal.

Portia - A commoner from the Maaka Institute of Cultivating Juniors. Anessa's friend. Commoner. Mortal.

Rhis Blackwood - Younger prince of the Blackwood Kingdom. Early Nascent Realm.

Roland Carlyle - Anessa's father and the patriarch of the Carlyle family. Late Sky Realm.

Rufus - Oliver's sentient sword that he received when he was two years old. He passed it on to Anessa shortly after they turned eleven years old.

Sarah-Knecht von Anessa (formerly Sarah Greensbaro) - Anessa's lady's maid. Once an Imperial Noble, she is now bound to Anessa for life through a slave contract.

Trish - Anessa's friend from Earth. Shows up in her dreams at times.

Veronica Nu Carlyle - Anessa's not-sister. Kristine and Julilah's daughter.

Wyn Blackwood - Older prince from the Blackwood Kingdom. Early Ascended Realm.

Yllia - Head maid of the Carlyle family.

Yukirei Truval - One of Gideon's love interests. She was antagonistic to Anessa when they first met, but has since warmed to her in realizing her mistakes. Somewhat of a tsundere. Early Sky Realm.

† - Deceased.

CULTIVATION TERMINOLOGY

Realm - A major steppingstone for cultivators to differentiate between one another.

Stage - A portion of a Realm necessary to advance. Typically, a Realm composes many stages.

Step - Denotes an even smaller portion of a Realm and subdivides Stages.

Dantian - A means for a cultivator to store essence within their body.

Divine Link - A connection with a god or goddess during an Awakening Ceremony.

Meridians - Similar to how veins and arteries carry blood, meridians carry essence.

Nexus - An organ within a cultivator that is used to control essence. It's similar to how your heart pumps blood, a nexus pumps essence. Different in that it helps you enact control *external* to your body.

Mortal - A non-cultivator. Equivalent to a normal person on Earth.

Nascent Realm - A cultivator who is in the first Realm. The weakest Nascent Realm cultivator is stronger than the average mortal (usually).

Ascended Realm - The second Realm. Most consider this Realm to be the real start of someone's cultivation journey. The Nascent Realm is like being on training wheels.

Sky Realm - The third Realm. At this stage, cultivators start to understand basic gravity and learn to counteract it. This is done innately, and they slowly move to temper their bodies for what comes next.

Ring of He - An enchanted ring which is capable of providing female couples with the means to have children. Cannot be used by someone under the influence of a Ring of She. Can be used by Mortals.

Ring of She - The opposite of the Ring of He. Cannot be used by someone under the influence of a Ring of He. Can be used by Mortals.

On-ma - The mother of a child in a female-female relationship.

On-pa - The father of a child in a female-female relationship.